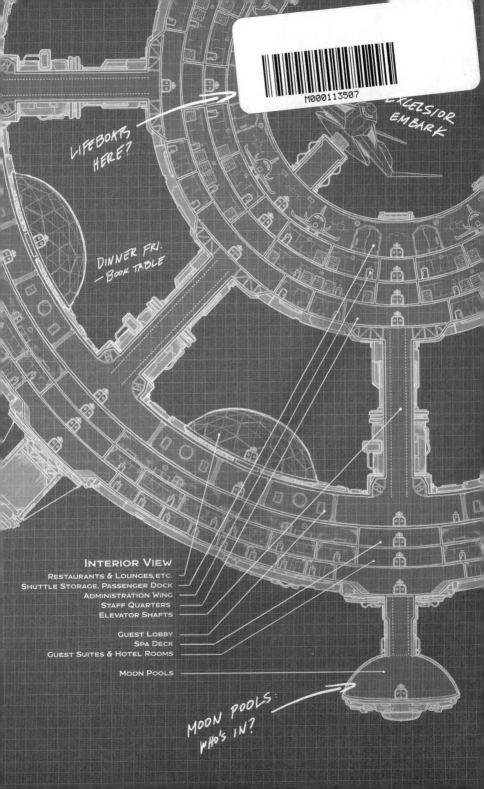

Escape Velocity

Also by Victor Manibo

The Sleepless

Escape
Velocity

Victor Manibo

EREWHON

an imprint of Kensington Publishing Corp.
erewhonbooks.com

EREWHON BOOKS are published by:

Kensington Publishing Corp.
900 Third Avenue
New York, NY 10022
erewhonbooks.com

All Kensington titles, imprints, and distributed lines are available at special quantity discounts for bulk purchases for sales promotions, premiums, fundraising, educational, or institutional use.

Special book excerpts or customized printings can also be created to fit specific needs. For details, write or phone the office of the Kensington sales manager: Kensington Publishing Corp., 900 Third Avenue, New York, NY 10022, attn: Sales Department; phone 1-800-221-2647.

Erewhon and the Erewhon logo Reg. US Pat. & TM Off.

This is a work of fiction. All of the characters, organizations, and events portrayed in this novel are either products of the author's imagination or are used fictitiously.

ISBN 978-1-64566-084-2 (hardcover)

First Erewhon hardcover printing: June 2024

10 9 8 7 6 5 4 3 2 1

Printed in the United States of America

Library of Congress Control Number: 2023944509

Electronic edition: ISBN 978-1-64566-085-9 (ebook)

Edited by Sarah T. Guan
Cover design by Samira Iravani
Interior design by Kelsy Thompson
Author photograph by Sean Collishaw

To my mother, Ramona

But outer Space,
At least this far,
For all the fuss
Of the populace
Stays more popular
Than populous

—"But Outer Space," Robert Frost

Chapter 1
Schrödinger's Spaceman

The stars blurred into curved lines of silver, crisscrossing the spaceman's field of vision as he tumbled and spun. He flailed his arms and legs, his grasp searching for something, anything to arrest his motion. Which way is up, Henry Gallagher asked himself. There was no "up" in space, but when one is in a free fall, rationality takes a dive as well.

He awoke in that state, shaken by a floating piece of debris. A rock, or more possibly a torn-off hunk of satellite. The loud thud to the back of his helmet roused him from unconsciousness just as much as the spinning that immediately followed. Soon enough, his movement had slowed to what felt like stillness, his body having found its own orbit.

"Comms," Henry called out weakly. The inner screen of his helmet came to life with icons and graphs.

⟨*Communications System Out of Range*⟩

"Find Altaire," he stated. Even as his screen zoomed in on the station, he could barely see it. Space Habitat Altaire floated far beyond him, at the edge of the Earth's horizon where much of Asia slowly disappeared from view.

The screen flashed a directional arrow and a number too big for him to comprehend.

"Holy fuck," he muttered under his breath. "How did I get here?"

He got no response; apparently, the smart suits weren't as smart as he'd been promised. All it told him was that it was Saturday, October 10, 2089. 5:53 p.m. station time.

He pulled up his vitals, which showed his oxygen saturation, his pulse and breathing rate, his blood pressure. All stable, all things considered. Most importantly, his tank had enough O_2 for another three hours and change.

Henry knew that the Altaire orbited the globe about eighteen times in the span of a day, and he assured himself with this fact. The station would circle back around to where he was well before he ran out of air. He checked that his signal beacon was still transmitting, then pulled up his coordinates to see when this flyby would occur.

The display told him that he was 1,400 kilometers above sea level, on an orbit well below the Altaire's. The station could float directly above him and he would still be too far to establish comm range.

Blind panic began to set in, but all was not lost. Henry reached for the control arms of his jetpack. All he needed to do was propel himself toward the Altaire's orbit, close enough for its scanners to pick up his signal beacon. Cheered by the prospect of rescue, he held on and pressed the buttons on the jetpack controls, only to be deflated by the display on his screen.

<Propellant: 0%>

"Fuck!" Henry screamed. As he did, a crick in his jaw radiated pain.

Instinctively, he raised a hand to feel his head. He'd been knocked around, and not by the slight piece of space junk that shook him awake. He'd sustained some sort of blunt force injury, and if he weren't marooned in space, Henry might have been more afraid. As it was, the only emotion he could muster was confusion.

He checked his reflection in the glass and saw a reddish bruise on his left jaw. He saw, too, that instead of the standard base layer for an EVA suit, he wore a spread-collar button-down shirt and a black bow tie. Even his spacesuit was wrong. He was wearing a standard-issue silver-gray EVA suit with the Altaire logo. One of the station's loaners. Why would he have this on? He had a custom designer suit—bright red, with racing stripes running down the sides.

Henry attributed the memory loss to a head injury, but he at least remembered his civilian aerospace training and all the math that it required. Having a computer helped too. Judging by his straight-line distance from the Altaire and his distance from the station's orbit above him, Henry estimated that he'd been off the station for about an hour. The Altaire's orbital speed was constant, and so was his; he may have gotten knocked around by debris, but the impact wasn't too fast or too forceful to have changed his position by much. Looking back now, Henry thanked that piece of junk for having just the right size and velocity to wake him up without throwing him farther off course.

His angle was the bigger conundrum. To end up in an orbit well below the Altaire would have required sustained thrust—and someone intending to steer him into a trajectory that diverged from the station's.

That explained the empty jetpack.

He was shunted off the station. He had to have been.

Henry drew some satisfaction in answering at least one of his questions. He'd get his answers soon enough, but for now he needed to focus on one: how to get back to the Altaire.

The station had light shuttles for this exact scenario. Regardless of how the brochures touted the safety of space tourism, there'd always be a risk that guests or crew might go overboard. Altaire Security would have been alerted the minute he left the station's range, since his EVA suit would have been relaying his last known location until it lost contact. Once someone realized he was missing, a shuttle should have no trouble locating him. Untethered with no propellant and no means of communication, his best bet was to wait.

Yet Henry also knew that the Altaire wasn't his only bet. He asked his suit to run a scan for nearby bodies: a probe, or a satellite, maybe another luxury orbital. If he came close enough, he might be able to communicate with it. If it were crewed, it could send rescue.

His own field of vision gave him nothing, and the screen indicated two weather probes below him, both farther than Altaire, and a satellite overhead. That last one had enough modules to be crewed. Henry asked the suit to identify the craft, but it had no information aside from its orbit, location, and speed. No information meant defense sat. In any case, it, too, was too far above him.

He patiently watched his screen as it scanned for other crafts. Space is crowded, he told himself, this small part of it at least. More crafts would come around as he transited around the planet. It was only a matter of time.

4

In the lull of waiting for a flyby, Henry's consciousness reassembled the moments that led to his stranding. They came to him mostly as whispers of sense-memories, slowly cresting above the louder thoughts in his mind: calculations of elevation and distance, comm range, etc.; projections and readouts from his helmet. Underneath the data and the noise, the murmurings of his recent experiences made their presence known.

Like the spacewalk he'd taken that morning. The view of the sunrise, the feel of his husband's gloved hand in his. They returned to him in flashes. The black bow tie too, the one he still wore now, and the feel of Nick's hand as he adjusted it, made it straighter. Henry had never been able to tie one right the first time, and Nick always knew to check. He made sure the butterfly ends were level yet askew enough to evince an air of sprezzatura. He made sure it was tight. Henry felt that constriction now. The sense-memory suffocated him even as he stared at the loosened tie reflected on the glass of his helmet.

The world turned beneath him, and Henry found himself straddling the line that bisected the Earth between day and night. Half the planet basked in the glow of the sun and the other slumbered in shadow. The line was narrower than he remembered from prior spacewalks. Starker, with little gradation on either side. One moment an island was there, and the next it wasn't, swallowed by the dark. As he hovered over that twilight meridian, Henry felt himself bisected too. Schrödinger's spaceman: in the same moment both alive and dead.

His orbital path soon passed over to where the sunlight never reached, over an ocean that had been sapphire blue, but now was black as jet. Plunged into the darkness, Henry was overwhelmed by more sense-memories. He smelled the hickory of their suite's fireplace. He felt the thrill of a hand under the warm waters of the Moon Pools, the rumble of the shuttle engine as they rocketed off the launchpad. He tasted champagne on his tongue, as when he toasted the Altaire's captain over dinner. Then, above all these sensations, a melody. Cymbals and trumpets and strings.

Henry heard the sound so crisply he thought he was hallucinating. His consciousness chased after it, clutching at it, and once caught, Henry found it to be more than just a disordered cacophony in his jumbled mind. It was the opening notes to an overture. The sound began to swell into a song. He remembered now.

Summertime. The theater box.

His final moments aboard the Altaire.

Henry gasped as he realized what had happened. He gasped like someone who had just been brought back to life.

Then, from beneath his multilayered gloves, his fingertips tingled with a burning sensation. First on his left hand, then his right. This felt different from the blunt impact on his head. This felt like fire.

Henry knew it wasn't external, not a tear in the suit. He didn't need to see his hands to know what they looked like now. This was a sensation all too familiar. His palms throbbed violently, and he gritted his teeth as the heat flowed in his veins, like his own blood had transformed to acid, searing him from within. The pain moved up his arms, his shoulders, his neck. He caught his reflection in the glass and saw, through welling tears of agony, that his entire face had turned an alarming shade of red.

Chapter 2
Arrivals

Tom Lazaro III was having a fitful flight. He couldn't tell why, but he figured it was the disorientation from his view windows. The HLV Excelsior kept its portholes shielded, obstructing an outside view from the shuttle during its upward journey. As a substitute, the cabin system projected onto each window a "hyperrealistic" real-time view of space as seen from the shuttle's exterior.

Laz groaned. He'd actually seen space. This filtered, panoramic projection was too sharp, too lifelike; it came back around to looking fake.

That was probably what made him feel queasy. It wasn't zero-g; that had never been a problem for him before. He had the best drill times back in high school, and he'd maintained his training certifications since then. He had also racked up a handful of trips to other orbitals, though only for a day, and nowhere as grand as his current destination.

He didn't want to admit it, but deep down he knew the cause of his unease: It was the reunion itself. The thought of reliving his days of youth pained him, knowing that things would never be as they were. That they would never be as *good* as they were.

His helmet's comm announced their final approach toward the station. Instantly, his port screens opened. Muffled cheers came from passengers in the neighboring pods. Laz gaped in awe, his eyes wide at the sight of a space orbital larger and more majestic than he'd expected.

Space Habitat Altaire was shaped like an eight-point star ringed by a massive, glimmering torus. Some called it a ship's wheel, but the comparison was a crude approximation of the orbital's design. The central hub was also a torus, smaller but no less impressive, and it housed the station's helm, staff and crew quarters, the medical bay, and all parts that made the Altaire function, including the shuttle ports that the Excelsior now approached. Along the docking bays, across a flat surface uninterrupted by windows or walls, two thick diagonals of brushed crimson steel converged at an angle. The painted lines spun with the rest of the station, like a compass head aimed at an ever-changing direction.

Each of the spokes that radiated from the hub were lined with solar arrays and acted as conduit between the hub and the shining halo of the upper torus. This outer ring contained the Altaire's amenities, including a full-size theater, a shopping pavilion, bars, lounges, and restaurants. A tree-lined promenade ran alongside the entire length of this ring, which also contained all of the Altaire's suites. Each had floor-to-ceiling windows with either a full view of the Earth beneath it or the starscape beyond.

Laz held his breath as the Excelsior approached its docking port in the hollow of the station's central hub. The shuttle slowed, keeling to align itself as the Altaire rotated. Once it docked completely, the shuttle's commander addressed the cabin with an inauthentic tone reminiscent of a weary tour guide.

"Rochford Institute Class of 2064, it's my distinct pleasure to announce that we have arrived. Welcome to Prestige-Class Space Habitat Altaire."

The cabin erupted in cheers and applause. Laz joined in, unable to help himself. As the other passengers did so, he unbuckled himself from his pod, rose from his seat, and took his helmet off. He craned his neck over the crowd in search of a familiar face and caught sight of an old friend, Henry Gallagher, beaming in breathless excitement. Henry waved at him, giving a winsome smile that hadn't changed in decades. He weaved his way through the crowd and upon reaching Laz, he leaned in for a hug.

"Are you ready for an unforgettable weekend, Ambassador?"

"As ready as I'll ever be," Laz answered, returning the gesture effusively.

"Twenty-five years, man. I'm feeling my age; are you?"

"You don't look a day over fifty," Laz quipped, earning him a playful swat on the arm. In truth, Henry looked as vital and refreshed as he always had. Unlike some of their class who'd let their hair thin and their midsections thicken, Henry's flaxen hair remained lush, and he cut a trim figure beneath his custom EVA suit.

"And you . . . you're looking good too," Henry said. "Chile agrees with you."

"If only that were true," Laz replied. He began to extol the cool climate of his current diplomatic posting, but quickly veered into a monologue about American interventionism and the political quagmires he often found himself in. Though his friend appeared rapt by his stories, Laz worried that he was boring Henry. A pang of fear returned to him like an echo from their boyhood days when he'd always been anxious for his friends' approval. In due course, Laz wound down his tale, promising himself that the rest of the weekend wouldn't see him quite so desperate.

"No plus-one?" Henry then asked. "What happened to that publicist I met at that wildlife benefit . . . Syll, was it? I thought she was lovely."

"It didn't last too long after that," Laz replied, impressed at his friend's memory. That had been almost three years ago.

Henry shrugged in commiseration. He turned back to his aisle and waved his husband to come join them. Laz took Nick's arrival as a chance to change the subject. "Was that seriously the last time we saw each other?"

"Well, with you down in Santiago, yes, it was."

"I jet up every so often."

"I really should make more of an effort," Henry replied. "It seems we only see each other every few years, and at stuffy galas and benefits too. We never have enough time to catch up."

"This reunion weekend is just the thing, then," Nick interjected, sliding an arm around Henry's waist. "Thank you, Rochford."

"And here I thought we were only here for the points," Henry jested, giving Nick a peck on the cheek.

Every year since the Altaire had been built, the Rochford alumni committee threw a lavish bash at the station, all expenses paid. Not that any of the Institute's students needed help in that respect—as far as boarding schools go, it was the best money could buy. These reunions were critical to cementing one's status; countless deals and marriages had been brokered at other Rochford reunions. That alone was reason enough to go, but the greater enticement was the chance to advance one's Mars applications.

Laz pretended, to others as much as to himself, that this reason was foremost in his mind. Well before his invitation arrived, he'd done a mental calculation of his MERIT score. A single trip to low-Earth orbit was worth three points. A weekend on the Altaire, with spacewalks and other extravehicular activity could give him as much as six points. On top of his advanced training, multiple degrees, and health background, this reunion all but ensured that he'd be granted Mars settlement rights. Laz suspected his classmates felt the same.

"Imagine," he replied after a pause. "In a little over a year, we might all be having this conversation on Mars."

"Fingers crossed," Henry said, gesturing in earnest.

As soon as the Rochford class was cleared to go through the airlocks, everyone quickly queued up for the passenger lifts. No one put up the pretense of cool, Laz included. His heart raced as they waited to ascend from the Altaire's hub to the upper torus. Unable to endure the anticipation, he finally turned to Henry and opened the subject.

"I don't think I saw Ava on our flight, did you?"

"No, I don't think so," Henry said breezily. He turned to his husband, who shook his head. "Have you talked to her lately?"

"Not in a long time. You?"

"We do, once in a while," Henry replied, clearing his throat. "The company does a lot of business with Khan-Powell Financial."

"She's been busy, that's for certain." Laz felt relieved that even the golden boy hadn't heard much from Ava in a while, yet Laz still couldn't shake off the distinct feeling that she had been specifically avoiding him.

Henry leaned in closer and swung an arm over his friend's shoulder. In a low tone, he told Laz, "I know that look."

"What look?"

Henry narrowed his eyes. "Come on, man. It's me."

"I have no idea what you're talking about."

"Yeah, I'm sure you haven't heard of the divorce."

The news of Ava Khan's failed marriage reached Laz with barely enough time for him to get recertified for space travel. At the time, nothing had been finalized yet, but a friend of a friend told him that Ava's wife Fallon had lawyered up and decamped to the couple's Loire Valley chateau. The timing felt fortuitous. He immediately RSVP'd for the reunion, counting down the days until he could see Ava again.

"Fine, you got me," Laz admitted. "Can't blame a man for trying, right?"

"No, never." Henry grinned, almost giddy. "I think this is sweet, for serious."

"I'm keenly aware of what a massive cliché I am."

"Cliché or not, I'm rooting for you," Henry said tenderly. "I just . . . wouldn't get my hopes up. You know how it is." He gestured around them, at the queue of Rochfordians impatiently waiting for their turn at the lifts. "If she's avoiding *us,* what are the chances she'll want to see these people?"

"It's been twenty-five years," Laz argued. "Surely everyone's moved on by now."

"Have you?"

Their lift arrived. Laz stepped in, looking back at the rest of his classmates, wide-eyed and eager, absorbed in chatter. He began to remember how vicious they'd all been. How vicious they all could be, even now. Beneath the smiles and the childlike fascination in their surroundings, Laz understood, for the first time that weekend, that he was entering a nest of vipers.

Henry entered the Altaire's reception lobby with the calm serenity of someone who belonged. From the moment he walked out the elevator doors, his peers turned toward him, greeting him with the warmth of their smiles. Henry never relished their esteem, and deserved though such esteem may have been, what truly gratified him was their acceptance. As long as he maintained them at arm's length, privy only to the bullet points of his curriculum vitae, Henry felt secure that he would never be cast away.

Right beside him, his husband pranced into the atrium, basking in the attention. Nick was the plus-one but by the way he acted, one would think he shared the same Rochford pedigree as Henry. Nick nodded at those who waved and smiled, made noises of surprise or glee upon seeing passing acquaintances. Already he was enjoying himself, though Henry also knew that his husband's eyes roved the crowd, searching for one person in particular.

"We need to talk to the Architect," Nick said once outside everyone's earshot. "Tonight."

"We just got here, love. Can we enjoy this moment and save the scheming for later?"

"We don't have the luxury of time, *love*. Arrangements need to be made."

This had been Nick's refrain ever since the UN Mars Settlement Agency announced that the first civilian habitats had been built. Applications were opening in six months, and he was determined to garner as many points as possible and submit their applications the second the online portals would let them. "Top points mean top chance," he always said. "And first to file means first in line." Of course, millions of people had the same plans, but Nick took every step to ensure that he and his husband would not be outclassed.

In fact, coming to the reunion had mostly been Nick's idea. Sure, it was Henry's high school reunion, but he might not have gone if not for Nick's insistence. Rochford was best left in the past, and Henry wasn't thrilled to revisit it. His husband, however, was relentless.

"It's five MERIT points, each. Minimum. That's more than any one thing you and I could achieve in a single weekend. Everything else we've been doing pales in comparison," Nick had argued, and he was right. Besides, the couple needed to offset the "gay penalty," and despite the many points accorded to two healthy, well-credentialed men, the system penalized them for their "inherent inability to produce offspring."

"I have a plan," Henry told his husband now, steering him by the arm. "But the more you press me, the more I'm gonna make you sweat."

"You're seriously going to make me suffer?"

"I'm gonna make you enjoy yourself," he replied, patting Nick reassuringly. "Because I have no intention of making this weekend be all about business. Now stop thinking of the Architect. That's an order."

Henry understood that his husband's anxiety came from the disparity in their individual MERIT scores, a detail that he'd learned to sidestep whenever the two of them discussed their plans. As an eminent neurosurgeon, Henry's career was classified as a Tier A occupation. It didn't matter that he barely spent any time in an operating room anymore, or that his duties as CEO of GDX Pharmaceuticals, the Gallagher family empire, occupied his days. A doctor was a doctor, and Mars could always use more of them. Meanwhile, Nick was in Tier C. Hollywood executives were not needed on a newly-settled planet, no matter how many record-breaking movies they worked on. Nick had other handicaps too: he didn't graduate from an aerospace-affiliated school like Rochford, and compared to Henry, he only had a handful of shuttle flights under his belt.

The disparity stung Nick's ego, but his larger concern was that the MERIT system weighed a married couple's scores together. Nick couldn't stand being the reason that the two of them might miss their opportunity at Mars, even though they both knew that, worst come to worst, if one of them stood to sink their joint application, it would be Henry.

Presently, a young Altaire crewmember weaved through the guests to approach the couple. He wore a navy-blue uniform, and though he was in his late-twenties at the most, already he had earned bars on his shoulders. A deck officer, with the stiff bearing to match.

"Mr. and Mr. Gallagher," he said. "My name is Pio Asuncion, and I'll be your personal liaison during your stay with us here at the Altaire."

Henry's brow knitted. A crewman as valet, and an officer no less; that seemed excessive. He shook the man's hand and startled at his viselike grip. He looked at the valet's name plate. Philippines. That's the fourth one he'd seen so far. He wondered how many of them staffed the station.

"I'm sorry it took us a while to get here," Henry said. "Got waylaid by small talk. And please, you can call us by our first names."

"If that's what you prefer," the valet replied with evident discomfort. "May I take your bags?"

"Pio. Sounds like C-3PO," Nick said, pronouncing the name with overextended vowels. He handed his satchel over. "That'll be easy to remember."

"Yes, exactly like the robot," Pio replied with a solicitous laugh. "But I'm here for more than just protocol. Whatever you need to enjoy your stay, I'm your man."

"We should head up to the suite," Nick told his husband, then turned to Pio. "We're on a bit of a schedule. Things to do, people to see . . ."

"Of course." Pio promptly led them toward a receiving station and took out two thin metal boxes. Along their top edges ran an engraving of each guest's name. Inside were a communicator earcuff, a ring of lightweight steel, and an implant injector.

"Do I really need all of these?" Henry asked.

"Your phones will work while you're on board, but all financial transactions on the Altaire are conducted via the ring or the cuff. The subcutaneous implant is for location services and contains your security access level that will allow you to move around the habitat. You may choose between the ring and the cuff, but I'm afraid the implant is not optional."

Henry blew out a deep sigh.

"If you have data privacy concerns with our location trackers, I'd be happy to address them."

"Oh, no, it's not that. I know it's federally mandated on orbital stays," he replied. "It's just that I'm . . . feeling a bit unsettled from the flight up."

"Yes, it's been quite an adjustment for him," Nick added. "Would it be all right for him to do it himself once we're settled into our suite?"

"I'm sorry, but the doors on the station are implant-activated, including that one." Their valet gestured at the glass doors that led out of the welcome lobby and into the atrium. "I couldn't admit you even if I wanted to."

Defeated, Henry pulled back his shirt sleeve, baring the inside of his left arm where he had a modest tattoo of the Southern Cross constellation. The valet gently took his forearm, searched for a firm spot, and jammed the implant device against his skin. A hiss and a subsequent beep indicated that the tracker had taken hold.

"Don't worry," Pio told Henry. "It will dissolve and be eliminated from your system by the time you leave on Sunday."

Once done, the valet escorted the Gallaghers into the main atrium of Altaire, an oblong dome with a vaulted ceiling and thin tapering windows. In the center was a sunken garden with four rows of cherry blossom trees in full bloom. On both sides of the garden were viewing platforms, where thick glass panels rose from the floor all the way up to the dome's apex. Some guests gathered excitedly on one of these platforms, catching a god's-eye view of the Earth. The other platform, the one that showed a view of empty space, was not quite as crowded.

Pio gave the couple the introductory spiel, sweeping a hand toward the platforms, the trees, the two bistros that lined the hallway leading to the promenade.

"His English is perfect," Nick said with no attempt at concealment. Henry hoped that the valet, who walked some paces ahead of them, didn't hear. "Unaccented too. If I didn't know better, I'd say he was born and raised in the Midwest."

"Don't sound so surprised, love. They all speak English over there," Henry answered in a hushed tone, a look of reprimand on his face. "They're very well educated."

"I didn't say they weren't," Nick replied defensively. "I'm just pleasantly surprised, that's all. He even gets classic movie references. We have loads of Filipino-American friends, but the crew here, they're all from the homeland. Isn't that right, Pio?"

"Yes, Sir Nick," Pio said. Henry bristled at the title, clearly the young man's workaround to the use of first names. "And most of the staff as well. Made in the Philippines. But we all trained in Singapore or Tokyo before heading up here."

"And did you go through accent training as well?"

"Maybe you can tell us more about the crew," Henry interrupted. "I noticed the flags on your name plates."

"Well, Sir Henry, the staff and crew of the Altaire come from all over the globe. As you might guess, the captain and the top brass are all American, but the rest come from seventy different countries. As for my country, we make up about a third of the people who make this station run."

"Why so many?"

"It's just like how it is planetside. Most of the hospitality staff for hotels and cruise ships are from the Philippines. Been so for decades. They say it's the English skills," the valet replied, turning to Nick. "But really, it's because we're the most hospitable people on the planet. We can't help but please. It's in our DNA."

"Well, I was just telling Henry here how I admire your fluency," Nick replied. "For a Filipino, you sure could pass for a Minnesotan."

The valet paused before turning back the way they were going. "Thank you, Sir Nick," Pio said with a proud look on his face. "That's really nice of you to say."

Henry sighed, and Nick shot him a look that he knew only too well: the smug look of a husband who had just won an argument.

Past the cherry blossom trees, the atrium split off into passages, the most inviting of which was the outermost hall, the promenade. The few guests who weren't mesmerized by the stars instead marveled at the lush landscapes that lined the Altaire's upper torus. The central garden was inspired by the Kenroku-en in Kanazawa, Pio reported as they ambled out of the atrium, personally designed by the landscape artists from the famed garden itself. The Altaire rotated this display every year, and next year's atrium would feature the Florentine Boboli Gardens. He then gestured toward the first section of the promenade: rows of roses in full bloom, hedges of camellias and geraniums, their foliage vibrant against the void of space, separated only by a pane of glass. Every few steps, a marble statue in the Roman style stood on a pedestal amidst the shrubbery.

Henry inspected one of these—a stately woman wearing a flowy gown, cradling a cornucopia under one arm and raising a sheaf of wheat with the other. He leaned in closer. *Abbondanza.* He touched the plinth and was surprised to find solid marble. Most landscapes were enhanced with holograms these days, to make them seem fuller, more prolific than what the climate might allow. As they walked on, Henry ran his hands through the bushes, grazing the blossoms, pleased to feel real life in his fingertips.

It was then that Henry saw him. The liquid folds of his iridescent kimono-suit glimmered in gradients of citrine and emerald and oil-slick black, and its low-cut lapels exposed his chest, his solid pectorals, a slight peek at his abs. An obi of copper lamé cinched his waist. He seemed taller than when they last met, until Henry noticed the man's three-inch platform heels.

"Hello, Sloane."

"Henry!" he replied excitedly, almost in overcompensation. "Lovely to see you."

"It's been a while." Henry reached out a hand. "Have you met my husband, Nick?"

"Not formally, but it's a small world," Nick replied, saving Sloane from trying to find an answer. "I believe we know many of the same folks in New York."

"You do look familiar," Sloane said before rattling off names and events, this one soirée in the Pines, this one weekend out on the Cape. Henry let the two carry on as though he wasn't even there. His husband seemed charmed by Sloane, and Henry was not surprised. Sloane always had a way with words. He'd been more reserved in their youth, but Henry recognized that now as it was then, Sloane's silver tongue could spin words into gold.

"That settles it," Nick announced after a while. "We should have drinks ASAP."

"Absolutely. I'd love to catch up," Henry replied.

"There's a lot of ground to cover," Sloane said, arching an eyebrow. "First, tell me—what have I missed?"

"It's been, what, four years since we bumped into each other?" Henry started. "Got married and got GDX, those are big ones."

"Your folks finally gave you the keys to the kingdom!"

Henry smiled uneasily and quickly unloaded his burdens about running a conglomerate, the soulless tedium of board meetings and earnings calls, desperate to downplay what he'd usually consider his crowning achievement. The complaints weren't false, and he did miss his former life of running hospitals and saving lives; most days he wished to return to it. Yet Henry had never spoken of that desire to anyone besides his own husband. Did he now express his complaints in consideration of Sloane's feelings, knowing his circumstances and his history? Possibly. The more Sloane listened to him whine, a patient but knowing look in his eyes, the more Henry understood a greater reason altogether: he could never pretend with the people who knew him the most.

"What I'd like to hear more of," Nick said when he found his chance, "are stories about Henry in high school." He turned to Sloane. "Was he always this . . . humble?"

Sloane paused for a moment and Henry held his breath. "Yes, he was," Sloane finally replied. "Everyone bought into the hype around him, but he himself never did. He never cared about petty high school politics either. He was a good friend to everyone, no matter who they were."

"See, when I hear someone was class president and prom king and valedictorian, I get a different picture in mind," Nick answered. "And since Henry never tells me anything about his life at Rochford, the gaps find themselves filled by my imagination."

"Oh, I'm sure there's nothing I can share that you don't already know," Sloane replied. "Besides, everyone was all over Henry's business back then. You won't have a hard time finding people on this station who would be happy to fill the gaps for you."

"That's what I'm here for. The more embarrassing stories the better."

Henry laughed. "Oh, is that the real reason why you wanted to come?"

"One of many."

To Henry's relief, Sloane soon excused himself, promising drinks and more stories before the weekend was over. Nick was thrilled by the teasing, and Henry gamely shooed his friend away, laughing. He cast Sloane a sidelong glance as he left. Sloane and alcohol had always been a combustible mix, and no matter how honest he'd been with his husband, Henry still dreaded the stories that might come out if his friend made good on his promise.

Charles Sloane IV loved a grand entrance. No sooner had he disembarked from the Excelsior did he find the nearest guest lounge in which he could liberate himself from the unflattering layers of an astronaut suit.

Once he'd changed into designer duds that showed off his physique, he slinked through the Altaire's atrium like a snake among the cherry blossoms, hoping that the folds of his ensemble caught the light as well as his classmates' attention.

He took such measured steps that it appeared as though he was gliding. His sense of fanfare was only one reason for this. Another was his outfit's copper sash constricting his posture and arresting his walk; the heels didn't help either. Mostly, though, it was Sloane's acclimating sense of balance. The Altaire's rotation was imperceptible, yet he feared he might suddenly get thrown into the air along with the guests and their monogrammed luggage, the flowers and the sculptures and the trees all around them. He'd been a competitive rock climber and he always preferred feeling the firmness of the Earth beneath his feet.

Sloane felt a semblance of that security upon meeting Henry. The two of them relied on each other for so long and the remembrance of their childhood friendship gave Sloane an anchor of sorts. The routine small talk of a high school reunion transported Sloane to their times at Rochford, when he and his friends dreamed of becoming spacemen, training for missions, living on Mars. What would the Sloane of twenty-five years ago think about this moment now, he wondered, feeling a slight thrill at being in space, on the Altaire with old friends.

Yet the man he was now, the one who'd had to grow up too early too fast, stifled this flutter of excitement. His circumstances were inescapable, had been so since his last year at Rochford. His father made sure of that when he squandered the family fortune, along with all his clients', and had the poor sense to get caught. Everyone witnessed the Sloanes come into ruin. They shunned the teenage Sloane, his mother, and his older brothers, all of whom worked for his father's investment firm and were widely believed to be complicit in his crimes. After their mansions were seized and their assets frozen, his family's fall from stratospheric heights all but assured that Sloane would never step foot on the red planet.

A Rochford diploma helped, but he did not have a degree, or any sort of skill that earned points on the MERIT system. He knew several languages, a necessary skill in the line of work he chose, but that helped little with his score. More so when he was competing against the Lonsdales or the Gallaghers, who regularly went to space to rack up points.

There they all were now, racking up points by mere dint of their presence aboard the Altaire. Sloane knew his classmates well enough to be sure that they all had their scores in mind even as they tried to talk around it. He, too, couldn't deny that it helped his application, but that's not why he'd decided to attend. Sloane had been looking forward to the reunion for years, eager to obtain new names for his client list and the secrets that they brought with them. A single conversation, well executed, could set him up for a while.

It was in the service of one such conversation that Sloane excused himself from Nick and Henry, who appeared relieved at his departure. Altaire staffers fanned out of the atrium bearing chargers of champagne flutes, and Sloane helped himself to one before waltzing across the lobby in the hope of catching a certain woman's eye. He did not have to wait too long.

"Charles Sloane, as I live and breathe," she greeted, the deep timbre of her Georgia drawl immediately recognizable.

"Isobel Hayes. It's been ages." He leaned in for an air kiss. "Did I get that right, is it back to Hayes, or are we still using Lonsdale?"

"Still Hayes-Lonsdale," she answered with a wave of the hand. Rumors swirled that she and her husband were on the brink of divorce, and while she acted as though Sloane's remark meant nothing, her thin smile told him otherwise.

"In any case, this weekend's the perfect opportunity to take inventory," Sloane teased. "I would fight for this station if I were you. Don't let Julian get it in the settlement. Get half at least."

"Oh, Sloane. Always looking at someone else's bowl," she replied coyly. "Have you been on the Altaire before?"

"First time."

"Splendid! There is so much to experience."

Isobel yammered on about the station's amenities, and in that moment of unguarded excitement, Sloane saw a glimmer of the old Isobel. The guileless headmaster's daughter had always been kind to him, though he often didn't deserve it. On the surface, all the Rochford kids took the same courses, wore the same uniforms, lived in the same stately dorm rooms, but Isobel didn't belong the way everyone else did. She wasn't old money, and no one made her forget it, Sloane included.

That all changed once she started dating Julian Lonsdale. His father would never deign to send his own children to an American school, opting to board Julian at a highly selective collège in the Swiss Alps, but the senior Lonsdale did matriculate at Rochford and so bestowed upon it a hefty endowment and an aerospace training facility. This brought the headmaster's daughter into Julian's orbit, and Isobel Hayes gained a level of respectability among the class, and more importantly, among their families.

Right around the time Sloane lost his.

"So, what have you been up to?" Isobel asked him before taking a sip from her flute. The two hadn't exchanged words since senior year, though they surely kept tabs on each other in the same way everyone in their social circles knew exactly who was doing what. Isobel's question was no innocent inquiry.

"Not much. Living la dolce vita, one might say."

"Seriously, what do you do now?"

"I'm a bon vivant, same as always."

"That's not a job," she answered.

"Neither is philanthropist, though that seems to be your official title, right next to your name every time I see it in print."

"Fair enough. Charles Sloane—international man of mystery."

"I wouldn't go that far."

"You've met Julian, surely? It's been hard to keep track," she said.

"At one party or another," he replied. "Can't remember when exactly. Though I'm not sure he'd remember me."

"Your presence isn't so easy to forget," Isobel replied earnestly. "And in any case, I know my husband would welcome being reacquainted."

There lies her true title, Sloane supposed. Wife to the great Julian Lonsdale. Directing a world hunger nonprofit certainly required most of Isobel's time and considerable talents, and the Hayes-Lonsdale Foundation had all but managed to transform Earth's warming tundra into arable farmland, but they wouldn't have done so without solar satellites from Lonsdale Aerospace. It all came back to Julian. That was her real job, and a sweet one at that. If only she knew that Julian was Sloane's job too.

"I don't see him around . . ."

"Oh, he's probably hiding in our suite," Isobel answered conspiratorially. "Now that everyone's come aboard, he expects nonstop meetings and pitches, and he'd rather avoid them all if he could."

"I see. Well, I hope our paths cross at some point," Sloane said, even though their rendezvous was all but assured. Julian had insisted, and even if Sloane's accounts weren't running too low for comfort, he still would have agreed. No one says no to a Lonsdale.

"He'll show up for the weekend's festivities, I'll make sure of it. The parties are not to be missed," Isobel replied. She lowered her voice. "Especially the one after tonight's welcome dinner."

She had a glint in her eye, and Sloane didn't know whether to take it as an enticement or a warning. He smiled slyly. "I hear it gets pretty decadent."

"My dear, decadent doesn't even begin to describe it."

On a promenade level that overlooked the atrium, Ava Khan watched the paths of her old friends collide with each other. She'd known they were all attending—one of the perks of being the CEO to the Khan-Powell Financial Group, a major investor in the Altaire, included access to the guest list and passenger manifest—but Ava needed to see with her own eyes that the three of them had actually arrived. She sipped her champagne as she observed Laz, Henry, and Sloane fumbling through the motions of reuniting for the first time in years. The awkwardness was palpable even from her perch. She would have to wrestle with the same awkwardness when she herself met with them, and she only hoped that a sense of goodwill or nostalgia would follow soon enough. After all, she only had two days to get what she needed from them.

Yet even at the possibility of coming closer to the truth, Ava held doubts about her attendance. Rochford had caused her too much pain, too much loss. Over the years, she'd conducted business with people from her class (it was unavoidable; their circle was small and incestuous) but only with the rare one-on-one encounter, delegating the bulk of negotiations and glad-handing to her staff. This reunion was different. All these people, together in one place? It would be like high school all over again. The disdainful looks, the hushed whispers. Everything Ava achieved outside Rochford's hallowed halls changed little of how they viewed her. She would always be twin sister to Ashwin Khan, the heir to the family dynasty brutally murdered by Ava's own lover, the girl from the wrong part of town. The question would loom over every encounter this weekend, the one question all her classmates had been asking for the last quarter century.

Did Ava do it?

Wouldn't everyone love to know.

"Ah, the masses have arrived," said a voice from beside her. The man joined Ava in leaning over the promenade rail, looking down on the rest of the Rochford class as they trickled into the station. "The fun can finally commence."

Julian Lonsdale and his wife had been aboard the Altaire since the prior weekend, having decided to use the reunion as an excuse for a week-long getaway. Ava had arrived early too, hoping to ease herself into the toll that the event would no doubt inflict on her. To her dismay, she'd had to spend the last few days dodging the Lonsdales around the station.

"I don't know about fun," she said. "This is a work trip for me, as I'm sure it is for you."

"Your board made you come, huh?"

Ava nodded. She had managed to avoid the Rochford ten-year reunion, but the KPF board couldn't excuse her this time. She was the head of one of the world's largest investment banks, and missing such a networking opportunity would be tantamount to mal-feasance. Why, her attendance alone would raise the company's stock price a few points before she even shook a single hand. Being chummy with the CEO of Lonsdale Aerospace, the primary contractor for the Mars habitats, didn't hurt either.

"Well, I'm happy to be the plus-one, for once," Julian replied.

"Fewer names to remember, fewer meetings to take."

"It's Isobel's reunion, and she's in the driver's seat. I'm just the date."

The fact that he was talking to her now proved that to be a lie. At some point soon, Ava expected Julian to court her, to float a proposal for another venture that KPF could bankroll. She didn't resent this; that's how most of her interactions went these days. In fact, she even welcomed it—Julian's need ensured that he would play nice with her. She couldn't say the same about the station's recent arrivals.

"What was it like, with your reunion?" Ava asked him. "It was here on the Altaire too, wasn't it?"

He nodded. "Back when this had just opened. I can't wait to see how Rochford parties, but I gotta say, the Desmarais reunions set a high bar."

"I've heard stories," she replied. "Like how the fate of the World Bank was decided on a literal pissing contest."

"That wasn't my graduating class," Julian replied, chuckling. "Ours was the one with the brawl over the cybersecurity consortium." With unabashed relish, he recounted the intricate dealings and motives that drove twelve full-grown men to an all-out slugfest. News outlets never picked up the story, of course, nor any of scandals that inevitably occurred at these parties. They knew to protect their own reputations and had the power to do so. Yet Ava knew of these stories, everybody in their social set knew, and she allowed herself to enjoy gossip that for once did not involve her.

"Well, let's hope no one comes to blows this weekend," she said.

Julian raised his flute and clinked hers. "At least not unwelcome ones."

"You know, you're making me feel like this reunion won't be as bad as I think."

"I walked away with two things from my own reunion," he replied, smirking. "Well, three if you count a fat lip."

Ava laughed. "And what of the other two?"

"The first one is the knowledge that all adults are just children with money, and we act even more childish the more money we have."

She sipped her drink, sighing in agreement.

"The second is the realization that the past is never as good nor as bad as we remember it. It's always a little worse—and a little better."

From below them, Isobel Lonsdale waved at her husband. Julian beckoned for her to join them, and for a moment Ava worried that she would. It had been a comfort, talking to someone who wasn't from Rochford, who wasn't part of that history. To her relief, Julian instead chose to meet his wife downstairs, leaving Ava with the weight of his words.

She had recently started seeing a therapist for this exact reason. The intrusion of her memories had remained so persistent even after all these years that she feared she'd have to endure them for the rest of her life. She'd recall the suffocating dark of a cramped locker every time she took out sheets from the linen closet. Whenever she cooked, the gleam of the knife blade reminded her of the many times that Ashwin ran a blade through her skin. She still felt echoes of pain from long-healed fractures. This was common in cases of abuse, her therapist explained, especially given the complicated sibling dynamics of twins. With time and therapy, Ava learned to keep these intrusions at bay, never letting their recurrence color her view of what really happened. So, yes, in some ways, her past was better than she once remembered.

But sometimes, the past is missing context. Incomplete information. This, Ava resolved to rectify. There would never be satisfying answers to why

Ashwin hurt her the way he did. Ava wasn't even sure that she needed them. Yet questions surrounding Ashwin's death were left unanswered, and the version of the truth that comforted her had long lost its potency. Julian was half-right. Ava's past was never as bad as she thought. It was worse, she was certain, and before the weekend was over, Ava would get her friends to tell her how much worse.

Laz felt nigh delirious after going through the vacuum of the airlock, and his delirium further heightened when he exited the lift and spilled out into the welcoming bay, a lush green lobby filled with miniature palms and flowering vines. Along the wall of this circular anteroom stood a phalanx of station officers in their crimson and gold.

He instantly noticed how they looked like him. What he had heard about the Altaire was right: it was much like a cruise ship, and as on Earth, this ship was staffed by Filipinos. Each of them wore a badge with their names and titles, and next to them, a small icon: the colors of their homeland. More than half the staff bore the Philippine flag. It made him feel proud of his heritage, and proud of the people who served on the grandest luxury orbital in the entire solar system.

That surge of patriotism permitted him to ignore the cringe that crept up his spine, one borne of an indelible childhood moment when, at his lolo's retirement party, a guest mistook him for the waitstaff and asked him for a refill after handing him an empty snifter of bourbon. Over the years, Laz had convinced himself that the mistake was easy enough to commit. His lolo staffed his mansion exclusively with Filipinos, and they were well attired for the occasion. Never mind that Laz was wearing a bespoke Savile Row tux while the servers wore standard-issue navy; the guest, who'd probably been on his third or fourth drink, could just have easily confused a waiter for the senator's grandson. And being the gracious grandson that he was, Laz didn't bother with a correction; instead he made his way to the bar to fetch the old man his next round.

Laz understood that no one would make the same mistake this weekend. Everyone at Rochford knew who he was, and despite the schoolyard barbs of his youth, none of his peers would make him feel so small now. Yet that murmur of cringe remained, especially as he was approached by an Altaire staffer.

She was a peppy young woman whose warmth and energy belied a blithe disposition that hadn't been battered by time. She reminded him of a distant cousin, which made Laz feel at ease.

"Ambassador, allow me to be the first to welcome you aboard the Altaire. My name is Cielo Mallari, and I'm the head of Guest Relations." She shook his hand firmly, then escorted him toward a receiving station. "The rest of the staff is here to attend to all your needs, but during your stay, I will be your personal liaison."

"Oh, that's not necessary. I'll manage fine on my own."

"Yes, of course. Nonetheless, I am at your beck and call for the weekend. Whatever you need, I'm only one tap away," Cielo replied, presenting him with his Altaire earcuff and ring as she walked him through the tech briefing.

"How was the flight in, by the way?" she asked. "I trust everything was to your satisfaction?"

"Great," he lied, still feeling lightheaded. His queasiness heightened as his liaison implanted him with the Altaire's all-access tracker.

"And with that, Mr. Lazaro, we can start our tour."

"Well, we can start with you calling me Laz," he replied. To the Rochford class, he'd always been Lazaro or Laz, in the same way Henry was called Gallagher as often by his first name, or how Sloane never went by Charles or Chas or Chuck or Charlie. It was one of those boyish private-school affectations, the type that came with the spiffy uniforms and vaguely military traditions. Also, though no one admitted it, everyone knew: last names made it easier to impress your value on others. At Rochford, some tried to be creative by using their numeric suffixes instead, but then four boys in his class all wanted to be known as "Trip." Juan Felipe Tomas Gonzalez-Lazaro III was one of them.

As they walked past the sunken Japanese garden, Cielo described the technical specifications of the habitat, which held no interest to Laz. He already knew these details. His liaison's voice gradually faded to ambient noise. He gave her a smile, made sure to glance her way every so often, but his attention was elsewhere. Soon enough, he linked his handheld with his earcuff and pulled up a multilevel floor plan of the habitat.

"I appreciate the tour," he finally told Cielo, "but I think I can find my way around. Do you suppose my bags have been delivered my suite?"

Cielo paused and stared into the middle distance, waiting for a prompt from her earcuff. She nodded.

"If there's anything else you need, feel free to call." She then escorted him to the other end of the atrium, where the walkways split off into several wide corridors that led to the marble staircases up to the stateroom levels.

Laz returned to his handheld, reviewing the map and tracing a path toward his suite. He needed to change into clothes that weren't rumpled and get a dose of motion sickness pills. Half an hour should be enough to put himself together. Transfixed by his screen, Laz absently bumped into another guest, and as he turned, he came face to face with Ava.

"Laz!" she said. "Are you all right?"

He tried to recover his balance with a smile. Ava leaned in for an air kiss, which he received, managing a faint hello in response.

The first thing he noticed was not the deep wells of her hazel eyes, nor the softness of her hands as they landed on his arm. No, it was the smell of lilacs in bloom: crisp, clean, with a sweetness that was barely on this side of cloying. His nose had been so desensitized, enclosed in a vessel of compressed air for the last few hours, that her scent overpowered every sensation.

"I didn't see you on the Excelsior," he said.

"Oh, I arrived a few days ago. I had some business to attend to. Were you headed to your suite?"

"Yes, they've just brought up my luggage and I wanted to—"

"Or we could maybe head back downstairs, see the viewing platform?"

This surprised Laz, who assumed Ava wouldn't want to be so exposed so soon. Save for their small clique, she never held anyone at Rochford in high regard. He would have thought she'd want to avoid all the curious eyes and wagging tongues.

Ava led him back toward the atrium. The two of them walked past half-forgotten faces, names remembered only after some effort. He politely nodded back at those who acknowledged them, trying to ignore the thoughts that nagged at him as they walked: They're judging me. Judging us. The unease almost soured the fact that Ava had let him take her arm.

Laz studied Ava as they moved through the crowd, and if she noticed, she never let on. The eager waves, the air kisses, the let's-catch-up-laters. She was faking it. He wondered what exactly this was supposed to mask. Was it the agony of being among these people, the kids who hated her, now grown into adults who no doubt hated her still? Was it the shame of the divorce? Or was it the shame of being with him?

"This isn't so bad, is it?" he whispered. Ava dropped her head and shot him a look that said, *You can't possibly be serious.* That single glance reminded Laz of how deeply she knew him. Their unspoken bond may have slackened as they aged, but it was still there.

His feelings for her were as strong as they'd been when they were children. The years hadn't changed that either. Through her transition and after, through their short-lived relationship, Ashwin's death, and the varied detours their lives had taken, he always came back to her.

"I heard about Fallon," he said. "I tried to call."

"Sure, yes, of course. I'm sorry, the last few months have been hectic. I meant to get back to you."

"Oh, don't worry about it," he replied, waving it off sheepishly. "You had a lot to deal with."

"I haven't been a good friend to you in a long time, have I?"

"We're here now. That's all that matters." After a while, Laz said, "We should have dinner, get the group back together: you, me, Henry, Sloane. Maybe after the welcome reception?"

"Perfect," Ava replied, more eagerly than he'd anticipated. "We all have much to talk about."

Chapter 3
Twenty-Five Years Ago

No one knew that Ashwin Khan had been murdered
until he had already been missing for two days. In the
grand scheme of things, not such a long period of time,
but the Rochford Institute was a closed environment.
It was fairly easy to spot when one of its students went
missing, but it was fairly difficult to find them. The
campus sat on forty square miles of desert, mountains,
and woods. The boundaries were enclosed and mon-
itored by security pylons, which tracked the comings
and goings of every creature. Within the perimeter,
surveillance drones took to the skies to do periodic
sweeps of the area, while on a level above them, a different type of drone hovered, the ones that blocked spy
sat intrusions.

Security first noticed that Ashwin's badge hadn't
been swiped in at any of his classes. That in itself was
not uncommon for seniors coasting through their final
year, and especially not for this senior, who notoriously
skipped more classes than he attended. But when the
system showed him missing six meals, and no swipes
through any of the building gates for forty-eight hours,
the prefect was alerted. Soon, the entire school learned
that one of their own had gone missing.

The campus-wide announcement went out on a Sunday morning. It was the first time an emergency broadcast had ever gone out to all of Rochford, and Laz didn't understand what was going on at first. He didn't know where the beeping came from, nor what it meant; all he knew was that nothing should have woken him up so early on a weekend.

The holoprojector descended from the ceiling in front of his dorm room bed. The curtains drew open, bringing in the searing light from his east-facing windows that looked out onto arid landscape. He rose sluggishly, and before he could wipe the sleep from his eyes, the headmaster appeared before him. His message was short and simple. Ashwin Khan was missing and students were requested to share any information on his whereabouts. For a fear-stricken moment, Laz thought he heard Ava's name, but a 3D rendering of Ashwin's face corrected him.

Laz was certain that Ashwin probably just bypassed security and was up to no good. Wasn't it only two months ago that he got suspended for disappearing after an ayahuasca trip in the desert? This was the same thing all over again. For all his faults, Ashwin at least knew the outdoors; worst case was he'd be dehydrated or injured, with his comm devices drained and unable to call for help.

Still, he had to check in on Ava. Ashwin was a dick, but he was still her twin brother. The animosity between brother and sister was deep and unhidden, but if her twin was missing, Ava would surely be devastated. Laz never understood why Ava always looked out for him, especially given what he knew about Ashwin's abuses, but he supported her all the same.

Laz called Ava, but her in-room comm went to voice-mail. So did her handheld. She hadn't left any messages for him either. He quickly changed into halfway-decent clothing and headed to her suite. His knocks went un-answered. Though unlikely, he checked next door to see if Ava might have sought comfort from her neighbors. All three of her closest friends—Henry, Sloane, and himself—lived two buildings away, and she might have settled for whomever was close at hand. None of her neighbors had seen her though, not since last night.

Henry found Laz as the latter made his way back to his dorm. Both felt relieved at the sight of the other.

"Ashwin's been missing since Friday, and the security systems haven't been able to find him," Henry said, briefing his friend as they walked. "Rochford kept it under wraps, but it's gotten to the point where they need everyone's help. Have you heard from Sloane?"

"You know the world's dead to him when he's up a cliff face," Laz replied. Those days, odds were low that he'd be in bed past five AM, even on a Sunday. He'd already be out on the crags for his morning rock climb. "What about Ava? I've been trying her, but she's not picking up. It's not like her."

"She's with her parents. They flew in from DC last night," Henry replied. "She's safe, man. She's all right."

"I want to talk to her."

"You will, soon. Right now, we gotta find Sloane so we can get started."

"Get started with what?"

Henry looked at him with chagrin, as though the answer should have been clear as day. "Someone's missing, Laz. We're forming a search party."

Henry took command of the auditorium despite the other adults in the room. The headmaster, the head of security, and several teachers were on hand, but it was Henry whom his classmates listened to. As student council president, he'd been working with the Rochford administration since early that morning to draft an action plan and he implored anyone who had information to come forward. He also encouraged volunteers to join the search-and-rescue party. At that point, he still believed Ashwin to be alive, and he inspired the student body to hold out the same kind of hope. By the time Henry finished his speech, the overall mood had turned from confusion and fear to one of stern determination. More than half of the student body signed up, including everyone who was at the top of their field training classes.

The volunteers were divided into teams and then assigned search grids. For this purpose, the security chief projected a topographical map of the Rochford campus onto the hall screen, zooming in and out of each team's designation. The map also showed a live feed of drone search locations on its outer edges, while the inside areas were partitioned and labeled.

At the northern border of the campus lay the Rochford Flats, a vast salt plain artificially created for the sole purpose of equipping the Institute's students with aerospace skills. Rocketry simulations, land speed tests, and emergency preparedness training were all regularly conducted there. Four teams were needed to cover the area, the hottest and most undesirable of the search grids. Henry's hand was the first to shoot up following the call for volunteers. Always the hero.

Later they would all learn that that Sunday was the hottest on record for 2064, but well before then, Sloane and Laz already begrudged Henry for roping them into his team and then signing up for the most arduous assignment without consulting them.

Sloane drove the buggy to the salt flats. The circuitous route went through narrow desert canyons, all of which he knew from memory, taking much the same route going to his favorite climbs. Laz, with top marks in field training across all modules, rode shotgun, navigating the dash-screen while simultaneously scanning the terrain with his smart goggles. Meanwhile, Henry sat in the back doing coordination and gear check. He should have done so back at the auditorium (what he had begun to call "HQ" and "home base"), but he didn't have time between briefing the other search teams and the security staff.

Laz tried calling Ava again. Still no answer.

He began to wonder whether her parents were holding her captive. Their attitude toward her differed from Ashwin's only in degree, and though they never hurt her the way her brother did, they had hated her ever since she came out. Even in their childhood, when Ashwin hit Ava, berating her for acting soft, her parents never protected her. They explicitly justified Ashwin's treatment as the sort of "character building" that Ava needed. Laz now worried that he and his friends might be looking for the wrong Khan.

The buggy's shades darkened once they reached the salt-white desert. The flatness extended in all directions. It was close to noon by the time they entered their search grid. The heat haze was thick and gave everything in sight a surreal shimmer.

"Maybe we could sweep the grid without leaving the buggy," Laz suggested. Despite the heat and lack of shade, at least the flat terrain had no obstructions for miles. "It'll be a lot faster."

"That would be unfair to the other volunteers who are doing this on foot," Henry replied.

"Plus we might miss something if we stay in here," Sloane said. "Especially if the dusty winds come in."

"There aren't any elevations or crevasses," Laz argued. "Between the three of us, how likely are we to miss anything?"

"Listen to me, bud—Ava will be fine," Henry replied, sensing Laz's true intention. "Ashwin's probably in deep shit and we shouldn't rush this."

Sloane gave Laz a look of reprimand. The decision made, the three friends reviewed their maps again. Once their visors and comms were uplinked, they then set out of the buggy and stepped into the arid white sea.

Rochford's aerospace curriculum gave Laz the best possible simulation of a true Mars training program, not to mention the best chance of being selected for a slot in the off-planet habitats. Alongside World Literature, French, and Inorganic Chemistry, his classes included Astrophysics, Orbital Mechanics, Wilderness Survival, and many others. None of those classes prepared him for this.

The ground crackled underfoot with every step he took in the desolate wastes. The heat stung his skin, and sweat pooled along the outer rim of his goggles. Laz found himself regretting that he was friends with Henry. His heart was always in the right place, but how many times had Henry enlisted Laz to do work that could have been outsourced? All the legislative phone banking last summer, all the extra-credit calibration tests at the gravitation lab, all the school dances Laz had to help organize. Sloane, sweet summer child of the outdoors, had always been the more pliable one, and between his go-along-to-get-along tendency and Henry's leadership skills, Laz shouldn't be surprised that he found himself in full field gear in the middle of the Rochford Flats at high noon looking for the most detestable guy he knew. Not surprised, but resentful all the same.

Sloane estimated that they should cover the whole grid in two excruciating hours. The trio fanned from each other to cover more ground. Their search began silently, each boy engrossed in their displays. Aside from the temperature and air pressure readings, the only objects their scopes picked up were each other and their buggy behind them.

Laz was the first to get bored. Knowing that this quest required eyes and not ears, he was also first to speak up.

"What do you think happened to him?"

Sloane only gave a noncommittal snort. Henry was just as hard to get talking. Ignored, Laz toyed with his own thoughts, theorizing the many different mishaps that might have befallen Ashwin Khan. It wouldn't be unheard of for him to sneak in some outsiders past the security pylons for a weekend bivouac; everybody knew that he hung out with sketchy characters from the nearby town. He and his friends might be camping out here somewhere, naked and passed out in a tent after a heavy night of psychedelics. In any event, they would not be here in the flats. With every passing minute, this assignment seemed more and more futile.

"When was the last time you guys saw him?" Laz asked, a renewed bid for distraction. Henry gave him a sharp look in response, and Laz immediately knew.

Wednesday afternoon. The three of them and Ashwin, behind the Rochford sports arena. The fight was still fresh in their mind, and so was the pain in Laz's own knuckles.

He turned to Sloane, asking if Wednesday was the last time for him too. All three of them hated Ashwin, but Sloane slightly more than the other two. Ashwin always picked on him; beat him up a handful of times too, especially after news broke about Charles III's embezzlement scandal. It was bad enough that Sloane got it at home, with his father's drunken rages worsening as the criminal trial hurtled to its conclusion.

"Think so," Sloane replied with a shrug.

"Must have been Friday for me," Laz said after a pause, turning the question onto himself if only to fill the silence. "Now that I think about it."

Henry stopped in his tracks, and at first Laz thought they saw something in their scanners. "What time Friday?" he asked. "And why didn't you say anything back at HQ?"

"I'm just remembering now," Laz said, wiping the sweat off his brow. "Friday afternoon, right when I got out of Orbital Mechanics."

"I thought the profs said he hasn't been to class since Wednesday?" Henry asked.

"Well, he wasn't in class per se," Laz replied. "He was talking to Ava by the courtyard. Saw them after class was over."

"What time?" Henry asked again.

"Orb Mech ends at four, so around then."

"Don't you also have Orb Mech?" Henry asked Sloane. "Did you see the twins?"

Sloane mustered a half-hearted maybe.

"What do you mean, maybe?"

"Well, yes, I did." Sloane paused, giving Laz a stern look. "She and Ash were arguing."

"We need to tell HQ," Henry said with finality. "As soon as we finish sweeping the area."

"Tell them what exactly?" Laz asked in protest.

"We need to establish a timeline," Henry replied. "Don't you get it?"

The trouble was that Laz did get it, and so did Sloane, and so did Henry. They knew what it meant, to have someone go missing so soon after a fight.

"No, we need to talk to Ava first," Laz said.

Right then, Sloane raised an arm and pointed northward. An object lay about eighty meters from where they stood. The ground was flat and dusty white as far as the eye could see, and the dark, amorphous mound rising from the salt bed was the only thing that interrupted the landscape.

Laz ran first. Scope zoomed in on the mound, he forgot the heat and the stress, speeding toward what he feared he would see. As he drew closer, he saw the hiking boots, then the military-grade tactical pants, then the thick head of jet-black hair.

Ashwin's lifeless face looked ruddy, burnt, in the pale red-brown shade of untreated leather. His lips were cracked, caked with fine grains of salt around the edges. Salt collected, too, on his long eyelashes, like what happens with snow on a frigid winter's day. His eyelids were only half closed, the dark of his eyes peeking through.

Laz thought he might still be alive. He crouched down to feel for a pulse, but Sloane pulled him away. "He's dead."

"And this is a crime scene," Henry added. He pointed toward a band of purpled skin that wrapped all the way around his neck, underneath the red bandana that hung loosely across his chest.

A singular thought came upon them as they all stood there in silence. None of them spoke for what felt like an eternity, mute sentinels towering over the corpse of their enemy. Laz regretted the next words out of his mouth. He would later find that he'd regret those words for the rest of his life.

"What has she done?"

THE HEIGHT OF LUXURY

By Celeste Arnault-Lane

Also appears in the September 2084 issue of *Condé Nast Traveler*

In recent years, space orbitals have formed a new constellation over our skies, and soon, a new star will join the firmament. Opening in the spring of 2085, Space Habitat Altaire promises to bring us to the height of luxury as we've never seen before. The Altaire Group has invited me aboard in advance of its inauguration, and I'm thrilled to report that the world's newest prestige-class orbital is perfection in every way.

The Altaire is what happens when a mega-successful lifestyle and hospitality empire combines forces with the leading name in aerospace, defense, and information security technology. Every detail, from the high-speed shuttle flight to the station's impressive exterior design to the lush resort amenities, showcases the opulence that the Altaire Group is renowned for, paired with the technical expertise of Lonsdale Aerospace.

From the second I stepped foot in its atrium, I could tell that the Altaire was light-years ahead of the orbitals we have now, or any we might have in the near future. The Sky Citadel, having launched three years ago as the first space habitat open to civilians, cannot help but suffer in comparison to the Altaire's sheer size: it holds 225 executive-class, four-room suites (no cramped cabins here!), four Michelin-rated restaurants, nine bars and lounges, and an entire wellness complex, complete with two gyms, steam rooms and saunas, a thermal suite and a cold suite, a spa pool, and skin and muscle treatment salons.

My personal favorite: the Moon Pools, a lunar paradise where I had the pleasure of bathing under the moonlight. Here is where you really see the perfect marriage of the Altaire Group and Lonsdale Aerospace. I could scarcely believe how the physics of water works in space, let alone seven large pools simulated to look like lunar craters. If anyone can do it, certainly the people responsible for providing water to our Martian settlements can!

I was joined on my tour by Academy Award–winning actress Xiomara Harris, who recently inked a multiyear, multimillion brand partnership with the Altaire, the biggest endorsement deal on the planet and beyond. What follows is a condensed version of our conversation.

First of all, congratulations! How does it feel to be the face of the Altaire?

Thank you, it has been exhilarating! For ages, I've been waiting for the Altaire to get built, along with the rest of the world, of course. I only ever dreamed of being able to visit, so to be its brand ambassador is definitely a dream come true. I've been in sci-fi blockbusters before, and I've stayed at ultra-luxury hotels all over the world, but this place is beyond anything I've ever experienced. I still pinch myself sometimes!

What's your favorite part of the station?

The Floating Gardens, for sure. It's such a sight to behold, all those tropical plants floating among the stars. Since we haven't officially opened yet, I get to spend some alone time there, and it is transcendental.

What about less solitary activities? Which ones do you enjoy the most?

The spa. (laughs) The massage therapists here are the best, and the gravity differential is like magic on my muscles. I've also enjoyed seeing the dress rehearsals of our theater troupes; we're really giving Broadway a run for its money. I think our guests will be wowed by our revival of *The Phantom of the Opera*.

Speaking of wow, let's talk about the spacewalks.

Yes! Have you gone? There's no feeling like looking down on Earth and seeing the world from that point of view. Some have said it's a religious experience. I'm an atheist, but I can relate. Plus it's perfect for raising those MERIT (Mars Emigration and Resettlement Index of Trait) scores. That's another thing that sets the Altaire apart from the rest: unless you're an astronaut or have your own aerospace company, you can't do a spacewalk or a shuttle ride anywhere else.

The Altaire truly is a jumping-off point for Mars.

It's not just luxe, life-changing experiences that we provide, we also present an opportunity to boost your Mars applications. Visiting the station and using our amenities can help with one's points for space-worthiness. That's another thing that makes the Altaire unique.

Not to mention this station's pedigree.

Absolutely. Lonsdale Aerospace was among the first companies to build the Mars settlements in the late seventies, and they built almost all the ones still standing now. The Altaire Group designed the habitats used by not only American astronauts, but all astronauts living there. And so this resort that we're in, this is what life on Mars will be. In a few years, the first civilian settlements will open, and there's no better preview than a stay at the Altaire.

Hollywood's still quite divided on Mars. Your former co-star Trey Brockburn recently came under fire for comments about the Altaire, saying it provides a loophole to the MERIT system and that he hopes the station "sinks just like the Titanic." What do you say to him, and to others who might feel the same?

Trey and I are old friends. We haven't spoken in a while, but I'd like to think that he was speaking out of misinformation. I'm sure he regretted those comments.

The Titanic reference isn't new; they've been saying that about the Sky Citadel and Wonderland. I suppose it's a bigger deal now because the Altaire is a much bigger deal. I like to think that the Altaire is more like the Mayflower. It's a way that we can ensure the safety and prosperity—the future—of humankind, using the best technologies that we have. I'm all for Mars. It's where we belong, with the stars.

For those who still have some doubts about the station, let's talk sustainability.

The Altaire is very green: ninety percent of its power is provided by solar energy; those are all the mirrors you see on the station's spokes. Half the materials used to build this superstructure was mined from the Moon: titanium, aluminum, iron. Water is still imported from Earth but it's recycled and purified in the same way as the Mars habitats. We grow our own vegetables, fruits, and herbs in a cutting-edge hydroponics facility, which is also the largest that's ever been built in space. Because of superior technology, this station is more energy efficient than most hotels and cruise liners on Earth.

Even the interiors are sustainable. I was told that the faux fireplace mantel in my suite was made of wood from Venetian piers.

Yes, we use reclaimed materials wherever we can. Every suite has moldings and decor and furniture with a rich history to them.

The station's fully booked through 2086, and people are dying to know: Who's among the first on the guest list?

For the opening, we have a few heads of state, including the president, a couple of crown royals too. The UN Mars Settlement Agency will have a sizeable contingent as well. Of course, the biggest names in global entertainment will be there too, but I can't name names just yet.

What's next for you?

I have some film projects lined up, but it's mostly the Altaire for the foreseeable future. The inauguration and the first few years will keep me quite busy. Besides, I can't really plan too far ahead, with Mars applications opening up. Hopefully, in five years I'll have enough points to qualify for a residence there, and then I'll get to have an early retirement someplace as grand as the Altaire.

Chapter 4
The View from Downstairs

This is how a single grain of rice makes it to space: It grows from mud, maybe in Assam, or Gansu, or Ifugao, the seedling doesn't know where, or care. As long as it survives the drought, or the typhoon, or the pestilence, or all three, if it's a particularly bad season. Once the stalks grow tall and laden, the harvester rips them out of the soil to be threshed. In some places this is still done by hand, farmers flinging their bundles against the ground to separate the grain to be brought into the mill to dry. The huller follows, another separation, another stripping, this time the husk from the kernel. Along with the rest of the harvest, the grain is graded, the first of many times in its short life. Have the grains been damaged in the threshing, in the drying, in transport? Have the husks been removed completely? The grading continues after packaging, at every loading dock, where one sack out of many is torn open for inspection. Are the kernels the right color, chalky, broken? Have they been mixed in with other varieties? Because this shipment is for the ports in Jeddah or Rotterdam, and they want this kind, or that; no long grain for this market, only long grain for the other. Weighed and measured at every stage, from the dockyards to the warehouses for distribution, the bags found wanting cast off, if not sold at a deep discount. The best ones go to the specialty purveyors, who send them off to the palace complexes, the restaurant conglomerates, to the launchpads that load them onto supply shuttles for the resort orbitals. Another inspection, another grading. Are these pallets all rice, and nothing more? Has millet been mixed in somehow? Probably not, as the shipment comes from a trusted supplier, but the ground crew still needs to check. After all the prying eyes are satisfied, it is time for liftoff. Close to the end of this arduous journey, the kernel faces its last grading by the sushi chef running the grains through his fingers. He inhales the scent. Yes, *this* is the premium rice we asked for. On to the cooker with a bit of sugar, salt, vinegar, and then formed into mounds under a thin cut of raw fish, only to be quickly dunked into a pool of soy sauce and popped into the mouth of a guest, untasted, undifferentiated from all the other grains and textures and flavors. Then shat out into a toilet and into space.

Most days felt like that to Cielo Mallari. A series of measurements, an unceasing gauntlet of tests to prove her worth, only to pass unappreciated. Then, she gets to do it all over again the next day and the next, and the next. That Friday morning was no different.

She started her day in a haze. Her wake-up call sounded louder than usual: she'd forgotten to take off her earcuff after the previous day's twelve-hour shift. She'd also fallen asleep wearing her uniform. At least she'd managed to take her shoes off.

Station time: 5:01 a.m., said the earcuff's monotone voice. Four hours' sleep should be enough, she thought as she felt her way to the bathroom, her eyes still adjusting to the dark and windowless cabin.

The day's schedule scrolled on her mirror, asking her to confirm receipt. She pressed the glowing green check mark without giving the timetable a read. She knew what it said—the same thing it had always said since the start of her contract term. Staff scrum, desk duties, concierge services, guest activities, and special events. Two fifteen-minute breaks, a half-hour lunch. She knew the drill and what she didn't know, she'd catch up on later.

After four years on this station, days and nights and shifts had completely melded into one another. An endless cycle of groundhog days. Yet she had much to be grateful for. Her quick promotion to head of Guest Relations afforded her some comforts. For one, she no longer had to sleep in a bunk bed, sharing a cabin with three other staffers (though her bathroom was still cramped, and she still had to shower on top of the toilet). She also got direct interaction with guests and spent more time on the suite floors instead of the hub of the Altaire, where the lower gravity never quite agreed with her. The bump in pay was nice too: five percent was five percent.

As she took the lift from the hub to the hotel level, she thought of those comforts, plastering on a smile that she would have to wear for the next twelve-hour shift.

For a variety of reasons, she'd been looking forward to the Rochford reunion since it was booked. It was her first exclusive event since the promotion, and the full buyout of the Altaire meant that she had fewer guests than usual to attend to. They expected 242 guests all told, which included the Rochford alumni and their plus-ones. Each alum also had an allotment for "personal staff" who would be staying in the staff bedrooms on the upper torus. For some this meant their executive assistant, or their nurse. For a couple of guests, the slot went to a "blood boy," from whom they harvested rejuvenating transfusions of young blood. For others, this meant the third in a romantic triad, but for most, this was for the guests' security detail. As though the Altaire didn't have enough already.

Still, that number was only about half of the Altaire's guest capacity. And the best part about it: no children. An all-adult weekend came with obvious hazards, and these exclusive events tended to spiral out of control, but grown-ups Cielo knew how to handle, even if they were of this particular kind.

The rare gift of being overstaffed allowed Cielo to assign each guest their own dedicated Altaire liaison from the station staff and crew. Rochford and the Altaire head office gave Cielo dossiers containing guest bios, food preferences, special requests, and medical information, and she made sure that the matches were perfect.

Which is how she ended up with Tom Lazaro III.

After the ambassador cut his private tour short and headed to his suite, Cielo returned to the welcome lobby. Most of the new arrivals and their Altaire liaisons had begun their own tours. She approached one of the crewmen still waiting for his guests.

"They haven't come up yet?" she asked the younger man.

"Yes, they have, ma'am," he replied, then pointed out the Gallagher couple as they paraded amidst the crowd. "But they're busy right now. I'll wrangle them soon."

"I told you to stop it with the 'ma'am'."

"Sorry, force of habit."

Ordinarily, Deck Engineer Machinist Second-Class Pio Asuncion would be in the bowels of the engine rooms, maintaining the solar inverters or the radiation shielding. This weekend the young man was essentially a valet. A gofer. He still kept his rank, of course; VIPs liked it when their help bore stripes. It made them feel more special.

Pio turned to Cielo excitedly, "I saw one of them's Filipino."

"Yeah, an ambassador. I'm handling him myself. He's one of the Lazaros, major donors and close family friends with the US president. His lolo was a senator before he got dementia, and now his dad's in Congress."

"Wow, political dynasty. How very Pinoy," he joked.

"They've been in America for decades, but some things never change. Doesn't matter where you build your power or how, you gotta keep it in the family at all costs."

"Well, what do you think of him?"

"We've all seen their dossiers," she answered. "You know what I think."

"Yes, but now you've talked to him."

Cielo pursed her lips as though tasting something pungent. "This one is uneasy with himself. He treats the staff the way he thinks we like to be treated. Too ingratiating. But the entire time we walked around the lobby, he looked like he was ready to jump out of his skin."

"Ah, one of those."

"He exudes that fake warmth from being our kababayan," she continued. "You know the type. He's trying to relate to us, but you can clearly see the fear. Fear that he'll be thought of the same as us."

"Well, he is."

Cielo knew what he meant, but in truth, she and the ambassador were worlds apart. She did the math herself when she saw Tom Lazaro's dossier and his MERIT score. They were in the same age group, and both had no health, genetic or fertility issues. Yet their similarities ended there. All her aerospace training, licenses, and work experience were worthless because they were obtained through a staff training program, which were exempt from the MERIT score system. It didn't matter that she had everything that Mars needed in a new settler. She was the help, and the system was never meant to help the help.

"No, Pio. You and I are the same. He is one of them," Cielo said firmly. Whatever empathy or goodwill the young machinist might feel toward this guest needed to be choked in the cradle. "And to them, you and I and everyone else in uniform are the same. That's how you should see them too. It doesn't matter how he looks or talks or acts. There are sides, and Tom Lazaro doesn't get to straddle both. No one does."

Pio nodded, his pensive eyes cast toward the guests filing out of the welcome lobby, their mouths agape at the marvels in the atrium. Once the crowd had thinned, he took the chance to check in.

"Did Benita make it?" he whispered to Cielo.

"Yes. With some of the relief crew and the actors for the show. But the full shipment didn't make it."

"What? How much then?"

"One crate. But we'll make it work."

"How?" Pio asked, his panic palpable.

Cielo shared the same fear that showed on the young man's face, but she couldn't afford to let hers show. Fear breeds mistakes, and she'd promised herself that Pio would make it through this unharmed. She'd uphold that promise, even if it required the occasional lie.

"I'll think of something," she told him. "We'll have a new plan before the night is over. For now, you just take care of your part."

Before Pio could respond, Cielo gave him a reassuring nudge toward the Gallaghers, who had by then found themselves in a quiet, unguarded moment.

"Make sure everyone thoroughly enjoys themselves, you hear?"

"I'll do my best."

"Remember: ignorance is bliss . . ."

"Yeah, yeah," he replied, waving her off as he walked away. "And bliss is ignorance."

Chapter 5
Grand Designs

When they reached the Gallaghers' suite, Pio pointed to Henry's forearm, reminding him of his implant. "It transmits a signal unique to each passenger," the valet explained. "So no need for keys or cards or magic words." Henry waved his arm over the access panel, and the chrome double doors slid open.

Beyond the opulent interiors, the mahogany credenza, the supple leather of the couches and chaises longues, the curio table and the objets d'art cluttered over it, a glass wall spanned an entire length of the suite, showing an endless vista of stars. Nick walked toward the edge, ensorcelled by the million pinpricks of light that shone down on them.

"You have completely undersold this experience, Mr. Gallagher."

"I'm glad you like it, Mr. Gallagher."

"Why did I wait to do this again?"

"You were too busy with world domination."

"Yes, but this . . . you should have taken me sooner," Nick replied, a rare expression of awe on his face.

Henry himself had almost forgotten how it felt, looking out at the stars from space for the first time. The decades had done its work in flattening the memory, but he now found it revitalized as he watched Nick's own wonderment. Henry pulled his husband closer and rested his head on his.

Pio cleared his throat, bursting their bubble of bliss. "Shall I start putting away your luggage?"

"Yes, but no need to open them," Nick responded, untangling himself from Henry. He ordered the valet around the suite, directing where each suitcase was to be laid out for the couple to unpack later.

"He can do all that for us, you know. That's what he's here for," Henry whispered.

"I don't want some stranger pawing through our stuff."

Once he was done situating the suitcases, Nick dismissed the valet, reminding him to return shortly before they needed to dress for the cocktail hour.

Henry tried to bring Nick back to their view of the stars, attempting to prolong their shared experience of wonder. He spotted at a constellation and rattled on about it. "You should take a closer look," he said encouragingly, pointing to an ornate standing telescope on the far corner of the den. An obvious antique, although it probably still functioned.

Nick sauntered toward it, on his way running his hand over the fireplace mantle. He assessed the holographic flame, tilting his head in approval as the fake wood crackled and set off lifelike sparks. The room smelled of hickory. Nick cupped the tube of the telescope and bent over the eyepiece. He had scarcely begun to appreciate the view when an incoming message beeped in his earcuff.

The den brightened as the suite's holoprojector came to life. Threads of light flickered to form a simulacrum of a woman wearing a flowing gold gown and an enticing smile.

"Good day, Mr. and Mr. Gallagher. I am Xiomara Harris, and on behalf of the entire staff and crew, I welcome you aboard the Space Habitat Altaire." The holo-woman then delivered her spiel of announcements: event schedules, the station's various amenities, safety information. After a while, Nick asked it to pause.

"What a personal welcome," he said with sarcasm.

"I'm sure she's busy," Henry replied. "She'll come by soon, I expect."

"She wouldn't be here if it weren't for us, you know."

Henry braced himself for another one of Nick's monologues about the lengths he goes to for his clients. How he plucked the aging model-actress from near oblivion, how he revived her career with art house films and summer blockbusters. How he lobbied with the Altaire Group to make her the face of the finest luxury orbital the world had ever seen.

"Don't get started," Henry warned. "We both know you weren't doing it out of altruism."

Nick scoffed, staring into the hologram's frozen, dead eyes. "Sure, everybody got something in the end. That's the way of the world," he conceded. "A show of gratitude would be nice, is all."

"We'll see her soon enough, and then you'll get the groveling you so desire."

Nick tut-tutted, finally shutting off the holoprojector. "Speaking of groveling, will you now tell me what your plans are with the Architect?"

Henry groaned.

"I've gotten us invited to the Captain's Table to-night," Nick continued. "But you can't expect to wheel and deal over dinner like that. You'll still need a private audience."

"And I shall have it," Henry replied. "You're not the only one with strings to pull."

"Oh, I know you have strings. It's your reticence to pull on them that needs improvement."

"Fine. If you must know, Tobias Coen was in fact my first order of business," Henry explained. "I'm supposed to see him within the hour. Happy?"

"Extremely. Where? And how?"

"We'll have to change early for the welcome reception," Henry replied. "We need to make a quick stop on the way."

Nick's excitement was palpable. "Remember what we talked about. Lay the groundwork, make him see sense. He's our best chance at a secured spot."

"I know."

"You have to make this happen."

"You don't have to keep reminding me."

"Of course, I'm sorry," Nick replied. "The pressure is getting to me, per usual. The more points we gather, the closer it feels, and I can taste it. It would be a waste to have done all this only to be disqualified."

That last word landed with a thud, as intended. Points be damned, they both understood that if they were shut out of Mars, it would not be because Nick went to the wrong schools and pursued the wrong career. It would be because of Henry. He was the reason they needed to bypass the MERIT system altogether, and he thus had no choice but to obey his husband.

The helm of the Altaire looked less like a navigational flight deck than a military war room. Floating screens lined the long oval room on all sides, displaying star maps and satellite charts, as well as video feeds of every angle of the station's exterior. A sophisticated security module, set apart in a glass-enclosed alcove, showed multilayer surveillance of the station's interior in an array of high-definition grids.

"Mr. and Mr. Gallagher, welcome to the bridge," greeted Captain Edmonia Williams as the Gallaghers arrived. "It's nice to see you again."

The captain cut an imposing figure in her officer's whites, and despite years of running a luxury orbital, she still retained a naval commander's bearing. Yet she'd also found ways to adapt to her civilian role. She knew how to hobnob with the elite, and she understood the nature of her duties to these guests in particular.

"Thank you for spending some time with us," Nick replied as he shook her hand. "And I'm sorry to hear about your mother's passing. Henry tells me she was quite the individual. His favorite professor."

"A mentor, really. The most generous soul you could ever meet," Henry added, to the captain's clear appreciation.

She escorted the couple to the far end of the bridge, up a staircase that led to her office, a glass-enclosed room with a mezzanine platform that overlooked the command center. She pointed out which things did what, how each component and crew member made the Altaire run. Henry nodded knowingly, piping in here and there to explain terms for his husband.

"Quite the operation you have here," Nick told the captain.

"Yes, it's impressive, isn't it?" replied a booming voice from behind the trio. All three immediately knew who it was.

The white-haired man stood by the door, chin held high and back straightened. He clasped his hands in front of him like a tenor about to begin an aria. On his aquiline nose rested a pair of gold-rimmed spectacles, an outmoded device that seemed more like affectation than an actual aid for sight. The old man stepped into the room without waiting for an invitation, and Captain Williams rushed to the man's side, as though catching him from a fall.

"What a lovely surprise, Mr. Coen. I'm sure you know Henry and Nicholas Gallagher?" she asked.

"We've met."

"Last summer, if memory serves," Nick added, extending a hand. "At that wildfire fundraiser in New York."

"And your husband more than once after that," he replied flatly.

Henry cleared his throat. "It's good to see you again, Tobias."

"Well, I suppose I don't have to tell you," the captain told the Gallaghers, gesturing at the view beyond the glass, "That all of this is only possible because of the Architect."

"Indeed," Nick replied with awe. "I'm so honored to be here in the heart of your creation."

Henry beamed at how well his husband hid his distaste. Coen was an engineer, and Nick found it unbearably pretentious to adorn the position with a self-appointed title that connoted artisanship. Quite often he remarked that Coen was little more than a mechanic.

"Yes, the Altaire is truly magnificent," Henry added.

Coen bowed at this politely and assumed one of the seats in front of the captain's command module, a half-moon array of screens that doubled as her desk. The Gallaghers' casual drop-in with the captain now gained a weighty air. More pleasantries were exchanged, inquiries about everyone's shuttle trip up, the typical post-boarding fodder. With a subtle lift of his brow, Henry told Nick what to do.

"Captain, I was wondering if you could indulge me in a small request," Nick said when he found a moment. "Might I use one of your communications consoles? I'd simply love to make a vidcall to my mother from the bridge of the Altaire."

The captain initially seemed bemused by the request, but at Nick's mention of his mother, she was ready to oblige. With a permissive wave of Coen's hand, Captain Williams left with Nick, telling the two men to help themselves to a drink.

The last time Henry was alone in a room with Coen, the old man seemed cool to his offer. It was in poor taste, of course, this quid pro quo of swaying the organ donor board in favor of Coen's ailing son, but the Architect didn't reject it outright. Coen knows how things get done, Henry told himself. One does not get to where he is without these kinds of transactions.

"I've given it more thought," the old man started as soon as the captain's door slid shut. "And I don't want to waste any more of your time. The answer is no."

"It's only been a few weeks, Tobias. It hasn't been a waste at all." Henry walked to the bar and surveyed the selections. His fingers danced around the bottles of brandy and rum before landing on a decanter of whiskey. He sniffed its contents. Japanese, if he had to guess.

"Single or double?"

"Pass," Coen replied. "On both the drink and the offer."

Henry poured himself a double. "I appreciate you keeping up appearances before the captain. It wouldn't do well for either of us to appear quite so . . . familiar."

"Well, you know what they say about familiarity."

Resistance is good, Henry thought. A lot better than outright apathy. Resistance meant the argument could yet be won. He slid his armchair closer to Coen. "I hear plans for the next orbital station are going very well. The first one over the Martian skies. How much longer until the Altaire Group gets approval?"

"Before the year ends, if all goes to plan."

"Such a shame you can't be there for the grand opening," Henry said. "But of course, family comes first."

Coen bristled. Henry left the suggestion hanging. Let the man take the lead. He was looking to be persuaded. Why else would he be here?

"Leighton's doing fine, by the way," the old man replied. "Not that you asked."

"I didn't have to. I've been paying close attention to your son's case. I'm glad he's doing better, despite his latest prognosis."

Coen considered this and continued after a pause. "I don't see what it is you think I can credibly deliver."

"All I ask is your best effort."

"I don't decide these things. I merely design them."

Is that what the old man needed, some flattery? That, Henry could handle. "Your designs made it possible for humans to live comfortably on Mars. The MSA might be the one officially deciding the applications, but the Altaire Group, Lonsdale Aerospace, every other outfit building the actual settlements—they all rely on your genius. I refuse to believe that your word could be impotent, when you can transform an entire planet at your will. That kind of power, why, it's nothing short of godlike."

Coen chuckled, pleased but not surprised. No doubt he'd received such adulation before. "What really nags at me is—why?" he asked. "You're not the only one paying attention, Henry. I know your MERIT scores, and your husband's too. Where your points stand, it doesn't matter how many millions apply. You're getting in, and even if you don't get selected in the initial round, your wait won't be long."

"We know the scores are great, but we don't want to risk it," Henry replied. "We want to be there first, and if there's any way we can be guaranteed—"

"Outside the usual channels."

"—outside the usual channels, then we'd be foolish not to take the chance." Henry took a sip of his drink. Coen all but acknowledged that workarounds exist, and implied that he might be one. This was progress.

Henry set down the lowball glass and stared directly into the old man's eyes. "However egalitarian the MERIT system claims to be, Nick and I are still at a disadvantage as a couple who can't have kids," he explained. "That's not fair, is it? Merely populating a new planet shouldn't be the be-all and end-all. And Nick's

Tier C status isn't fair either. Artists are just as valuable to society as doctors."

"We all know the system's flawed," Coen replied sympathetically. "But it's the least flawed a system we can make. Every person can and will find a cause for unfairness or a reason to claim exception. That's the nature of hard lines."

"You've seen the scores. We're more than qualified. So what's the harm in making sure we get what we deserve?"

"Ah, but it's not a question of harm, is it?" Coen replied. "And it's not about taking spots from someone more deserving. You're almost guaranteed to get approved. No, there's something else at play here, and I'm not in the habit of making decisions without the full picture."

"And I'm not in the habit of accepting less than perfect odds," he replied. "I've told you everything. We just need an extra push to overcome Nick's deficit and the gay penalty. That's it. There's nothing else."

Coen leaned back on his chair, giving Henry a once-over. "You know, some would call this extortion."

Henry scoffed. "That's such an ugly word. Inaccurate too. This is a negotiation. We're just trying to see how we could help each other. It's a win-win, no commitments. Your best effort is all I ask. Mine is all I offer."

"You're getting a lot more out of this than I am."

"Well, I wouldn't devalue Leighton's life quite so cavalierly."

"You said it yourself, my word can transform planets. If I'm as powerful as you think I am, my guarantee is worth more than yours, no matter your connections to the organ registry system."

"We each have our spheres of influence, Tobias. Mine might be smaller than yours, but it's the one that could save your son."

"Because I know you, and your father and grandmother before you, I'll be generous and believe that you didn't mean that as a threat," Coen said. "But be careful, young man. You are treading on thin ice."

"I don't make threats, Tobias. But I do carry out my plans."

With some effort, Coen pushed himself to stand.

"You called me a god," he said as he walked away. "And by your terms, then you should know: what a god can grant he can just as easily withhold."

Chapter 6
Risk and Reward

The Altaire's casino level was a gambler's paradise, and as someone who made his fortune with daring and a little bit of luck, Sloane felt right at home. In the flashing lights, the bells and whistles, the riffling of the cards before they were fanned out on the felt, he saw a wealth of opportunity, not only at the bets stacked on the tables, but at the bodies warming the stools. If he made the right moves, he could walk away with a windfall.

He stopped by one of the roulette tables, manned by a virtual croupier with robotic appendages. He summoned for some chips and placed a tall stack on thirteen, black. When the rest of the table finished placing their bets, the wheel began to turn. The croupier's articulated digits flung the metal sphere along the edge of the wheel, spinning rapidly past a blur of numbers that spun the opposite way. Black, red, black, red, black, red. The wheel slowed to a stop. The croupier called it.

Seven, red.

A man collected his chips on the other side of the wheel. "Better luck next time," he told Sloane.

He had readied a playful retort but then recognition dawned on him. The big winner was no other than Chris Sorrentino, all-around douchebag who, last he'd heard, recently inherited his father's sports media conglomerate. Sloane rolled his eyes.

"How've you been, Sloane?" Sorrentino said in a tone that belied his disinterest in the response. He took him in from head to toe. "You've changed quite a bit, haven't you?"

"Wish I could say the same about you."

"Guess it's not just your duds that got sharper," Sorrentino sneered. "I'd steer clear of the casino if I were you. Pit bosses don't like cheats."

The others gathered around them snickered. Sloane recognized all of them, the older, pudgier versions of his contemporaries who once respected him, even admired him for his athleticism and his good name. For as long as it remained good, that is.

"That's Sloane the Third you're thinking of," he replied.

Sorrentino leaned in, teeth bared. "Like father, like son."

"Well, your dad was a fool who got bilked out of billions, so what does that make you?"

The gasps from the crowd gave Sloane a sublime thrill. As he walked away victorious, he took the ornate steel tube of a pendant that hung on a long chain around his neck. He jammed it onto his forearm and the concealed cartridge hissed on contact.

He located the casino bar and ordered an Armagnac, neat. The bartender obliged, bringing his drink in a tulip glass on a floating tray.

"You don't waste any time, do you?" a voice from behind him said.

"Vita brevis," Sloane replied, raising his glass toward Laz. He wore a satiny tangerine jacket, which, under the sparkling displays of the machines around them, gave Sloane a buzzing headache. The heady mix of brandy in his gullet and star mist in his bloodstream didn't help. "Please don't be a scold. It's a party."

"I have to warn you—if you get into another one of your scrapes, I don't have jurisdiction in space to bail you out."

"Oh, I'm sure you can talk your way out of anything, Laz."

His old friend had turned a bit salt-and-pepper since Sloane saw him last, three years ago, down at his posting in Chile. Sloane had been on one of his jaunts in Valparaiso with the governor's daughter, Claudia something or other. She was fun, the type who got tangled up in diplomatic incidents even as the country was embroiled in its third coup in the last decade. How were they to know that the handsy lecher at that palace cocktail party was a military attaché? The pervert was lucky she and Sloane only threw their drinks at his face. That he then slipped on the marble and split his skull open was his own fault.

"How are things down at the banana republic?" Sloane asked Laz.

"Good. It's been two hundred and sixty-one days since our last coup."

"That's gotta be a record."

Laz asked the bartender for a glass of Syrah from an obscure vintner. Chilean, if Sloane had to bet, to support the local economy. Laz had always been painfully earnest like that. It could be endearing, if Sloane weren't such a cynic.

"I'm just glad things aren't as rocky as they used to be," Laz continued.

"Sure. Until another upstart general gets ideas."

"It's the farmers I'm more worried about. The water reserves are dwindling faster than our desalinators can replenish them, and the natives are getting restless."

Laz droned on about water imports and American aid policy, bureaucratic red tape and hydrocartels, which Sloane might have found mildly interesting, but he had other things on his mind. Where is Julian and why hasn't he been answering his messages? He checked his wristband again. Nothing.

As Laz explained soil degradation in the Colchagua Valley, an Altaire staffer approached, informing him that they've readied the secure satlink in the station's boardroom, which had also been reserved for his exclusive use.

"There's a developing situation in Santiago," Laz told Sloane. "The President wants me camera ready in case shit goes down."

"A boardroom seems excessive, but it's a good thing you have the inside track with the crew."

"Ah, it's nothing. They aim to please."

"Don't tell me they haven't given you special treatment," Sloane smirked. "Or that you haven't exploited the connection for some prime access. You know, speak to them in Tagalog, banter about the homeland, then ask for private time in the Moon Pools . . ."

"Come on, you know I'm not like that."

Sloane gave Laz an incredulous smile that faded once he realized his friend's seriousness. Laz didn't actually believe this, did he? True, he built his career as a diplomat right out of Yale, top grades and all, but no one receives a plum posting at the age of thirty-six. A backwater island nation maybe, and even then, those ambassadorships go to fat-cat campaign donors who want to retire somewhere warm. No, he got his post exactly "like that." Maybe not on his own doing, most certainly his parents', but Laz couldn't possibly think he wasn't the type to leverage connections to gain an advantage.

"Now that," Laz said, nodding toward a couple walking down a staircase. "That is special treatment."

Sloane first noticed the statuesque woman in a gown of gold brocade, its embellishments reminding him of gilded ivy. Xiomara Harris stood high above the crowd, her hair swept to one side like a dark cascade. The guests fawned over the actress, a goddess among her devotees.

Right next to her, in an impeccably cut tuxedo, was Julian Lonsdale.

Despite his frustration at the wait, Sloane felt equally ecstatic at the sight of him. The two of them hadn't been in the same room together, not since last year, when Julian invited him to dinner in London. Sloane had just been referred to him by one of his defense contractor buddies, and Julian needed to assess whether Sloane would suit his specific needs. Over a dinner of port and stuffed fowl, they revealed to each other their predilections, which aligned perfectly. By the third course, they settled on the terms, the most essential of which was no physical contact. Sloane demanded it. Keeping clients at arm's length minimized risks. The rule benefited Julian too, for obvious reasons.

Thus it was decided: no in-person meets, encrypted channels only.

Julian's insistence that they meet on the Altaire was a serious breach of their terms. Being in the same space presented risks, Sloane reminded him, not the least of which was the possibility of being discovered. Yet Julian made it worth his while to the tune of a million-dollar bonus.

"There's a legion of crewmembers on this station," Laz continued, oblivious. "And we each get one personal liaison. But Julian Lonsdale gets Xiomara Harris in addition to his valet, and he didn't even go to Rochford!"

Sloane nodded absent-mindedly, his eyes trained on Julian as he approached a baccarat table, where his wife Isobel was playing. She gave him a quick peck on the cheek. As she did, Sloane spotted that Julian had his earcuff on.

"Not that I'm complaining," Laz went on. "I'm just glad to have the free trip. The five points are gonna go a long way."

This fucking guy.

"Like it matters that the trip is free," Sloane snapped. "We both know you didn't need a handout to get on this station, and you don't need the points either."

"Whoa, easy," Laz said, palms upturned. "I'm just saying."

"I'm sick of your down-home folksy crap. Why can't you be real for once, huh?"

"Look, I don't know what you're on, but maybe you should slow it down, yeah?"

"This earnest act might work down there in your South American fiefdom, but I know you, Laz, and I see right through you."

"Yeah, and what about you? This . . . persona that you've crafted?" said Laz. "You can play the wild child party boy all you want, give the people something else to talk about, but I know who you are."

"You don't get to judge me or what I do."

"Oh, that cuts both ways, buddy," Laz replied, pointing with his drink in hand. "Especially after what we've done."

Sloane raised a hand, sending the wine glass flying into the air. It shattered it into a million jagged shards, the noise in the gambling hall barely masking the crash. Laz stared at him in shock, but the longer Sloane stood there, himself startled by his actions, his friend's expression transformed into one that he knew all too well: pity.

"Fuck you," Sloane said. He again jammed the pendant against his forearm and stormed off, crushing the shards of glass under the soles of his heels.

Sloane found himself an alcove off a low-traffic hallway, out of sight of the casino and the crowd that had witnessed his clumsy display. From his corner, Sloane spied that Julian had taken the seat next to his wife. He channeled his energy into the next lines he planned to say, and by the time Julian finally picked up his call, he was on fire.

"How dare you keep me waiting, you worthless piece of shit?" he asked through gritted teeth. "Where's my fucking money?"

Julian tilted his head uncomfortably. To the people around him, he appeared otherwise focused on the cards in his hand and not Sloane's voice piped into his earcuff.

"I am watching you, pig. You better get yourself away from those bitches and get me my money right fucking now."

Julian's lip curled, and then he swiveled around. Sloane felt a thrill. He pushed further.

"Listen, you disgusting bag of filth," Sloane snarled, "you're gonna do as I say and you're gonna do it now. You're gonna stand up, and you're gonna head to my suite."

The reason that the arrangement worked, and will continue to work, was because Sloane knew Julian. The whole business of milking someone for money and having them enjoy it came down to two things: fear and desire. On both counts, Sloane knew his client. He never said it, and never would admit it, but Julian had a debilitating fear of causing the downfall of the Lonsdale empire. In that same fear lay Julian's desire.

With enough experience, any dominant could have discovered this about him. A seasoned pro knew how to convert that inexorable mix of dread and desire into profit, a balm sold to the client to soothe their greatest anxiety: *Lose it now, see how it feels now, and know that it won't happen. Not really. It can't happen, not here. Here, you are in control.*

Julian shifted in his seat and signaled to the dealer. The robot dealt him another hand. Julian subtly scanned the crowds until finally he caught a glimpse of Sloane. He placed a larger bet on the table.

"You miserable piece of shit, I will destroy you. I am going to walk up to you, right this second, and I will blow up your entire fucking life."

Sloane had used the threat once or twice before, and it had always been hollow, but never before had the two of them been in public, and with his wife present too. Sloane hoped that this gave his words more force, or at least caused Julian to become more excited.

See, Sloane was not just any other dom. He and Julian had a shared history. The Lonsdales and the Sloanes were close business allies, once upon a time. The families attended the same functions, went on the same holidays and company retreats. They often summered together, either at the Lonsdales' palazzo in Capri, or the Sloanes' private island in French Polynesia. That history gave Julian a certain confidence that his arrangement with Sloane would be kept secret.

"I've had others before, and they were all discreet," he told Sloane during that first meeting. "But it's not enough that my dom's reputation and livelihood relies on discretion. I need someone who's part of the circle. One of us."

More than trust, the shared history also gave Julian a tantalizing reversal of power dynamics, one based not on their wealth, but on physical athleticism. As with many others with aspirations of Mars, he and Sloane were expert rock climbers. But while Sloane was summiting peaks with raw skill and natural talent, Julian did so with the assistance of coaches and aides and tech and prototype gear and every advantage his parents could afford. Yet despite those boons, Julian never came close to Sloane's skill, who completed the Seven Summits in his freshman year at Rochford. He won the World Climbing Championships in both lead and bouldering by the time he was a junior, and was guaranteed a spot on the US Olympic team. If his father hadn't messed up his life, Sloane would have gone to the 2064 Games in Istanbul and swept all the climbing events.

Julian craved to be dominated by someone who had actually bested him, and being a sub would only be worth it if he could feel, in some profound way, inferior. With his status and privilege, very few people could do that. Sloane understood this and harnessed it to his advantage.

"One word is all it takes, pig," Sloane said into his cuff. "You lose your good name, your wife, everything you ever worked for. You hear me? You lose everything, the way you always have, the way you always will. You'll lose it all to *me*. That day you always feared would come—that day is today unless you do what I say, maggot. Get off your ass now."

Julian shot up from his seat, flinging his cards away without so much as a goodbye to his wife. With hurried steps he made for the elevators at the other end of the floor. After a beat, Sloane followed, satisfied and ready for more.

Sloane opened the door to the suite and led his client into the foyer. Julian entered the drawing room and took the wingback chair, legs spread wide in front of him. Sloane didn't wait for the door to slide shut before he began.

"What took you so long, you dirty pig?"

The sound of his voice felt unnatural as it left his lips. Sloane had only done this over comms. He had never debased Julian face to face and in close quarters too, where every twitch and tic was visible, every sound impossible to ignore.

Julian's nostrils flared, and his breath became more labored as he hesitated to reply.

"Well, why are you just sitting there, pig? Say something!"

"I—I'm so-sorry, I—"

"You're so-so-sorry?" Sloane scoffed mockingly. "You're fucking pathetic. You can't even talk right, you piece of shit."

The longer Julian stayed silent, quivering ever so slightly, the more Sloane grew confident. He leaned into his client, bracing himself on the armchair.

"Talk!"

Julian raised his palms, surrendering as though confronted by a bear about to pounce.

"What, are you afraid I'm going to hit you?" Sloane asked, laughing. "Fucking maggot. You're a fucking worm, you know that?"

Julian hesitated, then slowly nodded.

"What are you?" Sloane asked, cupping a hand over his ear for emphasis.

"I'm a worm," Julian whispered. "I'm a maggot."

"That's right. Now give me my fucking money, you fucking maggot."

Julian swiped a command on his wristband, a platinum cuff with a thin rim lined with the emblem of some French fashion house. It was a hair on this side of tasteful. A beep confirmed the transfer.

<$250,000 Received>

It was a drop in the ocean of the Lonsdales' wealth, and Sloane wondered if he should have asked for more. He never wanted to do any of this in person, and that had to command a higher price. Besides, Julian could afford it. If Sloane had asked for ten times that, the transfer still wouldn't have warranted a second look from his actuaries.

"That's the beauty of this arrangement," Sloane had once told him. "You can afford this form of therapy many times over. It's impossible to ruin you financially."

"The best part about this, really, is you're still one of us. Kind of. The others needed the money. No matter how good their acting was, I could smell it. They reeked of desperation. It's a real turnoff."

Sloane wondered now if Julian got a whiff of his desperation. Did Julian know how bad things had been lately? How his reserves were drying up, how his mother's fortunes—hitched to her third husband, an Emirati petrochemical mogul—no longer kept him afloat? Is that why Julian was renegotiating the terms?

"Well, what are you waiting for, pig?" Sloane yelled. "We're done here. Get your face out of my fucking sight. You make me sick, you bag of shit."

Julian stood, the same look of dumb fear on his face, but made no motion to leave.

"Why the fuck are you still here? Leave!"

"Well, I—I was wondering . . . I know I've displeased you. I've been a bad pig," Julian whispered. "And I deserve to be punished."

"You haven't had enough?"

"I—I think I deserve to be spat on."

Julian raised a brow, and tension rose to Sloane's temples. What fresh hell is this? This was not part of the arrangement, a breach on top of another. Julian knew that Sloane drew the line at physical humiliation. That they breathed the same air was bad enough; any sort of contact was off the table.

"Master, I deserve to be spat on. Because I am a lowly, filthy piece of shit." Julian repeated, enunciating each word with an assured tone.

"Don't tell me what you deserve, maggot," Sloane yelled. "You deserve nothing. You get nothing."

He got in his client's face, their noses nearly touching. Julian's unblinking eyes conveyed an air of defiance. He wasn't leaving until he got what he wanted. In that moment, staring into the light gray pools of the man's commanding gaze, Sloane understood.

He cast his head aside, took in a sharp breath, and launched spittle onto face of Julian Lonsdale. Holding the stare, Julian slowly took the pocket square from his suit jacket and wiped the spit off his face.

"Thank you, master."

"You dirty motherfucking pig."

Sloane shoved him, without thought as to whether that contact crossed a line too. At that point, he didn't care. Julian retreated out of the room like an injured creature.

Sloane stood there, stunned and shamed. That wasn't how any of this was supposed to go. Fuck. Then, a beep came in on his wristband.

‹$250,000 Received›

He scrolled to check the time stamps, to make sure it wasn't a duplicate transaction. Another beep—a message from Julian—interrupted him to confirm that it was not.

Now that wasn't so hard, was it?

Chapter 7
Falling Bodies

Ava entered the observation lounge the way a stag enters a wood on the first day of the spring thaw: with guarded exhilaration. As she passed her peers, she met stares that ranged from amused to curious to hostile. Some gave her a smile or a polite nod in acknowledgment, which she returned. She fielded compliments on her ensemble, a midnight-blue ombré gown with a tiered skirt. Yet regardless of their reception, Ava scarcely needed to imagine what went through their minds. It was only ever about one of two things: her utility to them, or her brother's death.

Being one of the most powerful women on the station meant nothing to these people who still viewed themselves—and everyone else—as who they were when they were teenagers. For them, the pecking order was still what it was twenty-five years ago, which meant Ava was still an easy target. Walking across the lounge felt quite like walking down the halls of Rochford, and she located possible points of exit, an instinct learned from as far back as she could remember. Each time she entered a room, without cause or prompting, her first thought was always, *How can I escape?* She could slip out after a brief cameo, but at least an hour of the opening night reception had to be endured.

A sizeable crowd had gathered by one of the viewing decks. Some of them pointed at a glint in space. Ava followed their fingers and guessed that the Altaire was in an orbital position that had a view of Mars. A vapid young thing, a trophy spouse, clapped excitedly. On the edge of a low dais, lost in the stargazers, Henry Gallagher nursed a scotch. The golden sheen of his swept-back hair was unmistakable. While everyone lifted their heads to loftier sights, Henry's thoughts seemed to drown in his drink.

Back at Rochford, Ava often caught her friend in intensely quiet moments like this. He might be sitting in a library carrel, staring at the surface of an empty desk, or lingering a tad too long by the pool in the buoyancy lab. Whenever she disturbed these reveries, Henry appeared to remember himself, reinhabiting a role he briefly forgot. He became the confident and gregarious Henry, the brilliant, perfect young man everyone expected. As Ava drew closer now, her old friend did so again; once she caught Henry's eye, he instantly slipped on a new mask, one with bright eyes and a welcoming smile. One that fit in with the rest of the crowd.

"Ava. You're breathtaking, as usual."

"As are you," she replied, greeting him with an air kiss. "Always nice to see a familiar face."

"Everyone here is a familiar face. For better or worse."

"More worse than better."

"I'm glad you made it. It's been ages."

"I wouldn't have missed it for the world. How's Nick? I don't think I've spotted him."

"Oh, he's here somewhere . . ." Henry raised his head, searching. Ava gestured toward a corner booth where his husband sat with Xiomara Harris and a few Rochfordians.

"He fits in perfectly. You'd think he went to school with us," she said.

"He sure knows how to make friends."

"Can you imagine though? If he came up with us?"

"I don't think he and I would have ended up together if he did."

"Why not?"

"I was a different person back then, and so was he. We found each other at the right time in our lives."

"High school certainly wasn't the time for finding great loves," Ava replied. "Especially toward the end."

Henry only nodded in response, his veneer of cool deftly maintained. Ava pressed on. "I hate to admit it, but being here with all these people almost makes me miss our days at Rochford."

"Does it really? Those days are better left in the past, I think."

"But we can't escape the past, can we?" she said, feigning a weary acceptance. "Right before I came aboard, the program committee talked to me about Ashwin. They wanted my permission to hold a memorial segment during the banquet."

Henry sighed somberly. "Of course this weekend wouldn't be complete without commemorating him somehow. I could talk to them for you," he suggested. "Raya Morgan still owes me a favor and I could probably get her team to cut the segment."

"Thank you, but that's not necessary. Besides, I've already said yes. Ashwin was still part of our class, no matter how we feel about it." Ava continued, measuring her words. "Do you ever wonder what it would be like if things had been different? How we all could've done things differently? If Ashwin ..."

"I try not to think about it. Do you?"

"Sometimes," Ava replied, though that was far from true. She never stopped thinking about Ashwin's death and the disaster that followed. She replayed her final days at Rochford on an endless loop. "And the closer I came to this reunion, the more I found myself wondering. Asking questions."

"Questions like what?" Henry leaned in with cautious concern in his eyes. Ava saw this as concern for her, and not for whatever she thought Henry might be trying to hide. It was the same look her therapist gave her whenever she shared some of her more alarming suspicions.

"I've been thinking about how Ashwin . . . how I never knew that you three were the ones that found his body."

"I thought you knew," he replied, brow knitted. "In any case, we would have told you ourselves, if . . ."

"If my parents hadn't sent me across the ocean, away from the scandal."

"I'm happy to help you find the answers you need, but Ava, these what-ifs aren't healthy. You can't let past regrets haunt you forever."

She should have corrected him: her regrets were not in the past. They were here, alive, their consequences still felt to this day. She might have been powerless to stop Ashwin's death, or to prevent Daniela paying the ultimate price, but she knew more now, and now she had the means to discover what her friends had truly done.

Before she could continue, the tap-tap-tap of a heavy heel rang on the marble floor. It sounded determined, ruddered toward her. Ava hesitated to turn to see who was coming.

"Oh, Henry, always so serious," greeted Sloane. He slid an arm around Ava's waist and gave her a peck on both cheeks. "Ava, love, glad to find you. Finally."

"Seems like the party's already started," Henry sighed, sharing Ava's look of amused resignation. "Sloane, can I get you a water?"

"You can get me an Armagnac," he replied. He then reached for his pendant, but before he could take another hit, Henry placed a hand on his forearm, gently, like he was about to touch an open flame. The two exchanged a glance that told everything that needed saying. Sloane lowered his arm, his entire body loosening. He pulled Henry and Ava into a huddle, then exclaimed, "The gang's all here!"

"Well, not quite yet," Ava said.

"Right. Where is Laz anyway?" Henry asked.

"Saint Lazarus is around. Somewhere. Careful though, he's in a bit of a mood," Sloane replied with an exaggerated pout.

Unlike Henry, much had changed about Sloane since their days at Rochford. The boy Ava had known was reserved, an old soul. A far cry from the fantastical creature before her, with his colorful nails and outfit, the flashiest in a room already brimming with ostentation. The change was abrupt too, right around the time they graduated and went on their separate ways to college and beyond. She saw this new Sloane as a product of his family's circumstance, that the finery and the wild behavior were part of his armor. It would have been easy to leave Sloane behind following the scandal, though Ava supposed it would have been easy for him to leave her behind too. No, all four of them were bonded for life, whether they liked it or not. Nothing forges friendships better than tragedy, and in their small group, Sloane and Ava knew that best.

"By the way, I heard the news," Sloane said. "Sorry about Fallon, love. For what it's worth, I never liked her."

Henry tapped him with the back of his hand in rebuke.

"What? I've always told you how I felt about Fallon. The signs were there from the beginning," he added, with a slurry effusiveness. "Remember that thing with the thing at the thing?"

"With such specificity, how could I possibly forget?" Ava replied. "You've never liked any of our partners, have you? Fallon, Nick, whoever Laz is dating . . . you've always disapproved."

"I quite like Nick, actually," Sloane corrected. "And I disapprove of attachments, not specific people. Marriage is a scam anyway. We should do away with it completely." Despite his state, he detected a subtle flash of pensiveness cross Henry's face. "Oh my, is there trouble in paradise?"

"Not at all," Henry replied, waving into the crowd. "Paradise remains."

The other two turned to see Nick, still in his corner booth. The Lonsdales had joined him, and he beckoned Henry over. Julian did too, waving a whiskey glass like a reward waiting to be claimed.

"Well, I'm glad to hear it," Sloane told Henry, then gestured toward Ava. "Any sage advice for the recently dumped?"

She gasped, slapping him on his arm. "It was a mutual decision."

"Excuse me, miss," Laz asked upon joining them, deadpan. "Is this man bothering you?"

"Find your own date, Laz. She's taken." Sloane pulled Ava closer, planting a peck on her cheek.

Henry chuckled as he shook his friend's hand. "High," he stage-whispered to Laz.

"Oh, I'm aware," he replied. Sloane set down his empty glass and hailed a server for another glass of brandy. "Watch him," Laz warned. "He tends to drop things."

"Fuck off."

"Boys, did we miss something?" Henry asked.

"Well, the ambassador here . . ." Sloane started.

"We saw each other earlier at the casino," Laz said. "He slipped and broke a glass. No big deal." He leaned in and wrapped an arm around Sloane's shoulder, which he shrugged off like a chastised child. Laz turned to Ava instead.

"How are you doing, with all of this?"

For a while, the company of her friends had made Ava forget the rest of their peers. She appreciated Laz's concern, though she would have rather not had the reminder.

"You know you can count on us if you need anything, right?" he continued.

"I'm fine. It's not as bad as I feared."

"And besides, the weekend will be over before we know it," Henry said. He huddled closer, bringing the group around a high top behind a marble column.

Ava looked at the three of them and smiled. Back at Rochford, she could always count on her friends for interference in case a snide remark came her way, or if someone picked a fight. Henry did most of the heavy lifting, acting as both protector and PR manager, using his influence to rehabilitate her reputation. Sloane did his part too, in his own, more personal way. He held her hand, sat with her, helped her process her trauma as she did his. They commiserated in their common pain and gave refuge to each other in a way their other friends could not. But if she were asked, the one who helped the most was Laz. Like the other two, he also cared for her and fought the charm offensive on her behalf, but most of all, he loved her. He loved her even when everyone was saying that she murdered her own twin. She had never been able to return it, and she grew weary of the relentless way Laz expressed it, but that love sustained her.

That's why they did it, Ava tried to convince herself. Out of loyalty and an instinct to protect, out of a duty that they've taken upon themselves. Out of love. In the public eye, she was equally guilty as Daniela for Ashwin's death. Her friends lied, kept things from her and from everyone else, in order to save her. Yet as she delved more deeply into the documents that she'd recently unearthed, she saw the truth of her friends' motives: They didn't lie to protect her. They lied to protect themselves.

Suddenly, a series of beeps issued from high above the observation lounge. One tinny beep followed by two longer blares, repeated twice, then a long pause before the pattern began its loop. The din in the viewing area lowed to an expectant hush.

"Which one is that again?" Sloane asked. Naturally he'd already forgotten the safety protocols.

"That'll be a station-wide announcement," Henry replied.

The beeping abated, replaced by Captain Williams's calming voice. "Good evening, Space Habitat Altaire. This is your captain speaking. It appears that two sizeable pieces of debris are headed toward the station's orbit. Impact is expected within the hour, and evasive maneuvers might need to be taken. This, however, is no cause for alarm. As you may recall from your pre-departure safety training, such incidents are common, and Altaire has a full suite of defense systems to protect the station and its occupants."

A tense uproar issued from one of the corners of the viewing platform. Two light vessels ejected from the station's shuttle bay and coasted away. Henry slipped on his visor for a closer look.

"It's far enough," Henry said. "We should be fine."

"Are you sure?" Laz asked. "'Far' means nothing out here, especially if we're dealing with a cascade. One thing crashes into another, then another, and before you know it an entire barrage of debris is coming down on us like a hail of bullets."

"That's what the shuttles are for," Ava explained. "They have shields and laser capabilities to deflect debris or obliterate it completely."

"See, I expected that depth of knowledge from the nerd over here," Sloane said, cocking his head at Henry. "But you? This wasn't covered in our safety briefing, was it?"

Ava shrugged. "Khan-Powell has a stake in the Altaire, which means we get a first look at the station specs, including its shuttles."

"Well then, tell me more about the Altaire's secrets," Sloane replied, intrigued. "Is it true the greenhouse plants are fertilized with—"

"I didn't know the shuttles had lasers," Henry interrupted. "Seems excessive, even for debris."

Sloane snorted, suppressing laughter. "Is station security worried about . . . pew-pew space pirates?"

"If you have a view of the front of the station—that's the side facing away from Earth," the captain's announcement continued, "you'll see that I've deployed the Castor and Pollux to impede the oncoming debris. I will give you all another update soon, but for now, sit back, relax, and if you're so inclined, you can look out on the viewing platforms and watch our Safety & Security team in action."

"That's a relief," Laz said. "Looks like they have it handled."

"For now," Henry replied.

"The things we have to endure for five points. Good thing this trip is free."

"God, even your cocktail chatter is repetitive," Sloane told Laz with a look of torture on his face. "Did you have your speech writer draft this up?"

"Sloane, be nice," Henry replied, "or else I'll send you back to your room with no supper."

At the reminder, Ava did the quick mental math of her MERIT score. She had seventy-seven points all told, and a handful more by the time this weekend was over. She wondered how her friends fared. Laz certainly had a lot banked, and despite being unmarried, he was straight. Despite the happy marriage, Henry wasn't as fortunate, though given his careerist ways, not to mention his husband's, they no doubt more than made up for it. Sloane surely had a substantial deficit, without any sort of gainful employment. He might even have disqualifiers that Ava didn't know about.

"Look, the only reason this trip is free is so Lonsdale Aerospace can get its hands on big-fish investors," Sloane replied. "Do you think they shuttle every Rochford class up here every goddamn year out of the goodness of their hearts? Everyone has an agenda."

"And what is yours?" Henry asked jovially. "Besides where your next drink is coming from?"

"It's not Mars, I'll tell you that much. Fuck the points."

"Oh, if only they were transferable! I'd love to unburden you of yours," Laz replied with a laugh.

"Christ, it's not a resource to be traded. It's a made-up metric for a made-up system of fucked-up rules."

"It's an interesting concept though. A marketplace for points," Henry mused. "Let's face it, billions of people don't stand a chance of scoring high enough to qualify. Their points languish unused."

"They could revive that proposal. Didn't your dad talk about an exchange program recently?"

"I don't keep up with his work, you know that," she answered, flushed. Laz should know better than to bring up her father.

"That must be difficult," Henry said with sympathy. "I can't imagine myself not wanting to know what goes on at the MSA, especially from the man who gets to decide who settles on Mars."

"Well, he doesn't really decide anything," Laz countered. "He's a country delegate, and they all get an equal vote. Trust me, us diplomats have very little sway."

"The MSA's quite different though, isn't it?" Henry answered. "It's not some state department position serving at the pleasure of the President. They have a direct hand in the future of humanity."

Being reminded of her father cast a pall on Ava's mood. In the abstract, she understood a father's grief. And so she shouldn't have been surprised at what Ashwin's death had driven her father to do. He'd been a lawmaker all his life. Of course he'd want to make sure that criminals would never get a second chance on a new planet. Mars was reserved only for "the best of us." Ava scanned the observation lounge. If it weren't for her father and the people who believed as he did, no one in that starlit hall would be as close to setting foot on Mars as they were. Everyone there—herself, the people she loved, and those who loathed her—they all reaped the benefits of a system that was built out of her brother's murder and the innocent woman made to take the fall for it.

"Laz went ahead and booked us a table at the Altesse," Ava cut in, tiring of the talk of Mars. "Shall we continue this over dinner?"

"I'm afraid I can't," Henry answered. "Nick got us invited to the Captain's Table."

"Fancy," Sloane said with an eye roll.

"Same restaurant, just different company, is all. I promise to make it up to all of you. Also, this way, you get to talk about me behind my back."

Sloane feigned insult. "Us? Never."

"You're joining, right?" Laz asked him. "We'll aim to meet your alcohol requirement well before we get to the digestifs."

"I'll have to pass too. I need to make my rounds, rub elbows . . . you know how it is."

"Are you sure? At least give me a chance to make up for earlier."

"I'm sure you'd like that," Sloane replied, his tone softer. He leaned over for a hug goodbye. "I will see you all at the Moon Pools though, right?"

"Oh, I don't know," Laz said sheepishly. "Who's coming? Or should I say, who got the invite?"

"The right people. But most importantly, me."

"Nick and I will be there," Henry said. "I know the Lonsdales will too."

"And how about you, love?" Sloane asked Ava.

"Let me think about it," she replied. She did receive the invitation covertly delivered to her suite, but Ava never attended these sorts of parties. The boys knew that too, but they always asked, and she always hedged for their benefit anyway.

"It'll be fuuun," Sloane said in a sing-song way. "Might not feel like it at first, but before the end of it, I'm sure you'll enjoy yourself."

Right then, the viewing platforms erupted in a commotion. The four friends made their way closer to the panorama, nervous conversations overlapping as they approached the crowd. Something about the shuttles, an explosion. Ava rushed to the edge of the glass that separated them from the dead of space.

"The shuttles—they're coming back," shouted one of the guests. Smatterings of applause followed. "There were flashes of light and thought something bad happened," another told Ava. "But it seems like we're fine now."

Ava squinted to see where the woman pointed and spotted the Castor and Pollux. Their thrusters were fully engaged and speeding toward the Altaire. Ava realized then that the crowd's relief may have been premature.

"They're coming in too fast," Henry said, stealing the words from Ava's mouth.

"Is that a bad thing?" Sloane asked soberly.

"Only because they're rushing out of there. Which means that whatever they failed to intercept was either too big or too fast to contain."

"All right, there's no need to panic. We don't have the full picture yet," Laz said. He seemed in denial like the rest of the guests, some of whom still clapped as the shuttles came closer into view. Didn't all these people graduate from a space training program? Ava thought, annoyed.

Three loud blares rang from the speaker system, looping in a pattern louder and more urgent than the last. The lights that encircled the ceiling's perimeter changed into a bright red.

"Fuck. I need to find my husband." Henry scanned the room and broke off from the group. As soon as he did, Nick cut through the crowd, panting.

"We might need to follow the evacuation plan."

"But they haven't announced anything yet," Sloane said.

"It's better to be ahead of these things," Henry replied. Laz nodded in agreement. He wrapped an arm around Ava and led the way out the observation lounge. The others followed. Everyone beelined for the exits but then stopped in their tracks when the captain's voice came on again.

"Dear guests, we apologize for the inconvenience. The Altaire needs to make a minor evasive maneuver following our attempts at containing foreign debris. The maneuver will require us to engage the station's thrusters," she said amid gasps from the guests. "This should only feel like a gentle rocking motion and should be over in a matter of seconds. In any case, everyone should recall their safety briefing in the event of minor impacts. If you are in your cabin, please remain there for the time being. If you are not in your cabin, please situate yourselves wherever you are able to brace . . ."

"Looks like we're staying put," Sloane said through the announcement. The group retreated into one of the lounge's VIP booths, one tucked away underneath a mezzanine balcony. Laz sidled closer to Ava, holding her hand in reassurance.

"This is nothing," he told her. "It's just like airplane turbulence."

"Except instead of rough air, we're dodging a hailstorm of debris," Sloane snapped.

A hush settled as the alarm system died down, though the lights remained a distressing red. Everyone huddled into corners, waiting for their world to shift. The thrusters came to life with a low, constant rumble beneath their feet. The distress signal went off again, sending the hall into panic. Ava leaned back into her seat, feeling the slow and steady pull of a backward recline. Soon, everyone felt it. Yelps and shrieks came as the floor beneath them shifted, joined in cacophony by the sliding of tables, the breaking of fallen glasses. The creaks and turns of the Altaire's guts and limbs provided a dull bass line to the syncopation. This didn't feel like airplane turbulence, this was a magnitude-six earthquake.

The hall erupted into screaming as the whole station swiftly jolted, its gravity engines catching up with its momentum. Ava lurched forward, her chest hitting the table before she had a chance to brace herself. A searing pain overwhelmed her. She felt another rumble and quickly clutched the edge of the table. Head down and eyes closed, Ava braced herself for another jolt.

It never came. Instead, the rumbling finally stopped, and so did the station's motion. The distress alarm quieted.

"I think that's that," Laz whispered, wrapping an arm around her. "How are you feeling?"

Ava raised her head, disoriented. The lights in the lounge brightened, bathing the harried guests in a warm and dreamy glow. The Rochfordians emerged from chaos shaken but relieved, jubilant even. As she rose to her feet unsteadily, Ava saw herself apart from everyone else. She drew no sense of relief from having averted one disaster. All she felt was pain, and the dread of further misfortunes that this incident portended.

Chapter 8
Times Gone By

The Altesse was a time machine to the Belle Epoque. With its lush, neo-baroque decor, the ornate moldings, the chandeliers of wrought copper shaped into birds and flowering vines, one couldn't help being transported to the opulence of Paris at the turn of the last century. On its walls were immense frescoes, glimmering panoramas of French cityscapes. Its glass-and-steel dome ceiling, one of the few areas of the station that did not have an overhead view of the stars, featured an array of peacocks in rich purples, turquoise, and gold.

Laz gaped at the restaurant's splendid vault, enthralled in fantasies of that wondrous era abruptly ended by war. It allayed his disappointment at the table they had been assigned. Losing half of their party meant he and Ava needed to be relegated to a less central one, tucked in a corner, away from the long banquet table where select guests had the honor of dining with the Altaire's captain.

"Well, this definitely beats Paris," Laz said.

"Not a tall order, considering the state it's in."

"True," he replied, wincing. Overrun by riots on a near-constant basis, the city had long lost its allure.

"Lucky you and I got to see it before it really went to shit."

"Yes, that was a fun trip, wasn't it?"

"Simpler times." He tried to signal for a server, but he was easy to miss in the massive hall. "If only we could go back."

The last time they'd been there, they were two young lovers on spring break. A week in Paris, then another in Cap Ferrat, driving through the wine country along the way. It was one of his favorite memories, and its sweetness almost made up for the summer that followed.

"Careful what you wish for," Ava answered. "Afterward was not too simple."

"Ah, don't remind me. I've only just recovered from the way you curb-stomped my heart."

"How dramatic! I'd hate to see you before this alleged recovery." She laughed. "Things really took a turn that summer, didn't it?"

"In more ways than one. Everything before senior year was golden. Everything after . . ."

"Do you ever think back on that time? About what happened?"

"You mean, about us? All the time."

"Ah, there's not much to think on there," Ava replied dismissively. "I wasn't ready to be with you, Laz. I wasn't ready for anyone."

"Until you were—just not with me."

She sighed, shook her head. "Besides, I didn't mean us. I meant what happened to Ashwin."

Right then, a server joined them, much to Ava's consternation. It took her a moment to realize this was no ordinary server. It was Laz's personal liaison Cielo, and beside her stood a stout man in chef's whites, the Algerian flag embroidered on his chest.

"Ms. Khan, Ambassador," she greeted. "Pardon the interruption. Please allow me to introduce our chef de cuisine, Toussaint Bernave."

"Welcome to the Altesse," he said. Laz rose to shake the chef's hand. He praised the Kasbah of Algiers, which he had once visited on a family vacation. The chef smiled bashfully. "Ah, you're luckier than me. I myself have not seen the Kasbah, having left my country as a child."

Left unsaid was the fact that Chef Toussaint could never return. In his short lifetime, the heat indexes for a wide swath of the northern edge of the continent had rendered most of its cities uninhabitable. An awkward hush settled over on the party.

"Yes, Chef Toussaint bears one of the seventy-one different flags worn by our three hundred twelve staff and crew members," Cielo finally interjected.

"Half of them working with me down in the galley," the chef added in jest.

Shortly, a server approached bearing a tray of coupe glasses which he then set down before Laz and Ava. The cocktails fizzed and shimmered, their color a lovely shade of rosy orange, like the pale flesh of a grapefruit.

"Before Chef Toussaint regales you with tonight's menu," Cielo said. "Please allow us to give you a taste of our signature drink, the Ad Martem."

"Thank you, this is very kind," Ava replied. She recognized it for the gesture it was: an appeasement for the furor at the observation lounge. She looked around and found servers handing out the same drink to every single diner.

"What's in it?" Laz asked, sniffing his coupe. "I'm getting a hint of almond . . ."

"You have a good nose," the chef replied. "It has cognac, Campari, and champagne. The almond note is from the orgeat syrup, rounded out by a splash of lemon from trees grown right here on the Altaire."

"Chef Toussaint is a very involved chef de cuisine," Cielo said. "Not only does he oversee the galley and our beverage service, he also manages our greenhouse and aquaponics systems."

"Do you grow almond trees here as well?" Ava asked.

Chef Toussaint laughed heartily. "No, the orgeat is all organic, made from Spanish almonds. Difficult to source, but not as difficult as the champagne and the cognac. The top French vineyards have been suffering, as you're no doubt aware."

"Because of drought?"

"Blight. Invasive aphids."

"Yet that didn't stop us from delivering the best," Cielo interjected. "This cocktail was made from the freshest ingredients from planetside. No synthetics at all. That goes for everything that you'll be consuming here on the Altaire. Except for things grown in our greenhouse, eighty percent of the components of each dish and drink come from the finest sources on Earth."

"Shall we toast?" Laz asked, excited to partake. Ava lifted her drink, its bubbles lazily escaping to the surface. After too-long a pause, Laz spoke up. "Well, I suppose only one toast comes to mind: to Mars!"

Ava took a sip and detected a bittersweet florality. Laz smacked his lips. "This is exquisite."

"We're glad you like it," Cielo said. "And we hope you enjoy the rest of our special offerings for tonight.

I know the turbulence from earlier was quite unpleasant, but I hope we can make up for it during the rest of your stay, starting with tonight's service."

"That's very nice, but not necessary," Ava replied. "Space is unpredictable. We all signed up for this."

Cielo and Toussaint looked at each other and smiled. "Be that as it may," the chef replied. "I'm certain this meal will make you forget all about it."

The two took their leave, with promises of a dazzling first course to arrive in a few moments. Ava watched as they moved to another table across the aisle, where the diners already enjoyed their glasses of Ad Martem. She faintly heard Cielo begin the same spiel.

"That's your personal liaison? The head of Guest Relations?" she asked Laz.

"That she is." He savored another sip of his drink. "Why?"

"And she's able to attend to you, even with her other duties?"

Laz took a moment to consider this. "Surprisingly, yes. I haven't felt neglected by her—or any of the staff—at all."

Ava's own liaison, Faiza, was a wiry Sudanese woman who previously only did housekeeping duties on the Altaire. She seemed to relish the variety of duties that Ava entrusted to her, such as handling her schedule and booking appointments at the spa. Ava discovered that while she slept, Faiza still attended to duties in the laundry room, and yet somehow, she never failed to be present when summoned.

"I know what you mean," Ava replied, gesturing to the back of the restaurant, near the galley doors. Behind a translucent screen, Faiza stood by in case she was called. Huddled next to her were other personal valets, all standing ready. "I've tried telling her off, but she said she would get in trouble if I was dissatisfied in any way. So I could never shake her off now."

"You're not complaining, are you?"

"Not even my own assistants wait on me hand and foot like this. It's off-putting."

"Because of the optics? Yeah, they are a bit too servile for my comfort, especially given what everyone looks like," Laz replied. "I mean, look at them, and look at us."

"I guess it must be worse for you," she said, kindly.

Laz shrugged. Even with Ava, he tried to maintain his nonchalance, but Laz was constantly aware of the makeup of any room he was in. He picked up the habit from his parents and his grandparents. The Lazaros may have been old money back in the homeland, but in America, they were nobodies. It didn't matter how large their bank accounts were; they had to prove that they belonged. And though their political and business successes steadily purchased their acceptance, Laz never forgot: He would always be viewed as less than, and he could never be seen to be affected by it. Nothing is more gauche than insecurity.

"Having a Filipina liaison does put a fine point on it," he told Ava. "But I'm not bothered. I'm sure it was a co-incidence, given how many there are of them."

"That's not what I meant, though," she replied. "Optics aside, I have this sense of being watched, and I don't like it."

"She's just doing her job." After a beat, he set down his drink. "What's this really about, Ava? Do you want to eat elsewhere, somewhere with not quite as many people around? We have options."

She wanted to say yes. She had noted where all the exits were, made a mental note of the faces she'd seen as they were seated. Who was where and with whom, what were they likely discussing and why. The stress of being around Rochford folk hadn't subsided, and had in fact worsened following the mishap with the space debris. Leaving would be the easy thing to do. Yet she didn't have a lot of time, and here was Laz, already in her hands.

"You always know what to say, don't you?"

"I try," said Laz, beaming. "So, would you like to leave? I heard good things about the steak house, and it's probably less crowded too."

"And you've always looked out for me," she continued, with an edge to her tone. "Even when I didn't ask for it. You always knew what's best."

"I'm your friend, Ava. Of course I look out for you."

"It's always been that way, ever since we were kids. Why is that?"

"You know why," he said, then quickly added, "I've just told you why."

Ava took a sip of her cocktail. She winced at its acrid notes. "It took a long time for me to reckon with what happened, Laz. I thought it was only a matter of confronting the past, but it isn't."

"What are you talking about?"

"My family shielded me from all of it, shipped me off to London more out of shame than a desire to protect me. But they couldn't shield me forever, could they? And I couldn't avoid it forever either."

"Ava, I don't understand. Avoid what?"

"The truth about what happened to my brother. And to Daniela."

Laz blanched at the mention of the name. He hadn't heard it in decades, as long as he'd been trying to forget it. "What about it?"

Ava lowered her voice but her firmness remained. "I got a judge to unseal the records—police reports, court documents, autopsy records—everything. I thought that I could finally move on by getting my head out of the sand, but all I got were questions that I thought I already knew the answers to. Like how you all found Ashwin's body, which you never told me about."

"When could we have told you? When you were boarded up by your parents? No one could reach you for months." He sighed, not impatiently, but not quite agreeably either. "Besides, how would this have changed anything?"

"And then you lied to the police." The look of knowing remorse on Laz's face further confirmed what she'd discovered. "Why, Laz? What were you trying to cover up?"

"Nothing!" Guests from a neighboring table turned to them, and Laz lowered his voice to a whisper. "It was a mistake. I made a mistake. I—I only did it because I didn't want them to suspect you."

"Because you suspected me. You thought I did it."

"I didn't know what to think. It was all happening so fast, and I panicked. What does it matter? I lied to protect you, is that what you wanna hear? Because I'd do it again, Ava."

"Do you think I killed him?"

"What? Of course not," he replied, wounded but insistent.

"I want you to say it."

"I don't think you killed him. And I regret ever thinking that you did."

"So why did you lie?"

"Because I had doubts. *Had*. But not anymore."

"Laz, I want you to be honest with me."

"I lied to the cops, Ava, but I never lied to you. Not then, and especially not now."

"And that's it? There's nothing else?"

Laz reached for Ava's hand. She flinched, pulling away like she'd touched a live wire. His eyes threatened to well in tears. "I swear on my life."

Chapter 9
Daniela

Ashwin Khan's lifeless body, skin taut and cracking from exposure to harsh elements, looked like an exhumed mummy. The salt and sand and dry desert air aged him more than the two days it took to locate him, and by the time he was found, no one could tell how long he had been dead.

"She didn't do it," Henry said. "She couldn't have."

"We need to talk to her," Laz replied. "We can't call it in, not until we talk to her."

Henry and Sloane looked at each other wordlessly.

"Why?" Henry asked.

"To protect her."

"Protect her from what?" Sloane asked. "From knowing her brother is dead? Or from being arrested for murder?"

"We'll have to go back soon," Henry added, with the measured, official tone that he'd used earlier at the auditorium. "And we can't just leave him here."

Laz searched for a reason but failed. Bile rose in his throat as he inhaled a whiff of the corpse's putrefaction. "We'll wait. Just until we get a hold of Ava." He tried calling her again, but the line went straight to voicemail. "Goddamn it!" Laz stomped the ground, kicking up a storm of salt.

"Where's your head at, buddy?" Henry asked him. "Talk to us."

Laz recalled a conversation, not a week ago, when Ava came to him with bruises on her arm. *I wish he was dead.* "Look, we don't have to report it. Maybe . . . maybe we tell them we couldn't finish the search, that it's too hot," he said, begging. "We need to buy her some time."

"Listen to yourself," Sloane said, in an uncharacteristically sharp tone. "Protect her, buy her some time—what the fuck do you think happened here?"

"We're all thinking it, all right?" Laz yelled.

"Well, then say it." Sloane's challenge sounded more like a plea. "Do you think Ava killed him?"

Laz crouched next to Ashwin's corpse, careful not to move anything. He searched for something, anything to dissuade him from the answer he feared, but all he saw were the strangulation marks on its neck, the long bruises that he imagined were formed by Ava's fingers.

"She didn't do it," Henry repeated himself. The authority in his tone did nothing to ease Laz's fear.

"She was with him Friday afternoon. We both saw them," Laz replied, turning to Sloane and grabbing him by the arm. "How many times has she come to us crying? How many times have you yourself reset her wrist? Don't tell me you don't get it—you most of all."

"What the fuck is that supposed to mean?"

"You know what I mean," Laz replied. "You're no better than Ava at hiding your own bruises."

Sloane's nostrils flared. "Don't go there."

"You know what it's like," Laz said. "And if you'd ever gotten the balls to hit your father back, I would have protected you too."

Sloane lunged, landing a sharp jab on his friend's jaw, bones cracking on impact. Laz staggered to the ground. Henry put himself between the two, shielding Laz from Sloane's continued advance. Laz wiped the blood off his face, readying himself to hit back.

"Stop it, both of you," Henry yelled, arms outstretched. The two stepped back from each other, still seething. Laz spat, his split lip leaking blood into his mouth.

"Laz, we care about Ava too. But we gotta do what's right. We can't leave here without him." Henry gestured at Ashwin's corpse, then crouched down to gaze upon his face. "He's still a human being."

"Barely," Laz spat.

"Here's what we'll do," Henry continued. "We'll call it in and tell HQ that we found Ashwin. Then the two of you will tell the cops what you saw on Friday afternoon. We'll let them sort it out."

"Do we have to?" Laz asked.

"We need to help them put together a timeline," he replied. "Look, man, I don't believe that she did it. She's not the type to kill out of revenge. The truth won't hurt her."

"Lying won't help her either," Sloane said ominously. "Who knows who else saw the twins on Friday afternoon? And who knows what she told the cops?"

"Ava and Ashwin were talking after class—that's all you need to say," Henry added. "You don't have to imply anything else; you don't have to say that Ava looked tense or Ashwin looked pissed or anything like that. Just keep it factual. Don't speculate, don't embellish."

"We don't have to protect her, because there's nothing to protect her from," Sloane said, sounding almost convinced.

"And what about Wednesday?" Laz asked pointedly. "I guess we should tell them about that too, huh? Since we're being honest and all."

Henry and Sloane were struck silent, each waiting for the other to respond. They all knew how it would look. A schoolyard brawl days before Ashwin ended up dead? The three of them confronting him, coming to blows, the same three people who then find his body? They looked down at Ashwin once more, each searching for signs of their fight. Laz remembered landing a punch on his chin and was relieved to find no mark on the corpse.

"We have nothing to hide," Henry said.

"Don't we?" Sloane replied, giving him a stern look. "It was three against one, Henry. With a switchblade."

Laz shook his head. "I think it's best we keep that under wraps."

"No. We're not lying."

"Henry, he was a piece of shit, but everyone's going to treat him like a saint now that he's dead. You don't want to be one of the guys who ganged up on him right before he died." Laz was on a roll. "Best case, everyone is going to think *you're* a piece of shit. Worse case, we get suspended for fighting."

"Worst case," Sloane added gravely, "we're all murder suspects."

Henry took a beat and blinked. "Fuck. All right, fine. We don't tell the cops about Wednesday."

"Thank you," Laz exclaimed in relief.

"But we need to tell them about Ava and Friday afternoon," Henry continued. He placed a firm hand on Laz's shoulder, a gesture of reassurance that never failed to persuade. Laz nodded.

They radioed HQ and in due course, the police arrived to take Ashwin's body for processing. The boys were escorted back to the auditorium where more cops waited to take their statements. Laz was silent until he met with a detective, and by that time, after the travel through the salt flats, after the long wait in the hallway for his turn at interrogation, the swirl of dread and doubt had overcome him and he lost his nerve.

He didn't tell the cop about the fight on Wednesday night, but he couldn't follow through with Henry's compromise either. He had to make sure Ava was fine. Fuck the timeline. He decided to lie. Under oath, he told the detective that he never saw Ava and Ashwin Khan together on Friday afternoon.

By the next day, the whole of Rochford heard the news. Ashwin had been strangled to death, his body dumped in the salt flats. To everyone's horror, Rochford also found out, at the same time the three friends did, that the police had arrested Ava on suspicion of murder.

The friends learned, too, that a second arrest had been made. An alleged accomplice. They didn't recognize the name, but it was one that would haunt them for the rest of their lives. That searing Monday in their senior year at Rochford, Henry, Sloane, and Laz first heard the name Daniela Rios.

Daniela was born lucky, or so she'd always been told. Something about the stars and the moon and the day of the year and the saint on whose feast day she was born, some agglomeration of forces both celestial and religious. She was raised Catholic and grew up on Mayan folklore, but by the time she had a mind of her own, earlier than most other girls, her only lodestar had been the personal myth that her parents imbued her with.

She was a lucky one.

Perhaps that myth started because her mother had her later in life. She was forty-two, underweight and anemic, when Daniela was born. It was a miracle that she conceived at all. When Daniela was two, she survived, along with her parents and abuelito, the third resurgence of coronavirus. Their home the only one spared of casualties in the entire border county where they lived. That was when Daniela's mother began calling her their angel de la guarda.

She had that title tattooed on her nape when she was thirteen, with a swirly sketch of wings and a halo. She originally kept it under the sweep of her long black hair, hidden from view of her father, who would have found it blasphemous if he had known.

"I don't really believe in angels," Daniela told Ava when she first asked about it. By then, Daniela had chopped off her locks in favor of a sideswept undercut that revealed her tattoo as well as the sinewy lines of her neck. "Never did. I did it for my mom."

Ava listened to her story, the blend of beliefs that she was taught, the admixture of freedom and predestination that Dani had since grown to disbelieve. "There's no such thing as luck, either. Fortune doesn't favor the bold; it doesn't favor anyone. It's chaos all the way down."

Ava supposed that Dani's disillusionment started when her mother died of lung cancer. That might have been when she felt her luck had run out. Her father blamed the death on his heathen lesbian daughter, and by the time she was able, Dani left home, unable to endure the years of stewing resentment.

She moved into a small bungalow at the edge of the desert, living with three other housemates in their early twenties. Ava still remembered the squalor of the place—the haphazard configuration of uncovered mattresses, the stacks of beer cans and mounds of cigarette butts, the transient air of what was more a pit stop than a home—and she loved it.

Back then, Ava was too young to know what drew her in, but she didn't feel the need to question it. She was already sixteen, and she had just transitioned. The time for doubt was over. She trusted her gut, and her gut told her to go for it. One night, in the backyard of that flophouse bungalow, looking out onto the desert through a chicken-wire fence, Ava kissed Dani on the nape of her neck and said I love you.

Once she said it, she couldn't stop, and neither could Dani, who showered her with the words for the rest of the summer and the months that followed. They called each other every day, and they spent every weekend together, Ava leaving Rochford grounds as early as possible and missing the gate closures every night. Some days, when neither could wait, they would meet by the edge of the property, at a spot too far out for school security to monitor. Ava couldn't risk leaving school grounds, not without suffering consequences, so Dani would sneak in past the tree line, past the pylons with their mounted cameras, fearless of repercussion.

They carried on this way for a year, keeping up their secret trysts for as long as they could. The fallout from Ava's transition had not completely dissipated, and her family had been on her case ever since. A girlfriend, especially one with an unsavory reputation, would only make things worse, especially with Ashwin.

Of course, Ava wanted to tell her friends. She already had a script too. *Dani's great, easy to get along with. She's a hard worker, she works at the elder care home and does grocery deliveries on the side. And she's got excellent taste in music.* She knew her friends would like Dani despite her station, but she also didn't want to hurt Laz. They'd broken up only last summer, and she could tell that he hadn't quite gotten over it yet.

And so, she kept her secret.

Before long, Dani was the only person in Ava's life who truly knew her. She was the only one she could confide in about everything: the stresses of making the grade at Rochford, passing her eligibility tests, the battles raging in her body as she grew into womanhood, the sadistic pleasure Ashwin derived from hurting her. Dani comforted her, helped her with her meds, cleaned up her cuts, and covered up her bruises.

Most of all, she loved Ava, more than anyone ever did.

Ava often wondered how her life would be if she was never a twin. If Ashwin had never been born. Her life would certainly be less painful. Yet she also knew that she only had Dani in her life because of him. It was because of him that she and Dani first crossed paths, that day Ava stepped foot in the bungalow at the edge of the desert. If Ava hadn't insisted that Ash take her with him to score directly from the source, if she had trusted him to do it himself, then she and Dani never would have met. And that would have been a much greater pain.

The media circus was as swift as it was brutal: the heir/ess of a biotech conglomerate and his/her lesbian drug dealing lover in a grisly murder of the former's twin brother. The story wrote itself, sold itself, spread itself like wildfire well before anyone could catch up to the truth. Who was Daniela Rios? How was she involved? Was Ava a drug dealer? Did they kill him together? For what reason? Each new detail, filtered through sensationalized accounts over the news feeds, brought an unexpected revelation.

The hours following the arrests were the most confusing. Laz needed to know what was going on, to ensure that Ava was safe. He tried to get a hold of Ava's family, braving phone calls that went unanswered. Desperate, he sought his mother's help; the Khans and the Lazaros were part of the same DC elite, but even her calls were ignored. His friends were equally out of luck. After the body was discovered, the Rochford administration clammed up, and Henry couldn't get any details from them aside from what was publicly available. Sloane was useless too. He might have gotten the lowdown, if only his father hadn't been ousted from the Rochford board of trustees.

The three friends managed to attend their classes the following day, distracted by the news as much as everyone else. The teachers muddled through their lectures while the students feverishly messaged each other about the latest scandal.

So word is Ava killed Ash and Daniela helped dump the body.

No, it was the other way around.

No, they both did it. My mom knows the judge, that's what they're saying.

Poor Ash. He was a cool guy.

Daniela's got a gang and they killed him because he shorted her on a deal.

No, Ashwin didn't deal, he was just a buyer.

You got it all wrong, amigos. Ashwin ran the gang. Daniela was his outside connect.

How does Ava fit in? She's always been a good one.

You never know with those freaks. Trannies are sneaky.

I still don't get it? So Ava's also a lesbian?

Throughout these exchanges, no one talked about how Ashwin was a bully. No one mentioned how he sent Ava to the infirmary twice in the last year. As gossip traveled the grapevine's long and divergent tendrils, Ashwin got portrayed as an innocent victim, a driven young man with a bright future derailed by occasional drug use. This was the exact opposite of what Laz knew him to be: a nascent psychopath. Laz would have found it laughable if it weren't so sinister. He understood that the more Ashwin was idolized, the more Ava would be condemned.

As co-defendants, Ava and Daniela both faced second-degree murder charges for the death of Ashwin Khan. The evidence was sparse but apparently sufficient to secure an indictment: two as yet unnamed eyewitnesses placed Ava near the scene, and physical evidence in the form of narcotics was traced to Daniela.

Laz's world shattered when he read the news. How had he not known about Daniela? Who was she? Were she and Ava really together? Since when? After all the torment he put himself through, lying to the cops, lying to his friends, was his fear actually true? Could Ava have really done it?

The next day, news came of Ava's release on bail. Laz saw a glimmer of hope. He could come to her side and comfort her, support her through this ordeal. He didn't care that she'd been keeping a secret from him all this time, that she'd been with someone else, that she'd broken his heart. It didn't even matter if she killed Ashwin.

They'd get through it. Together. He would make sure of it.

The Martian Emigration and Resettlement Index of Traits (MERIT) System

Summary Guide
United Nations Mars Settlement Agency
For Public Dissemination
Last Updated: 6 January 2087

Protected Categories

In compliance with the Universal Declaration of Human Rights (UDHR), and to ensure conditions that will maximize the protection of these rights on Mars, under no circumstances may the following traits affect a person's MERIT score calculation, or any intermediary or final decisions on a person's Settlement Application:
- Race
- Colour
- Sex

- Sexual orientation
- Gender identity
- Gender expression
- Religion
- Political or other opinion
- National origin
- Property
- Birth or other status
- Political, jurisdictional or international status of the country or territory to which a person belongs, whether it be independent, trust, non-self-governing or under any other limitation of sovereignty

Ineligible Applicants

Pursuant to the Moon Treaty, the Second Mars Treaty, the 2065 Copenhagen Protocols and the 2067 Outer Space Treaty, no Settlement Application may be granted for the following persons, regardless of their MERIT score calculation:

Health Grounds

Persons determined, in accordance with regulations prescribed by the World Health Organization (WHO) and its affiliate institutes and agencies, to be afflicted with at the time of filing of the Application:

An untreated communicable disease of public health significance. Per WHO as of 6 January 2087, these include but are not limited to:
- Chancroid
- Gonorrhea

- Granuloma inguinale
- Hanson's disease (leprosy, infectious)
- Lymphogranuloma venereum
- Syphilis
- Tuberculosis (active and infectious)
- A serious genetic disease or disorder listed in Article 6, § 101.7 of the Copenhagen Protocols; this does not include the mere genetic predisposition to develop any particular disease, serious or otherwise
- A physical or mental disorder, and behavior associated with the disorder, which poses a significant threat to public safety, and which is likely to recur or to lead to other harmful behavior
- Persons who fail or refuse to present documentation of having received vaccination against vaccine-preventable diseases, which shall include the following diseases: mumps, measles, rubella, polio, tetanus and diphtheria toxoids, pertussis, influenza type B, hepatitis B, and COVID-19 and subsequent strains; and any other vaccinations against vaccine-preventable diseases required by WHO and UNMSA for off-planet travel

Criminal Grounds
- Persons who participated in Nazi persecutions or genocide
- Persons who are members of a "terrorist organization" or who have engaged or engage in "terrorism-related activity"; such terms as defined in Article 8, § 125.2 of the Copenhagen Protocols. These activities include, but are not limited to:
  - Kidnapping

- Assassination
- Hijacking
- Unlawful use of nuclear, biological or chemical agents
- Unlawful use of information technology to attack networks, computer systems and telecommunications infrastructures
- Persons convicted* by a court of competent jurisdiction of any of the following offenses, without regard to how such conviction is defined by the sentencing jurisdiction:
  - A crime that constitutes a violation of the UDHR, including, but not limited to:
    - Slavery
    - Torture
    - Arbitrary arrest, detention or exile
    - Extrajudicial killings
  - A crime that constitutes a Violation of religious freedom as defined by the International Covenant on Civil and Political Rights
  - A crime that constitutes an Aggravated Felony, as defined in Article 8, § 125.5 of the Copenhagen Protocols, including, but not limited to:
    - Murder
    - Rape
    - Sexual abuse of a minor
    - Child pornography
    - Trafficking in firearms and destructive devices
    - Trafficking in controlled substances, as defined by the 2031 Cairo Convention against Illicit Traffic in Narcotic and Psychotropic Substances

* This ground of ineligibility shall not apply in cases where the convictions were based on fabricated charges or predicated upon repressive measures against members of a protected category on account of said category, including purely political offenses.

The MERIT Point System

Persons not rendered ineligible by the above grounds may file a Settlement Application as soon as the UNMSA portal opens on 1 May 2090.

At the close of the Application Period on 1 August 2090, all Applications will be ranked according to their MERIT scores. The 2,000 highest scoring Applicants will be granted Resident status on Mars. In the case of tied scores, earlier-filed Applications will be given priority.

The MERIT score for a dependent minor child is weighted together with the Applicant Parent/s, and is subject to a separate MERIT points matrix, see Appendix I.

The MERIT scores for spouses are individually calculated, but subject to weight adjustments, see Appendix II.

N.B. Categories and points are subject to adjustment after the 2090 Application Round. See Appendix VII for a Points Calculation Worksheet.

Trait		Points
Age		
	18–26	14
	27–35	12
	36–45	10
	46–55	5
	56 and over	2
Life Expectancy		
Based on the most recent WHO Indexes for applicant's country of residence at the time of Application (adjusted for the gender gap)	10.01 years or more above global life expectancy (GLE)	8
	5.01–10.00 years above GLE	6
	0.00–5.00 years above GLE	4
	0.01–5.00 years below GLE	2
	5.01–10.00 years below GLE	1
	10.01 years or more below GLE	0
Family Relationships		
	Spouse of a current Mars resident	8
	Child of a current Mars resident	6
	Parent of a current Mars resident	4
Biological Capacity to Conceive a Healthy Child	Irrespective of sex, gender or gender identity * For Applicants with spouses, see Appendix II for spousal score adjustments	10

Educational Attainment		
	Doctorate degree, or equivalent	15
	Master's degree, or equivalent	10
	Bachelor's degree, or equivalent, including vocational training	8
	High school diploma	5
	Elementary school diploma	2
Employment History	Subject to Aerospace Labor Exemptions, for every year of work experience in—	
See Appendix III for full descriptions	Tier A occupation	1
	Tier B occupation	0.75
	Tier C occupation	0.50
	Tier D occupation	0.25
	Tier E occupation	0.10
Entrepreneurship	For every year of significant investment, ownership, and control of a commercial enterprise—	
See Appendix IV for full descriptions	Tier A industry	1
	Tier B industry	0.75
	Tier C industry	0.50
	Tier D industry	0.25
	Tier E industry	0.10

Language Skills	* Maximum of five points for this category	
As tested by individual member countries, such testing subject to accreditation by the UNMSA	Basic fluency in a UN official language (Arabic, Chinese, English, French, Russian and Spanish)	1.0 points per language
	Basic fluency in the top 25 languages in the world by number of speakers (excluding the UN official languages)	0.50 point per language
Fitness for Space Travel and Habitation	* Subject to Aerospace Labor Exemptions	
All criteria to be audited and certified by individual member countries, subject to standards set by the UNMSA	College education in an accredited institution for space flight or aeronautics	1 per semester completed
	High school education in an accredited institution for space flight or aeronautics	1 per year completed
	Advanced individualized training in skills listed in Appendix V	1 per course completed, maximum of 5
	Prior spacecraft travel to low earth orbit and beyond, such area as defined by the UNMSA	3 per trip
	Prior extravehicular activity (EVA), including, but not limited to: supervised or unsupervised space walks, Moon walks	1 per instance**

Chapter 10
Course Corrections

The Altaire's shuttles wrangled debris on a near-weekly basis, but today, Cielo felt a sense of impending and irreversible disaster. It was that intuition, that tug in your craw that her mother called kutob, the ineffable crest of dread. A hailstorm of debris was a sign, her mother would've told her. There could be no clearer sign for you to stop.

The atmosphere in the Altesse made the sense of foreboding easier to ignore. As Cielo faked composure, plying libations and flashy appetizers, the guests' obliviousness infected her. They mostly dismissed the incident as the typical cost of being in space. Indeed, some even found the episode thrilling, a surprise adventure that would doubtless feature in their cocktail chatter for years to come. The select few who got scrapes and bruises, and the ones who demanded to speak to the captain directly, were comped with private spacewalks, vouchers for the boutique pavilion, or a free trip back to the Altaire. On the whole, a small price to pay.

Once done lavishing diners with apologies and promises, Cielo returned to the observation lounge. It was empty, save for the Sanitation crew, who were sweeping up broken glassware and setting furniture and decor upright. She waited by the viewing platform, her kutob further hushed by the view.

"How are the Gallaghers?" she asked when Pio arrived.

"They're not the worst, but still pretty bad. They make the same stupid requests. Lemon wedges cut a very specific way, baths run at a precise temp. And the same stupid questions too." Pio shifted into a mock New England accent. "Where are you really from? How is your English so good? Are you trained for this? Do you know what you're doing?"

Cielo indulged him as he continued complaining at length. Clearly, he relished the opportunity to banter, something he never got to do much of in his normal posting. Outside the rare unauthorized party in the community hall below decks, Altaire crew and staff rarely associated, until recently anyway.

"I meant, how are they after the incident?" she interjected when she found a chance.

"It's like nothing happened. Right now, they're tipsy and full so there isn't much to complain about."

"And the mood at the Captain's Table?"

"Same. They talked about the turbulence for a few minutes but by the soup course, everyone had forgotten about it."

"Perfect." She hoped all the other Rochford guests recovered as easily as the Gallaghers did. "We don't want anyone being on edge or paranoid."

"Yes, I know."

"Will they be at the after-party tonight?"

Pio shivered at the mention. Cielo rolled her eyes. "Oh, come on. It's no different than our parties," she said. "I seem to remember you having a wild time only two months ago."

"That was different," the younger man said, somehow sounding both bashful and proud. "That was for ... crew morale." He laughed.

"Ours might not be in the Moon Pools, but it's the same thing, just with different people."

"And that's my problem with it," Pio replied. "These people. When they fuck, it's really to fuck each other over, or fuck other people over. It's never just about fun."

"Won't argue with you there. So, are they coming or not?"

"Hundred percent. They were all talking about it over dessert. It sounds like everyone's going to be at this thing."

"Good. Remember to keep them happy, and never leave their side."

"In the Moon Pools, that first part will be easy. The second part's ... trickier."

"You'll find a way," she replied with confidence. "The staff is invisible to them, except when they need something, and even then, you'll be another nameless face, one of many."

Pio nodded gamely even as he was reminded of his insignificance. The young deckhand always had this contagious lightness to his being, which was why Cielo always had a tender spot for him. It helped, too, that Pio reminded her of her own sibling, Delfin. They had that same childlike nature, a sort of innocence that was simultaneously fragile and unbreakable.

In a few minutes, the Altaire would turn and transit above Northern Australia, then the Indonesian isles and a view of home. As the sun rose ahead of them, Cielo thought of her early mornings in Manila, not much different from her early mornings on the station. Waking up at the crack of dawn to catch the two trains and a jeepney ride to university, sitting in hours of transit delays and traffic, just to make her eight a.m. classes. Right about now, Delfin would probably be leaving for school soon, braving the smog and grime and thick heat of the same old crumbling city.

Delfin was thirteen when Cielo started working at the Altaire, not long after their parents died. Going to space meant having to leave her sibling with their sole relative: an uncle who lived in a tumbledown shanty of corrugated tin and salvaged fiberboards in a squatter's area along the Pasig River. He never cared about Delfin, caring only about the money that Cielo wired him every month for his troubles, but they'd be rid of him soon. Cielo had saved enough to send Delfin to college, wherever that may be. Judging by their last conversation, it might be Singapore, where Cielo herself had trained to become spaceworthy.

Delfin always had dreams of being in space just like their big sister. On the rare occasion that she had spacelink call credits, Cielo would see the boundless wonder in her sibling's eyes and she'd gain the strength to endure however long remained in her contract until she could return planetside to be with them again. That look on Delfin's face certainly buttressed her commitment to her plans. She was doing this for them, she would assure herself. It was almost enough to soothe her guilt from making Delfin an orphan a second time when she left.

Of course, she had never told them that she was a glorified waitress, a fancified maid. She told them that she was a senior manager at the most glamorous space station in the world, and that if they studied hard enough, they could be up here too.

"And then Mars?" they'd ask with doe-eyed fascination.

"And then Mars," she'd repeat, knowing in her heart that it was a lie.

Cielo kept the flame of hope alive in her sibling, even as hers had been snuffed long ago. Mars would never happen for either of them, but the illusion was enough to motivate Delfin. It kept their grades up in school, made them plan for their future. The spell of that fantasy would eventually break, and Delfin's heart would break a little too. But they would find new dreams to pursue, more attainable ones. Worthier ones. Ones that would no longer require Cielo to lie.

She had assumed their conversation was over, but Pio remained, staring at her instead of the view of their country. "Was there anything else?"

"Yes, I . . . wanted to talk about this new backup plan. The others, they have . . . doubts. And Miren doesn't sound pleased either."

Cielo's role in their plan was as expansive as the term "Guest Relations" and involved just as much coddling. No one in their group answered to anyone in the strictest sense, and though the chief housekeeper was the indisputable head of the operation, Cielo was central to it more than anyone else. She needed to manage up and down and every which way, and in this operation, unlike the Altaire, all pressure fell on the center.

"No one likes it when their hand is forced," she answered. "But I've made her see sense."

"See it your way, you mean. What if it doesn't work?"

"It will." Cielo considered leaving it at that, but the young machinist seemed genuinely worried. "We still have enough firepower to secure our targets and make our escape. Yes, we were counting on more, but this setback is a blessing in disguise. It's forced us into a play that could avoid bloodshed."

"And what about on our side? Security will still have their guns, you know."

"That's what plan B is for," she explained. "We might be outmatched, but the debris impact was a timely reminder: They'll do whatever it takes to protect the Altaire and its guests. And we can use that to our advantage."

"And if that plan fails, we shoot them all."

Cielo shook her head. That kind of tenacity could save Pio, yet she disapproved of how misguided it was. She felt responsible for how their actions would corrupt him just as much as she worried about any harm that might befall him. "They're not our targets, and more importantly, they're still our people. We don't want them to be collateral damage, not if we can help it."

Pio lowered his head, in agreement or self-reproach, Cielo couldn't tell.

They stood together and watched the daylight unfurl over their homeland, imagining a better life when they returned. They both understood the ignominy of what they'd decided to do, accepting the risk for the reward, even though in reality that risk would be borne by another. Cielo hoped that when this was all over, she could live with the fact that the future she purchased for her sibling was built on deceit, tainted with blood.

Chapter 11
The Moon Pools

The Moon Pools were situated at the terminus of one of the Altaire's spokes, away from the hub and most of the station. Henry explained that this was for safety. Such a facility needed to be housed where the spin gravity is at its highest; no one wants giant globs of water bouncing around. Nick had been complaining about the long walk to their destination, and distracting him worked, usually. When Henry cautioned his husband about the slight change of gravity as they approached the walkway, Nick shrugged it off without missing a step.

It seemed to Henry that not even an exclusive invitation to the afterparty could improve his husband's mood. Nick loved parties and he loved being with these people, especially to the exclusion of others. Not everyone was privy to tonight's festivities and his invite was a status marker, the surest sign that he was not viewed as an outsider. He should have been more excited.

"There seems to be a problem with your doors," Nick told the receptionist after his tracker had refused him admission into the pool area. He waved his forearm over the sensor several times, to no avail.

The receptionist, a tall and angular Black woman, came to the gate from behind her desk, tablet in hand. "I apologize, sir. It might be a communications glitch. I'm happy to override it for you, if you'll please give me your name?"

Nick obliged pleasantly. Henry held his breath; he saw through Nick's smile and carefree tone. As the woman's spindly fingers scrolled through the guest list, Henry felt his husband's temper roiling. Two more guests entered the lobby to queue up behind them. The receptionist shook her head. Nick drew a sharp breath and repeated his name, enunciating each syllable in case the woman didn't get it right.

"I'm sorry, I don't seem to have it on the list," she answered, sighing. "There is a Henry Gallagher, however."

Henry raised his hand meekly. "He's with me." He flashed her a lopsided smile. "Our names should be together."

The receptionist shook her head. The couple behind them edged past, stepping through the gate with no issue. Nick narrowed his eyes at them. "There must be some kind of mistake. Could you check again"—he leaned over to read her lapel—"please, Dominique?"

Henry cupped the small of his husband's back, a preemptive way of soothing him before he escalated. He patiently watched the receptionist scroll up and down the same list again, noticing how uneasily she held the tablet and how she flicked her fingers with some effort. When her hand seized up, Henry saw it coming, as he did the tablet falling to the floor with a loud crash. Henry froze.

"Oh, my, are you okay?" Nick asked as the woman crouched down, awkwardly lifting her device from the floor. She held it across her chest as one hand massaged her other wrist.

"Do you need help?" Henry asked. Even as he bent down to help her, he felt a whisper of irritation, of impatience.

"No, I'm quite all right. I just need a moment," Dominique replied, her lips pulled tight. Another guest entered the lobby, a confused look on her face. Henry rose off the floor and withdrew his extended hand.

The receptionist followed suit, leaning against her desk as she straightened herself. Once upright, she pressed a button on the cracked screen of her tablet. "You should be all sorted out now," she said evenly.

The gate opened, and Nick stood dumbly before it. "Are you sure you're fine? Should we call someone?"

"She said she's fine," Henry replied as he steered his husband through the threshold. He turned to the receptionist, leaving her with an abrupt thank-you. The other guest scanned her forearm over the sensor and breezed past after them. The receptionist waved them all off, barely masking the pained look on her face.

The Gallaghers exchanged no words as they walked toward the changing rooms and disrobed. Nothing needed to be said, but each knew what the other was thinking.

As Henry showered, he palpated his hands, his wrists, the spot in his forearm where the Altaire's implant was lodged. He'd always been uneasy about putting things in his body, especially those that beamed his location to parties unknown. Who knew what other information it tracked and transmitted? He of all people understood the value of medical privacy. He tried, but he couldn't feel the implant under his touch.

It supposedly dissolved after a couple of days, right about the time he'd be back planetside, yet Henry had no way of confirming that either, did he? He rubbed his thumb over the spot, hoping his chip had already, prematurely, melted away.

After he dried himself off, he tried to help his husband do the same. Nick declined his offer. Leaving their robes behind, Henry reached for Nick's hand and they made their way toward the Moon Pools.

What lay before them defied all expectation. They'd seen the promotional materials, and their en-suite system played an advertisement for this amenity nonstop, but the place had to be seen to be fully appreciated. Before them stretched, in a magnificent vista, seven pools of crystal-clear water in high-lipped lunar craters. The floor that they stood on was smooth to the touch, cold and firm like marble, but projected from underneath was a lifelike textured hologram of the lunar surface. The same textures were projected backlit onto the calderas, which were formed in a hexagonal array. Each one bubbled with jets of warm water. Seamless windows stretched the whole length of the chamber, but most of the illumination came from above, where a large, round aperture bathed the room in cool, simulated moonlight.

A shiver coursed through Henry. Every hair on his body rose on end, despite the finely-tuned climate control. He turned to Nick, whose lips were slightly agape, the most he would ever come close to having a jaw hanging low in amazement.

"You know, the edges of the pool are intended to . . ."

"Don't ruin it," Nick said. "I've read the brochures. Artificial gravity and fluid mechanics and all that. The rotating joints and the pool design and hydro jets, I know what they all do."

This was bait. Nick was spoiling for a fight, an avenue for venting his rage about something other than physics. This was about the Captain's Table, which Nick was intent on relitigating. Henry held his tongue, refusing to give him the satisfaction.

Nick dipped a toe into one of the calderas, one that contained a steel heiress and her husband, wrapped in a torrid embrace. Next to them a threesome was similarly engaged. One of the women gave Henry a playful grin, asked them both to join in. He smiled, promising to return before the night was over. They then moved on to another pool, one occupied by a solitary wader all the way on the other side.

Nick oohed as he slowly dipped into the pool, its water reaching just above his knees. He reclined himself on the low stone bench that wrapped around the pool's inside perimeter. He offered a hand in invitation, and Henry hoped that this meant his husband was ready to play.

He raised his leg over the crater's edge, and his entire body tingled at the pleasure of warm water touching his skin. He stood before his husband expectantly. Nick swept his gaze from Henry's face to his chest, then to his manhood. Henry let his husband savor the moment before lowering himself in front of him. Skin to skin, their breaths grew heavier. Henry leaned in for a kiss. Nick flinched away from him.

"I'll fix it, all right?" Henry said in frustration. "It's not over yet."

"I don't know, love. 'Fuck off' sounded pretty final to me."

"What did you want me to do? Coen demanded to know why. I can't just blurt it out in the middle of a full banquet table."

"You wouldn't have told him even in private—that's the problem. Face it, we're in the weaker position here, and we must make some calculated risks."

Easy for you to say, Henry thought. They might be married, but the risk did not fall on them equally, not when the secret was Henry's alone. He and his family kept it for all his life, well before Nick even laid eyes on him. Every record of his condition had been destroyed, or altered, or fabricated into a less damaging narrative. Every witness had been bought off. Nurses, technicians, consulting physicians. If Nick had been the one whose body prevented him from going to Mars, he wouldn't consider confiding in anyone whom he couldn't control.

"You know I can't," Henry replied. It was hard enough to convince his family to tell his husband everything, which naturally involved revealing the decades-long cover-up they'd all participated in. Now, pressed to further disclose, Henry questioned whether he should have told Nick anything at all. "He won't be like the others."

"This is just an old man's curiosity. It gives him no benefit to tell anyone." Nick said, running a hand through Henry's wet hair. "And he's a reasonable man. On some level, he must understand how unfair it is to disqualify a person because of a genetic mutation. It also doesn't hurt that he's got a sick son."

"And if he talks?"

"Then we'll deal with it the way we always have."

Henry stared at his husband, resenting his glib over-confidence. Nick had always been the planner, the power behind the throne, and he treated their present scheme much like his film projects and production deals. He could afford to be ruthless because his life was not on the line, not directly, no matter how strong their marriage was.

The worst part about it was that Henry wanted Nick to be ruthless. It allowed him to maintain his innocence. It let him be the good guy.

More of the Rochford class arrived, entering the hall of pools in full nakedness. The staff roved around, offering flutes of champagne and other intoxicants. Wine and liquor freely passed from hand to hand, as did phials of stimulants and psychedelics. Everyone partook of the offerings, and of each other. Guests in the other pools had started to move on from understated foreplay to more explicit indulgence.

Henry ran his hand up and down Nick's back, feeling the slick warmth of his husband's body. He hardened, and before long he took Nick's cock in his hand. He slid closer, stroking him, leaning in to kiss his neck as he went.

From the side of his eye, Henry saw another Rochfordian enter their pool. In the faint moonlight, Henry couldn't recognize him, though he could see how he stared them down like a predator. Henry gave the stranger a wink. The stranger summoned an attendant, who presented a shining tray of injectables and pills. He looked away from Henry for only as long as it took to make his selection and jam a tube on his bicep. His eyelids fluttered, and beneath the surface, Henry could tell that he was stroking himself as he watched.

Nick lifted Henry's chin from nuzzling in his clavicle. "I want to save my energy," Nick said. He gave Henry a chaste kiss, moving his hand away from his still-hard cock. "The night is young."

In response, Henry took Nick's hand and wrapped it around his throbbing cock. He didn't see why he shouldn't have fun if Nick chose to restrain himself. Nick withdrew, giving him a reproachful stare. Apparently, the restriction extended to Henry as well. Business before pleasure.

"You're not punishing me, are you?" he asked, half in jest.

"Punishment helps neither of us," Nick answered. "But we need to focus. The Lonsdales will be here soon and we need to be in their good graces. How do you feel about Isobel?"

Henry shrugged, a muted response considering the pressure in his groin. "She's lovely, sure."

"I've seen the way she looks at you," Nick said encouragingly. "Julian too. You all were very chummy at dinner."

"He was talking business, not flirting."

"What about her? She might be our way in. She knows how to play the game. Look at how far she's come."

"It doesn't matter," Henry said. "A good fuck won't be enough."

"It's a start."

From afar, Henry saw Sloane descend the steps into the pools, wide-eyed in awe and probably uppers. His sense of style aside, Sloane's looks did not need finery to draw anyone in. He captured people's attentions with not a single thread on his body. Henry waved him over to their pool.

"You're just in time," Nick said. "Shenanigans have ensued."

"Well, Sloane usually is the harbinger of such things," Henry said, sounding more dour than he intended. Sloane splashed some water at his face.

"Your husband seems to be in a mood, Nick. Maybe you should have left him at home."

"I don't think his dinner is agreeing with him," Nick said with a grimace.

Sloane beckoned a staffer and gestured at Henry to take his pick of libations. He opted for a glass of port. A group of Rochfordians joined their pool. Henry saw that their watcher now had his hands full with women on both sides.

The Altaire moved away from a view of the moon and orbited toward the Earth's shadow. In synchronous response, the interior lights illuminated the pools with a faint silver glow. The music crescendoed to a slow, rhythmic beat. The vibe in the room shifted too: the kissing and writhing grew more fervid, the moans and grunts growing in volume.

Henry slid an arm around his husband. He gazed right into Nick's eyes, which gave him no indication of want. Henry pulled him closer, planting a kiss on his neck, right below the ear where he liked it. Nick reached out at him, past him, grabbing Sloane's arm, roping him into their embrace.

"Do you mind watching Henry for a bit?" He asked Sloane. "I need to stretch my legs." Sloane assented. Nick gave his husband a peck on the cheek, then whispered, "Keep an eye out for the Lonsdales, all right?"

Nick shot up from the water, and swaggered toward the farthest pool, the one tucked in a corner where light barely reached. Henry eyed him intently and saw the glistening form of Xiomara Harris heading to the same pool.

Henry sank back into the water, gazing up into the starry sky with limbs outstretched. He wanted to float away, either physically in this pool or mentally at least. "You'd do well up there," he said, remembering his company. "Mars."

"Would I?" Sloane asked. "I don't think the red planet's in need of libertines."

"Did you mean what you said before, that you don't care about your points? We've only been training for it since childhood."

"Mars isn't the dream it used to be. My life belongs down there, on that shitty planet."

"Everyone here has cushy lives down on that shitty planet, but even they know it's not sustainable, especially for their kids or grandkids," Henry said. "You don't want to be sixty and stuck on an oven of a planet, missing your chance at a spot."

"And there's that too," Sloane said. "I'm objecting to the MERIT system on principle. Who says an old-timer shouldn't have as much of a shot as someone younger? Or that guy right there, slinging us meds and booze? He's needed up there more than I am."

Believing he was called, a server approached Sloane and lowered his tray. Henry looked around at the other servers, the only people in the room with clothes on, and marveled at their stoicism. He hoped that they didn't feel violated, or worse, *get* violated while attending to his cohort. Sloane finished his drink and picked up another champagne flute.

"You're usually up for harder stuff," Henry remarked.

"You and I haven't gone to these things in a while, but I prefer to have my wits about me when I'm in an orgy."

"The last time we came to one of these, we ended up gossiping all night."

"Not all night. Some fun was had, if memory serves." Sloane smirked. "Besides, isn't gossip why one goes to these things? For example . . ." He tilted his head toward Max Donahue, whose family owned the world's largest fast-fashion chain. He marched in with two women on each side, neither of whom were his wife.

"Interesting choice in partners," Henry said under his breath. One of the women was Giannina Weiss, a top DC lawyer who also happened to be married to the Justice Secretary. "I think someone's trying to head off a federal investigation."

"Labor violations?"

"Antitrust. Their latest acquisition has put a big target on their back."

"I'm surprised Daddy Donahue would leave his lunk-head son with such a critical task."

"Well, Giannina sure seems receptive," Henry said as Max started fondling the woman's breasts. "And she certainly came into her looks, didn't she?"

"She was fine back in the day."

Henry scoffed in disagreement. The two of them went on like this for a while, trading gossip, speculating on who wanted to fuck who and why. Henry disliked the risk and transactional nature of these events, but they'd always had a larger, more comforting sense of security. The feeling of one's place being reaffirmed and protected and celebrated by people like him. That feeling was at its height when Henry was with Sloane. They knew how to make each other feel good, doing as they had since they were still living in the Rochford dorms. They learned much from each other in those days, and though they never confused their teenage lust for love, each understood that what they had was some form of it. A more stable, more dependable kind.

Henry slung his arm around Sloane's shoulder, his hand tracing the curve of Sloane's triceps. Sloane gave him nothing in response, his attention drawn to another pool where the Lonsdales had just arrived and held court. Henry's hands inched lower. Soon enough he felt a twitch as his fingers reached the curve of Sloane's ass.

"We're doing this, then?"

Henry gave him a devilish smile. "Like you didn't know."

"Not too soon, at least. Didn't plan on having you as the first on my dance card."

"You never plan for anything, Sloane. Especially not at orgies."

Henry held Sloane's cock and stroked as it hardened in his hand. His friend returned the favor, matching his pace.

"Just to the edge," Sloane whispered as he leaned back.

"Same." Heat welled in Henry's chest with each movement. He searched his friend's eyes and found that Sloane was searching in him too. "Just to the edge."

As he came dangerously close, Sloane gripped Henry's wrist, digging his fingers to stop the motion. Henry was almost there too. Sloane went slower, even as Henry's panting grew quicker, heavier. Sloane rolled his eyes, lids aflutter. They were both at the brink.

Henry felt himself let go. Sloane released him too, and as he did, Henry was filled with a surge of ecstasy. He fell back onto the pool, eyes closed. Every part of him pulsed, sending him into a near-unconscious trance.

After a while, his hand searched for his friend, to hold him and share in the pleasure. There was no one on the other end. Sloane had moved on to another pool.

How long was I out of it, Henry wondered, his euphoria subsiding.

Suddenly, his entire body began to burn up. Not from the jets of warm water bubbling around him, nor from the lustful heat that came with Sloane's edging. This was different. It felt like being boiled from the inside. Henry clutched one hand with the other as they both grew redder, his blood vessels glowing hot beneath his pale skin. His fingers throbbed, his wrists, his palms and knuckles, the color moving up to his forearms.

Henry whipped around to face the rim of the pool, searching in vain for a corner in which to hide. He then dropped to his knees, submerging as much of himself as he could. Gripped by pain and the terror of discovery, he nonetheless kept a straight face, his will battling with his body.

"Sir, are you all right?" an attendant asked, bowing over to him by the edge of the pool.

"Cramp," said Henry through gritted teeth.

"Do you require assistance getting out of the pool?" she whispered. "And then maybe I can help you stretch out?"

"I'm fine," Henry snapped. He couldn't get out; he would be red all over, and then everyone would know.

His only hope was that the attack wouldn't last long before someone else noticed.

Slowly, he leaned against the lip of the crater pool, thankful that he could rest his weight on his back instead of his limbs. He waited for his extremities to turn lighter. Soon, the pain ebbed, and he could plant his feet on the floor again.

Henry checked each part of his body, making sure they'd paled to their usual color. He scanned the room for wary, questioning glances, but the party had continued unaware.

All that pain, a preview of a fiery death, lasted but a minute. A minor, manageable nuisance. As though nothing had happened, Henry stood tall and rose from the pool, bare body dripping, ready to resume his night.

Chapter 12
All for One

Despite the climate control and the heated passion of the party in full swing, the first thing that Laz noticed was the cold. The view of the dark, empty space through the portholes didn't help, neither did the soft, silvery glow emanating from the skylight, nor the lifeless gray of the lunar surface hologrammed onto the tile under his feet. As he made his way down onto the pools, Laz hoped that the cold didn't show on his body. He checked to make sure his manhood remained unaffected.

He forgot this concern as hands made their way to caress him while he passed. Playful fingers flicked at his leg, his bare chest, his ass. These advances were likely more about cordiality than lust, but still, they made him feel good. Wanted. Under different circumstances, he might have succumbed to these enticements.

Instead he searched the crowd, soon locating Henry in the central pool, receiving hands-on attention from a shapely redhead. His friend raised a glass in his direction and waved him over, the redhead extricating herself as Laz hesitantly entered the pool and squeezed his way through the soup of nearby bodies.

Henry called on a server and handed Laz a cannabis injectable. When he declined, Henry jammed it in his own bicep instead. He handed it back to Laz with an encouraging stare, which left him little choice but to oblige.

"See anyone you like?" he asked Laz.

"Plenty," he replied with a vigorous nod to make up for the lie.

"I know you have a particular type . . ." Henry chuckled, his tone bordering on malicious. "But there are a number of options here. And if you're willing to shake things up a bit, well, you don't have to look far."

"I think things are shaken up enough for tonight, unfortunately."

"What do you mean?"

This was hardly the time or place, but after tonight's dinner, Laz couldn't afford to wait. He lowered his voice. "We need to talk about Ava."

"What? Here?"

"I think she knows."

"Knows what?"

"Everything," Laz replied. "She just told me she got the police reports, court transcripts, all of it. She got all the records unsealed, and you and I both know what's in them."

"No, we don't," Henry said with no hint of being in denial. "And unless she said she knows about the fight, then we're fine. Did she?"

"I think she was trying to get me to say it first."

"And you're smarter than that."

"Of course, I didn't say anything," Laz replied, pleased. He'd never quite outgrown his need for Henry's approval.

"Because there's nothing to say. We didn't do anything wrong. We didn't"—here, Henry lowered his voice even further—"kill Ash. We didn't hide any evidence, and we didn't lie. At least I didn't."

"I was trying to protect her, all right?"

"Yeah, and how did that help? Made the three of us seem unreliable, and made Ava seem more suspicious."

"And what about the fight?"

"Do you think admitting it to her would, what, win her over or something?"

"She's giving me the chance to come clean. I can feel it," Laz replied. "And if I don't take it, then I don't know if . . ."

"Look, man. Do what you want. But this is not how you get her," Henry interrupted. "And you gotta get over her. It's not gonna happen."

Laz almost didn't hear it. After all, how many times have his friends told him this? Henry's words skimmed off him like the water off his back.

"Don't you get it?" Laz replied. "She doesn't want us to come clean about the fight or the lying. It's the murder that she's really after. She's asking because she thinks we did it."

Henry laughed, shaking his head impatiently. "But we didn't. And honestly, I'm still not a hundred percent convinced that she herself didn't. This could be Ava trying to cover her tracks, for all we know."

"Fuck you, man."

"All right, lover boy, calm down." Henry scanned the pools, eager to end the conversation. "I know we didn't do it, so it doesn't matter what she thinks or what she found. I still think you shouldn't tell her anything," he continued. "Unless you're ready to tell her *everything*."

A chill came upon Laz, his skin turning to gooseflesh.

"I think that's what this is really about, Laz. Are you ready to do that?"

He knew the answer. She'd never be able to forgive him.

"I didn't think so," Henry said after a pause. He came closer to Laz, taking him into his arms in a firm embrace. Laz returned the gesture begrudgingly. "It'll be fine. We'll be fine."

All throughout their youth, people thought of Laz as all brains, no spine, and certainly no will of his own. Here Henry was, again calling the shots without calling the shots. Laz resented it, most of all because he knew that his friend was right.

Presently, Nick joined their pool, and behind him trailed Xiomara Harris, regal and resplendent, the fulsome waves of her hair kept safe beneath a silk headscarf.

"Have you met one of our most eligible bachelors?" Nick asked Xiomara. Laz reddened. He'd never been at ease with this title, and he heard it all too often. It hung on him like an ill-fitting suit, especially now that he was reaching the point where they became less of a compliment and more of a veiled insult, a springboard for gossip. Never married, at that age? What sort of damage does he have?

"Thrilled," Laz said. He kissed the back of Xiomara's hand, a courtly gesture that seemed ridiculously demure under the circumstances. "I'm a big fan."

"I saw you earlier at the casino. I meant to introduce myself."

"Well, now's a better time to meet anyway, wouldn't you say?" Nick interjected. He winked at her and cupped a palm under Laz's ass. "Take care of her, yeah?"

The other two laughed. Laz splashed some water in Nick's face, which the latter took as his chance to leave. He slithered toward Henry and led him away.

"I'm sorry, he can't help himself," Xiomara said once alone with Laz. "Even up here, he's still managing my life."

"That's Nick. He's always on."

"I did mean it, though. I've been wanting to say hello since this afternoon."

"Well, then. Hello." Laz chuckled awkwardly.

She slid closer to him, whispered her hello. He looked good, he knew that much, but he paled in the presence of someone so dazzling. What could she possibly see in him? This must be a trick. She could have sex with anyone in this room. Was she perhaps looking for something else? Perhaps she, too, felt the pressure of being single at their age, more so as an actress who was now too old to play an ingenue, and who had missed the boat on being a trophy wife by a decade.

"I hope the Rochfordians have been treating you right," he said.

"They have, so far. Might you want to keep that going?"

There was no use doubting himself. Regardless of motive, Xiomara Harris wanted him, and he did in turn. He wanted to serve her, to please her. It had been too long since he'd seen someone like her.

She was as close to perfect as he could find.

Laz escorted Xiomara from the pool and they settled themselves on a wide, circular ottoman covered in plush towels. He lay her down and knelt before her. He drank in the sight of this woman, seeing her fully but witnessing someone else entirely.

He climbed on top of her, tracing her lips and her cheekbones with his fingers. He nibbled on her ear and neck. He held her breasts, firm and taut, the way he remembered Ava's were, all those years ago. He slid his hands across her side, down to her waist, thumbing the prominent ridges of her hip bone. It felt the same way Ava's felt, simultaneously smooth and sharp. Xiomara smiled at him with a look of polite impatience. Laz looked up at her. Through the curves and ridges, the heaving of her chest, the well-defined chin, all he saw was Ava.

Laz entered her, starting slow but gaining traction with every thrust. He smelled Ava, heard her through the moans, felt her enfolding him. Xiomara raised her head for a kiss and Laz felt Ava's lips.

His pace quickened. His fingers teased the hair under Xiomara's headscarf. She swept them away. He kept thrusting, and in between grunts, he caressed her face, her temple. Once again, his hand went for the headscarf. Xiomara held his wrist, a baffled question in her eyes.

"Please," Laz said softly, plaintively. He drove himself deeper into her.

He couldn't recognize her expression as he pushed and begged. All at once she seemed dismayed, revolted, aroused, resigned. He closed his eyes and asked again.

"All right," she whispered.

She removed the headscarf herself. Jet-black waves of hair spilled out from their enclosure, framing her in a dark halo.

Laz grasped her shoulders in a swell of triumph. He heard himself say Ava's name, and he hoped it was all in his head, that he wasn't calling this woman by another's, but the pleasure kept cresting to the point of delirium, to the point where he didn't care, until at last, he came.

Chapter 13
The Scapegoat

It was the longest week of his life. Ava had been arrested, accused of murder, arraigned, and released, and Laz had not heard a single word from her. Little surprise that his heart almost stopped when her name popped up on his screen at the end of that week. His fingers fumbled on his phone, dropping it on the floor.

"Hello? Are you there?" she whispered, her screen dark.

"I'm here, I'm here," he said breathlessly. "I can't see you."

She brightened her screen a little, and though the view was still obscured by shadows, what mattered was that he could see her now. She appeared to be inside a coat closet, crouched under rows of furs and down jackets.

"I don't have much time."

"Where are you? *How* are you?" Laz asked, myriad questions fighting to leave his lips. "Can I come see you?"

"I'm fine," she said. "My parents have me on lockdown, so I have to be quick."

"Are you sure you're all right? I'm so glad you're out. That's a good sign, right?"

"It's a sign that my parents have enough money to pay for bail. The case isn't over."

"Is there anything I can do to help?"

"I didn't do it. You have to believe me," she said, as certain as he'd ever heard her.

"I know," he replied, mustering as much conviction as he could. "I believe you."

"And neither did Daniela."

His chest tightened upon hearing her name. "Who is she, Ava? Is it true what they're saying? That you two were . . . together?"

"Yes."

He drew a sharp breath, trying to stifle a cry. Ava didn't falter at all. She confirmed it with no qualms, knowingly dashing his hopes. She could be cruel when she wanted to and was crueler still when she didn't intend it. His voice stiffened as he continued.

"And she's a drug dealer?"

"She's a good person."

"Did you deal with her?"

"Ashwin had an arrangement with her. He got the goods from her, but when Ash got put on probation, he couldn't go in and out of Rochford as easy. He made me do the pickups."

"So, yes, you did deal with her," Laz said indignantly. "What the fuck? And with Ash too? After everything he's done to you? All the—"

"It doesn't matter now. What matters is we didn't kill him."

"Then why did they arrest you?"

"I was with Dani all night," she said. "We camped in the woods like we do on weekends. She and I were nowhere near the salt flats. But my lawyer says they found pills on Ash's body. They traced it back to Dani somehow, and to me."

"Well, what about you and Ash?" Laz asked.

"What do you mean?"

"I saw you that afternoon, right after class." He observed every change on Ava's face, cautiously measuring his words. "You two were fighting."

Ava bristled. "That's not what it looked like, Laz. It wasn't a fight. It was a conversation. I don't even remember what it was about."

"That's convenient," Laz replied, unthinking.

"You said you believed me."

"I—No, yes, of course I do."

"Then you have to help me," she pleaded. "Help us."

However much the revelations pained Laz, Ava needed him, and that left no room in his heart for anything but mercy. "What do you want me to do?"

"Dani's still in there. The bail's set at two mil. And her legal aid lawyer is crap."

His heart sank as he understood the implication. "I don't know how I can help with that, Ava. That's a fuckton of money."

"Don't worry about the bail for now. We need to get her a good lawyer first. The longer this case drags on without one, the more she's in trouble. That you can afford, right?"

Laz nodded hesitantly.

"And your folks would definitely know which firms to go to."

"They won't wanna get involved with this," he protested.

"Then you'll have to do it on the down low," Ava replied. "Please, Laz. Her housemates can connect you with her abuela, she lives close by. Go to her. She can act on Dani's behalf and answer any questions, sign contracts or whatever. Do *not* go to her dad, and most of all don't give him money, no matter how much he insists."

"This is a lot, Ava. And what about you?"

"I'll be fine. My dad's hired a battalion of big-shot lawyers. They said this will be over quick."

"But it just started," Laz replied, confused.

"They're going to get the charges dropped," she explained. "They're gonna say that Dani and I weren't a couple, that we're not even friends. She's a dealer and I'm just someone who got caught up in her business."

"What? But that's not true at all."

"They want to paint me as the grieving sister, and claim that I'm just as much a victim in this." She began to waver and every crack in her voice broke Laz's heart. "I'm just falsely accused, helpless, malleable. Mentally unstable, with the transition and all."

"What the fuck?"

"It's making me sick, and I can't do anything about it," she replied with defeat. "That's their strategy. That's how they intend to clear me."

"But Ava—"

"One thing I know for sure," she said with conviction, "I'm not letting them pin this on Dani. She doesn't deserve any of this."

"Neither do you."

"You have to promise me, Laz. Get her a good lawyer. Bail her out of there. Time's running out."

As the trial went underway, Ava's parents kept her under closer guard. Laz supposed it was inevitable. Funeral arrangements had to be made, legal strategies had to be implemented, wayward daughters had to be controlled. That call was the last time Laz would talk to Ava for weeks, and it was not nearly enough. He still couldn't make sense of what was happening. He needed more answers, and in his desperation, he sought them from Daniela herself.

He enlisted his family's driver, who also acted as his bodyguard, to accompany him. With a small bribe, the prison guards let the man pretend to be Laz's guardian. The two of them were escorted through halls of drab concrete and fluorescent lights to a large room with dingy glass-paned booths. A buzzer blared to announce the arrival of an inmate.

Dani looked nothing like the picture on the news feeds, which portrayed her as a tough, hardened child of the streets, with her denim jacket and her piercings, flashing what could be a gang sign, a graffitied wall in the background. The journos must have creamed their pants when they unearthed that photo from her online profiles. But here, in her faded brown jumpsuit, she looked emaciated, hollowed out. Dead woman walking.

Laz introduced himself as Ava's friend, and her face beamed at hearing her name. Like a light shone behind her eyes. He recognized that feeling, knew the effect Ava had on people lucky enough to get close to her. Daniela said she'd heard about him, about Sloane and Henry too, and this put Laz at ease somewhat. He told her he'd been sent by her, though in truth, Ava wouldn't have liked him coming to see her, to do what he'd planned on doing.

"Ava said you needed bail money and a decent lawyer."

"Yeah, I really do," Daniela admitted, to his surprise. He expected some initial reticence. "I don't wanna stay here anymore."

"Did you hear they dropped the charges against her?"

"I knew that might happen. She has good lawyers. See, we're from different worlds, me and her."

And so am I, Laz thought. "Listen, I want to help, but I need to know what happened. I still can't wrap my head around it. Why do they think you two did it?"

"Ava was running for Ash, been so for about a couple of months," she replied with no hint of mistrust. "I guess people in your school like to talk, and they knew exactly who to point the finger at."

"Do you know if she and Ashwin fought, the day he died?"

Daniela shook her head. "They always fight. But then they always make up, or at least Ava lets it go and does what he tells her to," she said, her tone getting sharper. "But no, I don't know for sure if they even spoke that day."

"And she was with you Friday night?"

"All through Saturday."

The words cut through Laz like a knife. He asked her more questions but by then, she might as well be nonexistent to him. All he saw in his mind's eye were Ava and Daniela out in the woods together, doing things that he and Ava used to do. He thought if he saw Daniela, heard her voice, got some answers from her, he'd be able to overcome his heartbreak. Yet all he found was more.

"So are you going to help me?" she finally asked. "I need to get the fuck outta here, and the sooner the better."

"Yes, I will."

Ava never showed up for any of Daniela's trial days. Her absence was conspicuous to everyone, to Laz most of all. He watched intently from the gallery as the lead prosecutor, a gray-haired woman in a pinstriped suit, embellished Daniela's criminal history in her opening argument. He wished he could ask Ava, *Did she really have this long juvenile record? Did she really associate with these gangs?* The accusations all sounded flimsy, as suspect as the rumors he'd been hearing for weeks, and he needed to know for sure. He wasn't getting the whole story, not from a prosecutor determined to convict, and he wanted Ava there to give him the other side. He wanted to believe that Ava didn't do it, and despite himself, he wanted to believe that Daniela didn't either.

The prosecutor explained the timeline of Ashwin's murder, and Laz wished Ava could walk him through her version of events. She could explain what happened on Friday, what she and her brother talked about. Instead, all Laz had was an overzealous advocate with her charts and graphics.

At one point, the prosecutor presented a witness, a Rochford sophomore Laz had never met before. She claimed to have seen Ashwin with a woman—she couldn't be sure who—as they rode off in one of the Rochford training buggies that fateful afternoon. Laz was sure there was more to this; the witness must have gotten it wrong, and he wished Ava could assure him so.

The Rochford security chief might have blinked, too, if Ava was present in the courtroom. The chief wouldn't have been so definite in his assessment if the threat of Ava's counter-testimony loomed. She would have said, *We weren't near the salt flats that night. Daniela entered school grounds a lot, and school security was lax about it.* This was an open secret. Outsiders went into the desert and the woods and the salt flats at random hours of the day to do god-knows-what. Ava would have testified to all that, but since she didn't, Rochford was able to uphold its unfounded reputation as a safe and secure boarding school.

A forensics scientist was brought to the stand, guiding the jury through the crime scene photos. The whole courtroom reeled at the images, and Laz craved to hold Ava's hand. He wanted to feel her fingers, and disabuse himself of the idea that those fingers had wrapped around Ashwin's neck. *I know her hands, and they did not make those marks.* The scientist spoke about the narcotics too. Ava could have been the one to explain what the drugs were, instead of the state's witness. She would know the relevance of these pills, the etchings on their surfaces. Were these trademarks the ones used by Daniela's gang? Did she help Ashwin deal these specific drugs? Without Ava, the jury seemed poised to accept the prosecution's answers to these questions.

Most of all, Laz wished Ava was there when Daniela finally took the stand, looking disheveled in her baggy navy pantsuit that was no doubt a loaner from her court-appointed attorney. Ava could have provided the answers that Daniela couldn't give on the stand. She could have corroborated everything Daniela said. Like when Daniela claimed that she never saw Ashwin on Friday, that she and Ava snuck off into the woods for a weekend tryst. That Daniela didn't know how to drive a buggy, and that Daniela didn't have a reason to kill Ashwin, because as much rancor as they felt toward each other, they made good money, and money always smoothed everything out. Ava herself told Laz all these details, and they might have sounded more convincing to the jury members had they heard it from a member of the renowned Khan family, rather than this poor, orphaned drug dealer who fit their preconceived notion of a murderer. Instead, questions piled one on top of the other, burying Daniela in a mountain of suspicion.

Finally, Ava could have cried out in protest as the jury foreperson said the word, sentencing Daniela to a future in prison. But Ava wasn't there. She hadn't been there this entire time, not since she was cleared of the charges, not since the woman she loved was left to face the justice system on her own. Laz told himself that Ava would be here if she could, that her parents kept her away for a reason. That she would have done anything to save Daniela. These were one of the many things that Laz told himself, assurances that did not quite manage to convince him, even by the time the judge banged his gavel.

After the verdict was handed down, Daniela was remanded into custody and sent back to the detention center where she'd been held during trial. Her sentencing was in another week, when the judge would decide exactly how long she would languish in prison.

The state had a sentencing guideline, which meant a convicted murderer looked at a minimum of fifteen to life. Where Daniela fell within that range depended on a points system. She didn't have any prior felonies but she had two prior misdemeanors. A petty theft and a marijuana charge that she could have gotten expunged but she hadn't gotten around to dealing with. Those got her two points. She had two juvie convictions, for a point per. In the last ten years, her longest crime-free gap was three years, which at least shaved a point off. One point each for the crime being gang-related and drug-related. Finally, because the judge thought the crime was "extremely cruel or depraved"—a term pliable enough to cover dumping a dead body in the salt flats to be eaten by vultures—Daniela garnered another two points. In sum, she had enough points to merit thirty-four years in lockup. That was a long time for someone who hadn't seen her twenty-first birthday.

The best her court-appointed lawyer could do was request a medium-security prison that was only a two-hour drive from where the Rios family lived. Daniela's priors made this request a longshot, but the judge acceded. It didn't matter in the end. She never got to see her new permanent address for the next three decades of her life.

The day before her transfer, a riot broke out in the showers of the detention center, and Daniela Rios was one of the casualties.

The MERIT system was engineered to favor certain people. Ava understood that most of all, knowing how the idea germinated in her father's mind in those months after Daniela's verdict. Back then, Gaurav Khan was still three years away from being appointed US delegate to the UN Mars Settlement Agency, but he already wielded considerable power as the senior US Senator for the state of California. And wield it he did.

Ava overheard all his frantic calls, his late-night videoconferences and committee meetings. She saw his draft bill well before it became "Ashwin's Law," in commemoration of "Ashwin Khan's love of space exploration." It was touted as a corrective to the earlier, more permissive US policy on Mars, promising a complete regulatory overhaul to ensure that Mars was reserved only "for the most deserving Americans." One of its key components was the criminal disqualification: any US citizen would be automatically disqualified from applying to the UN Mars settlement program if they had a "violent crime" conviction. The term was defined broadly enough to include minor assaults and yet narrowly enough to exclude white-collar crime.

Ava confronted her father about it, one of the few times that she deigned to speak to him in those days. "You selfish fucking prick! This bill is a fucking travesty. You're using Ashwin's name to fuck millions of people over."

"If your tales about him are to be believed, fucking people over was exactly what Ashwin was all about," her father answered. "Something good must come out of this tragedy. Why not a more robust Mars program?"

"Something that keeps the riffraff away, you mean."

"Your words, not mine." Her father tut-tutted. "You're forgetting who you are and where you come from, Ava. This is what happens when you associate with undesirables."

Ava fumed at the word, incensed by the way her father's lips curled as he said it. "I know exactly where I'm from and I hate it."

"When I was a teenager, I went through this phase too. Rebelled against my parents, rejected the 'system' that clothed me and sheltered me and educated me. I never went as far as you've gone, but you too will come around. Once you see how hard life really is, you'll thank me for everything that I've given you. Then you'll be doing exactly the same thing I'm doing now. Carrying on the legacy."

"I'd rather die."

"I'm afraid that's not an option. Now that you've . . . now that Ashwin is gone, you'll have to take over our holdings," he said bitterly. "And if I have to break you in like one of our horses, I will."

"Do your worst. I've been through it all. With you, with Ashwin, with everyone. I can take it."

"We'll see about that."

Ava never truly believed her father would carry out his threats until he fired his opening salvo. The very next week, he introduced an amendment to the draft of Ashwin's Law, one that deprioritized joint marital applications by non-child-bearing US couples.

The last-minute change was roundly decried as a "gay penalty," a pithy misnomer, since it punished all kinds of queer and trans people and their relationships. Yet the uproar was not too vociferous—for one, the amendment was not a strict disqualification, and for another, childbearing persons and families had always been privileged under the law anyway. Most of all, the Mars settlers needed to propagate the species; it was only natural that those who could do so be given priority. Circumstances on the new planet would be different, and it was just as necessary to birth new citizens on Mars as it was to save settlers from a dying Earth.

It didn't matter that queer people had been the freest and most prosperous they'd ever been in American history. New rules had to be drawn. The policy debates raged, dominating every conversation, but all Ava saw was her father's machinations. It wasn't enough to have Ashwin's Law be a tribute to her brother; it needed to be a direct assault on her too.

In the end, enough of the public agreed that the need to propagate outweighed the incidental, indirect harm. They can be queer anywhere, even on Mars, but they'll have to pay a small price for it.

The bill passed and was signed into law on June 1, 2067.

She should have seen it coming. Mars would be no different from the rest of the American project. Certain people will get chosen, and others will get left behind. Some people will live, some people will die, and Ava lived in abject horror knowing that her father was one of the people who decided the question.

The following year, before Senator Gaurav Khan could seek higher office, the president appointed him as the official US delegate to the UN Mars Settlement Agency.

The American delegate had little trouble bringing his ideas to the MSA; indeed, many others shared his ideology, regardless of what flag they carried. The act of picking and choosing, favoring particular traits, privileging one type of person over another, had not been as taboo as Gaurav Khan initially thought. At least within the halls of the MSA, the belief was widespread that Mars should be populated by only the best humanity had to offer.

For his part, Delegate Khan proposed Ashwin's Law as a possible blueprint for the MERIT system, along with similar laws from other countries that shared his values. Get two hundred people in a room and one might think it an impossible task to reach any sort of agreement, but these were no ordinary people. By the time the system was finalized, the combination of merit and demerit points had entirely shifted the Mars settlement program from "Mars for All" to "Mars for the Best of Us."

Far from the egalitarian origins of the decades past, the MSA's prevailing ethos became centered on meritocracy. The delegates' definition of it, at least: the best people should be the ones to settle the new frontier. We should all strive to deserve Mars rather than expect it to be our birthright.

Ava viewed the MERIT system as the opposite of a birthright. It was the burden she carried as a Khan: daughter of one of the founding fathers of the MERIT system, sister of the fallen innocent whose death inspired its worst features. Ashwin might have been her father's rallying cry, but to Ava, he was just another rich kid whose murder was blamed on a poor kid. Daniela had been sacrificed following his death, and now, people like her all over the world were going to be sacrificed too. No matter what Ava's father believed, that was the Khans' true legacy.

Chapter 14
As Above, So Below

Cielo liked to say that she knew the Altaire like the back of her hand, and she meant it quite literally. In her early days onboard, she oriented herself by splaying out her left hand in front of her. The back of her palm was the hub, the fingers the spokes that her duties required her to traverse. Standing by the door to her four-person quarters, she navigated to the supply stations and cargo holds where her index finger pointed. The middle finger led to the casino, in the opposite direction of the spa wing that cut through the lobby, and her pinkie pointed toward the main ballroom, and so on. Her system kept her from getting lost in circles, but that was years ago. This night, at four a.m. station time, with the hall lights dimmed and with her own faculties fading at the tail end of a twelve-hour shift, she still swiftly found her way toward the Moon Pools.

In the spa's lobby, the receptionist puttered around her station, appearing to finish up her shift. "Dominique from Dominica," Cielo greeted cheerily, despite her waning energy. "Quite a party, huh?"

"I've seen better."

"Oh, I know you have," Cielo teased. The lower decks saw their own share of parties, unsanctioned by

Altaire command, of course. The staff would take over the community hall to celebrate someone's birthday, or wedding, or whatever occasion provided an excuse to vent and recharge before returning to the tedium of their duties. During those gatherings, the staff and crew, so distant from family and friends and lovers for so long a time, forged relationships. Cielo herself had her dalliances; Dominique did too, one of which ended up proving useful to their plans.

"A guest called in a missing piercing," Cielo told her. "Did anyone turn in a sapphire stud, titanium setting?"

"It's as good as gone, if you ask me. You could ask the cleaners." Dominique didn't sound too optimistic. "Would have been nice to find it, though. How much do you think it'll fetch?"

Cielo shot her a look of amused suspicion. "Are you sure you didn't see it?"

The receptionist clutched her chest mockingly. "Why, Cielo dear, are you calling me a liar?" she replied, the dropped r of her accent coming through.

She laughed. "Fine, don't tell me. You can keep it."

They all needed the extra cash, but Cielo knew some needed it more than others. She didn't let the receptionist's bearing fool her. Dominique had a lot to worry about: aging parents, a deadbeat husband, three kids, all relying on her planetside. Cielo commiserated with her often and so knew what ailed her mother, how much her husband had lost on gambling, how expensive primary school was. The last they talked, Dominique had complained about construction prices. Her family's run-down homestead kept getting wrecked every hurricane season, and the Sisyphean task of rebuilding was draining her dry. Yet she made do, had been making do for the last four years, the hope of a bigger payday buoying her.

"No one's gonna get in trouble, are they?" she asked Cielo.

"I'll handle it. I'll tell the guest that the robovacs got to it and the stud's now floating across space."

"They'll believe you too. Guests are dumb, and this lot more so." Dominique yawned with some exaggeration.

"Don't worry, you'll get your beauty rest soon."

"Not for another six hours. Jenne is down with the flu. I'm covering half her shift, and Myra's taking over the other."

"How is Jenne? And did she report it?"

"She's taking it easy," the receptionist answered. "And no, she didn't report it. You know how it is. She'd get written up, then blamed if someone else gets sick. Dock her pay too."

"If I had any say over payroll, you know I'd give you and Myra overtime for this."

"I know. But I'm happy to cover. We gotta have each other's backs."

Dominique would have done well on Mars, Cielo thought. She knew how to weather storms; she came from an island dotted with volcanoes. Most of all, she had grit, and she cared about others—weren't those the traits that people need most to survive in a treacherous new land? Too bad they didn't measure those on the MERIT scale.

Worse, Dominique had sickle cell. Incurable and inheritable. An automatic disqualifier. Her condition's name gained a much graver meaning now that humanity was essentially engaged in a culling. She took care of herself, managed her pain crises, never took a sick day even at their worst, but none of that mattered. The kind of people who decided these things, who confused her island country with another one similarly named, would gladly let her aboard the Altaire as a servant. But Mars was out of the question. She could never be fit for the red planet, not even to serve drunk, rich people for a pittance.

The glass doors of the spa lobby whooshed open. Two heavyset Security officers stared wordlessly at Dominique. She flourished her finger languidly. "Lav's that way. Last stall." The officers trudged past them, their boots thump-squeaking across the floor.

"Blackout?" Cielo asked as they left. "Why didn't you notify me?"

"Two of them. Completely plastered. One's hugging the bowl with a plug up their bum," she snickered. "I figured I'd save you the sordid details until the morning."

"No need for medical though, yeah?"

"Don't you worry. No one's dead. Though that wouldn't be the worst thing," Dominique joked, but only barely. The crew held the guests in varying degrees of contempt, and this crop from Rochford were, in many ways, worse. They were exponentially richer than the typical Altaire guest, which meant they were more demanding, more entitled. They were legacies, the worst kind.

And what did they do on their very first night? They fucked each other the way monarchs of old fucked kin to keep the bloodlines untainted. These folks weren't trying to reproduce but they were propagating just the same. With each encounter they fed and they nourished, traded and bartered, coupling and growing their reach.

And as they do everywhere they go, as above and so below, they left havoc in their wake.

At least tonight's bacchanalia provided a galvanizing effect. As Dominique gabbed about what she'd seen and heard that night, Cielo sensed from her a swell of enthusiasm, a departure from one of the more nonchalant of their crew. Their guests' excesses were a sobering reminder of how entrenched they were. There was no way to escape them, and the only thing she could do now was take what she wanted by force.

The two officers soon reentered, carrying a half-conscious reveler by his arms. The knot on the man's robe hung precariously loose over his thick frame, threatening to undo itself. A third officer followed close behind, this one carrying another guest over his shoulder, a petite blonde.

"It's like a war zone back there," the man said.

"Thanks for taking care of them," Cielo answered. The woman hung limply over the officer, drool caked on the side of her lips. Through stringy hair extensions and mascara-smeared eyes, the guest stared at Cielo while being hauled out the door.

"What are you looking at, bitch?"

Remembering that she still wore her uniform, she put her hands together, gave her a cloying smile, and bowed slightly. "Have a good evening, ma'am."

Once the lobby doors closed, Dominique spat, "What a first-class cunt."

"Hazards of the job."

"You seem pretty chummy with them," the receptionist said, nodding toward the officers.

"Ah well, those ones aren't too bad. Which reminds me . . ." Cielo took out a slip of paper and handed it over. "I have some names for you. Do you think you can hand it off to your man in Security?"

"Tsk tsk. This'll be the third time I'm seeing Jin this week. The others are gonna get suspicious that I keep hanging about, if they aren't already."

"I'd do it myself if I can," she replied. "But I'm not the one who has a side piece down there."

"Side piece?" Dominique gasped. "I prefer to call him my paramour."

"Either way, I can't just go down there and start sucking face with Jin—now that'll be suspicious."

"Always with the jokes." Dominique unfolded the slip, her eyes scanning the names. "This about the shipment, or the debris field?" She emphasized the last two words furtively.

"Both. The crates didn't all make it and so we've had to make adjustments. I've come up with a new plan, and this list should still get us what we want without us losing our necks."

"And so what about these names then?"

"Tell your *paramour* to make sure that these are the ones who get into the shuttles."

"When?"

"Tomorrow. He'll know when the time comes."

"But both shuttles? What about our escape plan?" Dominique asked, eyebrow arched.

"It'll be there."

She tsked again. "Jin won't like this. And neither do I. You're putting him at risk if he doesn't see the whole picture."

"I'd tell you more but this is for the best," Cielo replied encouragingly. "In case one of us gets caught. You know that."

"You best know what you're doing."

"Trust." Cielo lifted her chin as she walked backward toward the spa doors, double-thumping a fist on her chest.

Terraforming Success Promises to Bring More to Mars Sooner

By Jurgen Zimmerman
April 21, 2089
This article also appears in the May 2089 issue of
Wired

The United Nations Mars Settlement Agency (MSA) announced Tuesday that this spring's Martian wheat harvest exceeded qualitative and quantitative benchmarks, a first in humanity's efforts at terraforming. The spring harvest yielded eighty tons of wheat, eighteen percent more than necessary to feed the thousand-odd inhabitants of the red planet for the next quarter. This also marks the third successful year of wheat harvest, and the first to produce a surplus. If these numbers hold steady, food security will be assured for the next three years, accounting both for the nascent settlement and for next year's influx of civilian settlers.

NASA Administrator June Shelley-Scott called the news a "triumph of international cooperation and ingenuity." Food production has long been the bottleneck in humanity's efforts to settle on Mars, terraforming technology being slower and harder to develop compared to high-speed reusable rockets, long-term radiation shielding, and equipment for extraction of water from Martian subsurface ice. "With this latest harvest, it's clear that the fourth pillar is all but conquered," Shelley-Scott added.

The news comes at a time when the global food crisis arrives at yet another tipping point. In recent years, solar satellite technology has successfully converted around eight million acres of the Earth's tundra into agricultural land. Yet the crop yields have failed to meet the demand of the world's populations. Julian Lonsdale, CEO of satellite giant Lonsdale Aerospace, continues to be optimistic, but hastened to add: "As much as we are investing on Earth, the terraforming news shows how investing in Mars is worthwhile, contrary to detractors. Maybe even more so."

Many share Lonsdale's one-sided optimism, viewing the food crisis as the latest sign that Earth is no longer salvageable. Heat indexes continue to rise, causing ecological collapses and agricultural failure, which in turn exacerbate the climate migration crisis. "We keep moving up but we're running out of 'up' to go to," said Humberto Torres, one of the community leaders in the latest migrant exodus at the US-Canada border. "My family has been moving north from Ecuador since my parents' generation. Every time we try and build a home somewhere, there's always a reason to leave soon after."

A year from now, "up" might not be North for people like Torres: on May 1, 2090, MSA's application portal opens for the first civilian settlements on Mars. In addition to the astronauts, engineers, and scientists living on the planet, some for six years now, the rest of humanity will have a chance to be one of five thousand new inhabitants for this first selection round. Although subsequent rounds have yet to be scheduled, the rapid developments in Martian agriculture could mean that the next rounds will follow sooner than expected. This latest terraforming success solidifies public confidence in the MSA as it spearheads this momentous phase in humanity's journey to Mars.

Ioannis Athanasiou, MSA Chief Administrator, issued this statement: "Throughout history, there has been no stronger unifying force than the will to ensure the future of humankind. Together, we have all built a thriving community on Mars, one that the rest of us here on Earth can soon join. I thank all our member states for continuing to make Mars more than a dream, but a reality for everyone."

In a little over a decade, Athanasiou has successfully managed to wrangle all of the world's nations into a cooperative agency, bringing its collective mandate and implementing it in their home countries. Every year that the Mars settlement successfully achieves its research and scientific goals is further proof that the MSA is not a toothless coalition but a true global alliance that produces results. In the wake of technological and political advances in the Mars settlement program, gone are the naysayers who likened MSA to UN agencies of years past.

Despite these advances, certain sectors remain critical of the Mars program's fairness. Representative Yadira Perez (D-Washington), a staunch and longtime critic of American policy on Mars settlements, has called it "an irreversible drain on international aid and natural resources." Responding to the terraforming news, she said that the MSA "supposedly prevented oligarchs from owning Mars, but it still ended up that way, and it continues to be that way. This is not about scientific advancement or the future of humankind. This is about systematized corruption paving the way for the colonization of a new planet, plain and simple."

Athanasiou responded to these criticisms with a familiar refrain. "Mars is the backup plan. It is an investment in the future, not a divestment from the planet we now have. Human expansion into the rest of the solar system is inevitable, and we are here to make sure everyone will have an equal chance at living on Mars."

Though the latest terraforming news is a clear technological achievement, it remains an open question whether equality can truly be achieved, on either planet. Jerome Young, spokesperson for the REMAIN Climate Foundation, pointedly asked: "People are starving here, right now. These people will never make it to Mars, because they will die of hunger. What good does this news do for them?"

Chapter 15
Spacewalk With Me

Henry made his way to the launch area first thing on Saturday morning. In one hand he had the carrying case for his custom EVA suit, and with the other he held his husband. Before them walked their valet, whose chipper disposition worsened Henry's simmering hangover. Officially, it was ten a.m. station time, and he'd barely had any sleep following last night's after-party.

"The spacewalk platform is the only point of egress accessible to guests," Pio said, "aside from the shuttle ports, of course. We keep this area highly secure, so I hope you don't mind me droning on about the protocols."

Henry replied with a grunt, seeming less engaged than he intended. He was well-versed in space station security procedures, and didn't he also ace the recertification course? That was only five months ago.

"Everyone will be provided with an Altaire EVA suit. It has everything you need to make sure your spacewalk is safe and enjoyable. The comms are easy to link and use, so you can chat with each other—and me—while we're out there. Of course, it's not a real spacewalk unless you have photos and video to prove it happened, and our suits have capture and recording technology. With your helmet, you can take as many photos as you want using voice commands. I can also do it for you if you prefer that."

Nick held his suit before him, searching for the camera and the light. Pio helpfully pointed them out on the sides of the helmet.

"The suit has eight layers of protection and an intelligent system that regulates moisture and oxygen levels. The helmet's smart display will show your vital signs and navigational information. The suit also has radiation shields and smart sensors that can detect oncoming threats. Not that you have to worry about that. We expect a two percent chance of debris activity this morning."

"You'd think they'd shut up about debris after yesterday," Nick told Henry under his breath.

"Very low odds," Pio said, without missing a beat. "But in the unlikely event, I'll keep you safe. I'll be with you the entire time."

"You and everyone else," Nick complained. "How many of us are in this batch again?"

"Ten pairs. You're lucky to have been scheduled early. The later groups tend to be bigger."

"I suppose we have to thank the captain for that," Henry said. "But still, I was hoping for a more exclusive walk."

"Don't worry, there'll be plenty of *space* for everyone," Pio answered jokingly. "By the time we're out there, we should see the sun rising from the horizon, with a clear view of Australia right beneath us. It's enough to make you forget everyone else around you."

The staging area was a wide, clinical-looking hall lined with silver spacesuits encased in glass and chrome lockers, where some guests had begun stowing their clothes away. Altaire staffers waited on their wards as they outfitted themselves with the suits.

"Each locker is tied to your implant and should open with a wave of your hand," he continued as he led the Gallaghers to their assigned spots. Henry moved his hand over the sensor and his locker opened with a smooth click.

"Aside from your implant, each suit also has its own tracker and navigational system that is solar powered and not reliant on the suit's battery. Not that you need to worry about that, of course. This excursion is scheduled for only ninety minutes, and the suit has unplugged power for six hours."

"Can you imagine spacewalking for that long?" Henry said, breathless. "The longest I've ever done is sixty minutes."

"We're pushing the limits of legally allowable civilian spacewalk time," Pio said. "As you know, guests here at the Altaire get special advantages."

"Speaking of which—I spoke with Captain Williams and had the tech team inspect my suit," Henry said, lifting his carrying case and giving it a couple of taps. "They gave it the all clear, I'm sure you've been told."

Pio nodded. "Yes, sir. You're not the first to make such a request, and as you know, we aim to please. You can wear your personal suit, but we'll have to install our tracker on it and equip it with our own jetpack."

"Equip away." Henry handed the case to the valet.

"Why don't you just use their loaners?" Nick asked as they changed into their base layers. "Using your own might be more trouble than it's worth."

"I trust that suit. I've walked in it thrice already. Besides, I didn't spend that much money on a custom suit to not use it."

"And it's in red," Nick said, teasing. "Should make for striking photos."

"You could've gotten one too, you know."

Henry helped his husband slip on his gear, secured his helmet, and walked him through the on-screen interface.

Pio returned, having changed into his own EVA suit, and handed Henry his suit. The valet then resumed briefing Nick about his gear while Henry changed.

"Everything can be done by voice command," Pio said. "Your display is also connected to the suit's wrist panel, in case you prefer interfacing that way. Video capture is always on during the spacewalk, so no need to worry about getting the perfect shot."

"And what about our jetpacks?" Nick asked.

"You won't need to use it," Pio said, brandishing a length of cord attached to his own suit, with two large carabiners hanging on its end. "Once we walk out onto the airlock, we'll all be tethered. Jetpacks are only for emergencies."

"Actually, that's what we wanted to talk to you about," Henry interrupted. "I've gotten the NASA special license, and I've done a ton of solo spacewalks before. Nick here hasn't, but I can take care of both of us out there." He screwed in his helmet, asked the smart system to download his certifications, then sent the details to Pio's display. "I know it's a guided tour, but I've completed the mandatory hours. Nick and I will manage without your help."

Through the sheen of the helmet's display, Henry saw the protest growing on Pio's face and decided to forestall it. "If you want, you can watch us from a distance, but just the jetpacks, please. No tethers."

"I'm sure watching us won't be necessary," Nick told Henry, clearly for the valet's benefit. "We're not children. Besides, if the captain signed off on it . . ."

"Did she?" Pio asked with relief.

"She did," Henry lied.

"All right, then. If she said it's fine. But I'll still be watching you from the deck. And I'll ask the other guides to keep an eye out, just in case anything happens."

After Pio finished his final gear check, he led the couple toward the airlock where guests and their valets waited, all decked in their EVA suits. The steel doors behind them came down and closed. Beyond them was another steel door, its windows providing an unobstructed view of space.

A yellow signal light flashed intermittently as air was vented out of the sealed chamber. The process only took a few seconds, but the wait felt endless. Henry clasped his husband's hand, sensing his nervous excitement. Once the air around them stopped whooshing, the signal light turned green. The door before them slid open, and the guests found themselves on an expansive platform, like a wide diving board.

Through their private comm link, Henry told Nick to get ready. He then stepped forward onto the platform, pushing off, weightless. He took Nick with him into a drift toward nothingness. The Altaire crew followed, assisting their guests and leading the tethers toward the edge. Henry visually checked his tether with Nick, not satisfied with his helmet indicator that told him they were double locked and secure.

"I'm going to propel us slowly," he said. "You'll feel a shift once we get farther from the station, but it won't be abrupt."

Nick managed a thumbs-up through his thick gloves. Henry pressed on the controls on his wrist panel, then gave his husband the signal. Small, short bursts of air shot out of the tanks strapped to his suit, pushing him forward from the platform, stopping on his command. Once his motion slowed to a standstill, Nick floated toward him, waist tied via the safety cord.

"Now we're talking," Henry said as he felt total weightlessness. "How are you doing over there?"

"Great. This is very different from the last time."

"Yes, well, the last time you were strapped to the station, and to an instructor too. That wasn't a real spacewalk. This is."

Henry jetted toward him. As instructed, Nick avoided any sudden movements to prevent collision or the tether getting tangled. Henry held out his hand and Nick reached for it. When they touched, their contact sent them on a spin.

"You all right?" Henry asked, holding onto Nick's forearms.

"Yes," Nick replied, bumping his helmet into Henry's. "This isn't my first rodeo."

An incoming message beeped into their comm systems. Pio. "Hello, sirs. Just checking in to see that everything's okay."

"We're fine," Henry responded. "Nothing to worry about."

"Excellent. I'll be close by, and if you need anything, please let me know." Henry's helmet display showed a line of coordinates and a visual marker. He followed the marker and found the crew attendant's yellow suit near the platform, tethered to a railing.

"Will do," Nick replied, before cutting the comm link. "It's funny how concerned they are."

"They're just doing their jobs."

"*You* could teach *them*. You went to Rochford, after all. What kind of training do those guys have?"

"I'm sure the Altaire Group only hires the best of the best. Besides, they do these excursions all the time. Hours and hours under their belt. I wouldn't underestimate them just because their training is on the job."

Henry took his husband's hand and led him closer to the rotating ring of the Altaire's hub. He held Nick in a loose embrace, their arms interlocked, and then propelled the two of them again. The Altaire logo spun slowly, the maroon of its upturned V looking like an arrowhead.

"Are we headed back?" Nick asked.

"I'm taking us to the other side of the station. The view's going to be better with the swarm of other guests out of sight."

"Good idea. Wouldn't want them in any of the photos."

Henry steered them away from the curve of the hub. His vitals rose as they reached a spot directly above it. Heart rate, O_2 level, respiration. Signs not of distress but of exhilaration. With the station completely behind them, all Henry saw was the Earth and the sun, its rays breaking through the horizon. The sun rose, and the world was suffused with its light and warmth, revealing the expanse of the oceans and islands and continents below them. The morning rays illuminated the Pacific, then Aotearoa and the Australian east coast.

"Wow," Nick exclaimed. A fulsome exhale fogged up his helmet. "This ruins every other sunrise for me."

Henry gripped his husband's hand, feeling an up-swell of ecstasy as they marveled at the sight.

After a while, Nick spoke. "So are you going to pretend nothing happened last night?" He asked calmly, a sure sign of an ensuing argument. Henry tried to read his face and failed, as their helmets had dimmed in response to the sunrise.

"Lots of things happened. You'll have to be more specific."

Nick signaled Henry to make sure their comms were completely set on private. "You had another episode, love. I saw you."

The pulse rate rose on Henry's helmet display as a dizzying mix of emotions overcame him: shame that he had been seen, fear that others might have seen him, distress from having caused Nick a moment's concern.

"It wasn't bad, maybe a two out of ten," Henry replied. "It came and went quickly."

"Well, if I saw you from two pools away, don't you think others might have seen?"

"Everyone was busy doing something. Someone. And of course you'd see me, you can't keep your eyes off of me."

"For good reason," Nick said, rebuffing Henry's attempt at lightheartedness. "This is exactly why we need the Architect. The sooner we have him in our pocket, the less we'll have to worry about being found out. You have to tell him. Otherwise, we'll have to move on to plan B."

"Yes, we can keep trying the Lonsdales. I think I made some headway with Isobel last night."

"No," Nick replied. "I mean Leighton."

"You can't be serious. We already agreed he's off limits."

"That's before Coen told us what he really thinks. It's time for the stick, love. We can have Leighton taken off every donor registry on the planet. Let's see how the old man feels once he's forced to hire some backwoods medic to transplant a black-market kidney into his kid."

"Jesus fucking Christ, Nick. Are you hearing yourself?"

"It's only a threat. We won't actually do it."

"It's absolutely out of the question. Even as a threat."

"Then give the man what he wants," Nick implored. "We don't have any leverage here. He wants you to make a sacrifice at his altar, so just do it."

"And if he talks?"

"For good measure, you could make him understand how this could affect your family too. No threats, but impress upon him how the Gallaghers are better allies than enemies, with everything going on."

Nick never fully grasped the import of keeping secrets that were never his, but he was nothing if not persuasive. Henry saw sense in his husband's words even as he felt manipulated into accepting them. Leighton was Nick's tool, if not as a bargaining chip against Coen, then as a means of getting Henry to do his bidding.

"All right, I'll talk to him again."

"Are you sure?"

"What did I just say?"

Nick cheered, wrapping his arms around Henry. He knocked his helmet against Henry's, the closest to a kiss that he could manage.

Through the visualizations on his display, the double panes of glass on their helmets, and the smart shields blocking the sun's rays, Henry tried to gaze upon his husband's face. The peaks of his cheekbones, the wizened eyes that seemed to belong to a much older man, the lines that bracketed his lips every time he smiled. Henry searched, but he could only see darkness.

"I knew you'd see it my way," Nick said. "That's why I took it upon myself to get us box seats to the opera."

Henry had forgotten about that afternoon's matinee. "What, orchestra center seats aren't good enough for you?"

"No, silly. I bribed a concierge to find out where Coen's box is, and asked to switch us to an adjacent one. He bumped off Shiliang Gao for us, can you believe?"

"Ah, he probably won't even show," Henry replied. The metaverse magnate was more interested in entertainment beamed directly into his brain stem. "Is that what you were up to before breakfast?"

"The devil never sleeps, and neither do I."

"All right, then," Henry said firmly. "Let's get our act together for the opera."

"There's the man I married."

Chapter 16
First Ascent

If he wanted to, Sloane could have gotten certified for a solo spacewalk. No tethers, no guide, no tandem partner. Just him and the wide-open space. He could have trained a lot earlier, taken the necessary tests and classes, and it might have been worth the experience, if not the additional MERIT point of doing it unassisted. He could have, but there he was now, a listless kite on a windless day, pulled on a string by an overeager attendant.

"How does it feel, sir?" asked Benita through the comms. "We have a lot more slack if you want to venture farther out."

"Sure. Let's get away from the crowd."

Altaire advertised that "everything is first-class" on their station, but as the weekend drew on, Sloane found that to be an exaggeration. Certain suites were roomier, some had grander views. Special dinner tables were harder to book; some couldn't be booked at all. The Captain's Table was invitation only, and so was the after-party in the Moon Pools. The spacewalk was no different. Some guests did their spacewalks unassisted, or assisted by two crewmen, or wearing custom designer suits. A few arrived a full hour earlier than he did to enjoy an extended excursion. Meanwhile, there he was, alone with one assistant, scheduled later than everyone else.

No, Altaire was not egalitarian, no matter how much their PR people tried to assert it. Things were the same up here as they were planetside, the same now as they were when he was a schoolboy back in Rochford. There remained the same cliques and hierarchies that his peers loved to maintain, and the one percent of the one percent continued to be stratified into thinner and thinner tiers.

"We could go higher, above the upper torus," his valet suggested. "It's a bit of a trek, but by the time we reach it, we should have an unforgettable sunrise view."

Sloane agreed, and Benita led their tether through the fittings on the station's hull to which they were attached. A part of him wondered if the spacewalk would rekindle in him the sense of awe he had lost, and cause him to rediscover a dream he once abandoned: the ultimate first ascent. He'd need a sizeable climbing team, gear that's specific to Martian terrain and climate, and months of planning, but he knew even at a young age that he would be the first person to summit on a new planet, on the highest peak in the entire solar system.

The tug of the tether reminded Sloane of his days as a climber, and the cord felt like the lifeline that secured him. He recalled those days fondly, as distant to him now as was Mars. His life had taken too many turns, and each of those turns brought him farther and farther from that dream.

It wasn't the crimes of his father and brothers, nor his mother's callous abandonment, that led to the choices he had to make. There was no one wrong turn that caused him to spurn Mars completely. They all accreted, both his actions and others', and he took from those experiences one lesson: nothing mattered. He tried to do everything right, and he still failed spectacularly. He would never make it anyway, so why should he bother spending his short life chasing a score?

"We'll wait here for a bit," Benita said as they approached the edge of the upper torus. "Do you want to pose for pictures while the view isn't obstructed by other guests?"

"I'd rather not pose. Natural is better. Just find my angles and make sure the light hits me right."

Sloane looked below him. *The Indian Ocean*, his helmet display read. It also labeled the long sliver of Java, and farther below, the Australian expanse. Its western coast smoldered in the dawn light as wildfires raged, inexhaustible, poised to swallow the continent.

"Holy shit," Sloane whispered to himself. He had never seen it, not from this angle.

"Yes, it's pretty bad. It's been going on for six months, I thought it'd be over by now."

"Everyone did."

"I promise to leave it out of the pictures," his attendant said, waving a hand to steer him into a good angle. Sloane followed her directions absentmindedly.

"That's the spot. Perfect."

Below them, other guests took their photos too, doing their tumbles and turns, pointing at the stars and the moon and the identifiable features of the Earth below. An immense surge of guilt rose within him. His display showed a drop in his breathing. It felt as though he could inhale the smoke, feel it saturate his lungs. Rome burned, and there they were playing the fiddle.

Sloane turned his head away from the fires. He stared at the curvature of the Earth and the sun rising in the distance. The shield on his helmet began to darken his view, but not before the glare had already stung his eyes.

He asked to be taken back inside. His valet obliged, and Sloane was relieved that she didn't try to coax him otherwise. She made quick work of leading him back to the spacewalk bay.

As he took off his helmet and changed, he spotted Isobel by a distant locker. She'd changed into a custom suit, a teal number emblazoned with the Lonsdale Aerospace logo. His chest tightened, thinking for a moment that the man who stood next to her was Julian, but he was relieved to find that it was merely another valet.

Isobel hadn't noticed him, too absorbed with fitting her gloves onto her hands. Sloane hoped he might sneak away without being seen, but the near-empty room gave no chance of that.

"Sloane," she greeted eagerly. "Done so soon?"

He handed his helmet to Benita and thanked her. The attendant took this as her cue and quietly left. "I've seen all I needed to."

"I'm afraid I got up a bit late, but my man here says I still get the full ninety minutes, so it's all good." From behind her, Sloane read the impatience on the crew member's face.

"That's generous of him."

"Well, they're paid to please. Speaking of which . . . I saw you giving Julian the eye at the Moon Pools last night."

Sloane suppressed the urge to run, to leave her and this conversation altogether. "I don't know what you're talking about."

"Come now, let's not pretend." She narrowed her gaze. "I know, Sloane. And I don't mind. Whatever gets his rocks off."

"How long have you known?" he asked warily.

"About the money, or the other thing? I've known for a while that he was your cash pig."

"And what's the other thing?"

"His new penchant for pain?" she answered. "I'm fine with that too, as long as he doesn't do it with me. I can't get off on that, and I told him to find someone else."

Sloane didn't mind or care that Isobel knew about the money. If Julian wanted to know that he was a cash pig, that's between the two of them. It wasn't cheating, not really. What bothered him was this new arrangement that Julian had tried to force on him. More than that, Isobel knew, and it might even have been her idea that Julian seek it from him.

"I don't do pain."

"Darling, everybody does."

"I don't know what you've heard," he answered coolly. "But my services are as select as my clients, and I'm selective because I can afford to be."

Isobel grinned at him like he was a precocious child. "Haven't you noticed how everyone on this station craves even a second of Julian's attention? Yet he wants you, Sloane. He trusts you. More importantly, I trust you. You're not like the rest of them. You're not trying to get to Julian through me."

"It's a job, Isobel. Nothing more. And my terms have always been clear."

"A Lonsdale's favor is priceless."

"I'll tell you what I told him earlier," Sloane said firmly. "No means no. I'll be his fin dom, but that is it. Next time he asks—"

Isobel pouted dramatically.

"—or sends you to do the asking for him, we are done." He edged past Isobel, not bothering to wait for a response. She held him back by his arm.

"He doesn't take no for an answer, you know that." Isobel lowered her eyes, a clear play for sympathy. Sloane figured he'd try the same tactic.

"I've given impact play a good try, a long time ago. It . . . didn't go so well."

He meant it too. The last time he'd been a dom, he was in his twenties. Youth had given him a false sense of emotional invincibility, and he assumed that he wouldn't get affected. That every slap and shove would bring him more pleasure, that the act would replace the pain ingrained in his psyche. He wasn't as strong as he thought.

He hadn't been the one on the receiving end of the paddle and the whip, hadn't been the one shoved to his knees, his hair pulled back so hard that it burned his scalp, and yet the experience inflicted him with an exquisite kind of pain. That night ended with Sloane a naked ball of raw nerves, weeping in a fetal position on his client's zebra-hide rug.

"And it's not about the money either," he continued. "It doesn't do anything for me. And I don't do anything I don't enjoy."

Isobel edged closer, almost leaning for a hug. "Is it because of your . . . history?"

Sloane froze. She continued. "There were rumors, and I'm a pretty observant person. I remember the casts and the bruises. It ain't all from climbing."

"Don't believe everything you hear." Denial had always been his first instinct when it came to his father's abuse, but for a moment he considered revealing his true reason. Maybe doing so would make Isobel stand down and Julian find another. Yet he recognized, too, that he couldn't push Julian away too hard and risk losing the arrangement Sloane already enjoyed.

"Fine, it's nothing but idle gossip," Isobel replied with an unconvinced eye roll. "If it's not *that*"—she emphasized this last word—"and if it's not about the money, well, how about something else?"

"This is not a negotiation, Isobel."

"What about a spot on Mars?"

Sloane fell silent. That was not something he expected, nor something that they credibly could deliver. Right?

"How? Lonsdale just builds things. It's the MSA that decides the applications. And my MERIT score is in the shitter."

"Fuck the MERIT score!" Her attendant startled, and she waved him away. "You don't truly believe the habitats are handed out fairly, do you?"

"Look, I don't want it, and I sure as hell don't need it. I got no family, no kids. The future is me and only me, and the next however many years I get to keep living."

Isobel gave him a patient look of disappointment. "I've always felt a kinship with you, Sloane. We're both strivers. You lost your fortune and your privileges; I never had any to begin with. So I strived, and so did you. We made the best of things. Could I go to Mars on my own? With my grades and Rochford diploma, maybe. But now I'm a lock. You know why? Because merit only gets you so far, and that ain't never been far enough. At a certain point, you gotta play the game. Rochford taught me that."

"And your marriage is what, just gamesmanship?"

"Oh, honey. That's one hundred percent pure uncut love," she replied. "But I'm not blind to what that love gets me. The system's rigged, and you might think it's not rigged in your favor anymore, because of your family or your shitty score, or because of whatever sad-sack baggage is holding you back. But now I'm telling you: The one who's doing the rigging wants something from you. Why in the world would you fucking say no?"

Tantalizing as it was, Sloane abhorred the offer, especially after having given up on Mars all this time. The life that he built for himself planetside, that was all he really needed. The rest of the world might be on fire, but Charles Sloane IV was perfectly fine. Hadn't he convinced himself of that?

"All right, I'm listening."

Chapter 17
The Overview Effect

Ava minded Laz's tether more than she did her own. Spacewalks were second nature to her, having done them six times in the last two years. Training helped too, and she decided to attend the reunion with enough time to get several more simulations under her belt. She didn't need to check her displays or her gear as closely. She had a strong sense of balance and motion, unlike Laz, whose stiff movements indicated an attempt to hide his panic.

He drifted ahead of Ava, far enough to give him a sense of independence but not too far that he'd start getting scared. Hovering right by him was her liaison, Faiza.

"You all right there?" Ava asked him through the comms.

"Fine," Laz said, turning. "I think it's coming back to me."

"Just remember to relax."

"Oh, I'm relaxed," he replied unconvincingly. He inched toward the bottom rim of the station. "Ava, are you sure about this spot?"

"Everyone's heading to the peak, but down here is better. Away from everyone else."

She watched the other guests, tied to the Altaire like pet beetles on a piece of string. The less experienced ones, with their tandem tethers and guides, stayed mostly near the platform. The way Laz acted now, he might have been one of those too. Good thing Ava's skills made up for his lack. They could have space-walked unsupervised if she so chose, but the prospect of having to care for Laz—steering him, attending to him, being responsible for him—repulsed her, knowing what he'd done.

She glided closer, giving Laz a heads up as she approached. He held out a hand and caught her flight. Hand in hand they jetted to their destination, Faiza a specter that followed at a distance. Ava steered, the canopy of the spacewalk platform hanging far above them. She stopped her jetpack when they reached the underside of the station's outer torus. They arrived right on time.

"Oh my god," Laz exclaimed, every vowel extended.

This was what they saw: the curve of the Earth, a sliver of white-blue against the void, and then suddenly, a burst of light, blazing orange, breaking through the darkness, parting it in half, blanketing the view with a warm glow. Every cloud, every island, everything, more than what anyone had ever seen of the world at any given time, was visible in its resplendent beauty.

"The OE is real."

Ava nodded in agreement. Every nerve on her body tingled with life. This was always when she felt most alive: looking down on the world, basking in its majesty. All at once she felt infinitesimal and immense, alone in the universe, yet also attuned to every being in it. They called it the "overview effect", and if the feeling could be bottled up, it would make for the most irrepressible, incomparable high.

"Do you ever get tired of this?" Laz asked breathlessly.

"Never."

She could never tire of the awareness, the vision, the transcendental clarity that this view gave her. She would come up here every day if she could.

Laz drifted closer to her, his helmet lights on and shields undimmed. Judging by the expression on his face, he seemed to be on the verge of a revelation. The moment seemed right, too, with the spectacle of sunrise. Ava was the one who had brought them there—alone under the station, such emotionally charged circumstances—but if Laz had orchestrated this, the timing would be perfect for some grand declaration.

He disabled comms, giving Faiza an all-okay signal. Ava's valet did the same and retreated.

"I'm really happy you're here, Ava. I wasn't sure you'd want to see me again after last night."

"What do you mean?"

"It just felt . . . off. Talking about the past, about Ash—it didn't make for the best dinner conversation, did it? I felt like I let you down." He paused, waiting for affirmation which Ava withheld. He continued hesitantly. "I guess I'm saying, I'm glad we're here now. Because look at this."

He gestured widely at the rising sun, the new day dawning. Above them, the other spacewalkers had begun to amass, positioning themselves for photos.

"This brings back memories, doesn't it?" he said after a while. "Freshman year, under the bleachers, watching everyone watch something else."

"I remember it well." Ava recalled those times with bittersweet fondness. She'd usually rather avoid memories from her early teenage years; as far as she was concerned, the story of Ava began after she picked her name. Yet she also found herself comforted by those memories, her afternoons under the bleachers with Laz, fumbling on each other's arms, finding each other's lips, searching each other's bodies with inexperienced hands. She smelled the fresh-mown grass, the sweat on their brows. It was a time of carefree innocence, probably the only one she'd ever known.

"How was the after-party?" she asked him instead.

"You didn't miss much. Looking back, I wish I'd skipped it. They're never as satisfying as I think they'll be."

"Cocktails and dinner I can handle, but that kind of socializing . . ." She shook her head. "I can tell that Ashwin's death is still on people's minds and I just don't think I'd feel welcome."

"It's been twenty-five years. No one cares anymore. Besides, half the people here have done so much worse."

Ava knew this was meant as a salve, but the implication still stung. "Have been *accused* of worse, you mean."

"Yes, yes, of course," he stammered. "I was being glib, I'm sorry. The sentiment stands, though: You have as much right to be here as anyone else."

"But you weren't mistaken, were you? You've always thought that I did it. That's why you lied to the police."

"No, that's not what I meant. I've already said, it was a stupid mistake. I only did it for you."

"Stop it. You don't do these things for me, you do them for you," she said pointedly. "For you to have me, to possess me. You'd do whatever it takes, no matter the consequences."

Stunned, Laz struggled for a response.

"Daniela died, Laz. Because of you."

"What do you mean? She died in lockup."

"I asked you to help her," Ava replied, fuming. "To get her a good lawyer and help bail her out. You promised you would."

"And I did! I went to see her the very next day after we talked. She didn't want my help. Our help. She was too angry and too proud, and that's not on me. No fucking way."

For decades, Ava carried that burden like a tumor that slowly consumed her. Daniela hated her, Laz had said. He'd recounted that jailhouse visit, claiming that Daniela hated Ava for abandoning her, for throwing money at the problem and not even having the decency to do it herself. He'd described how Daniela spat on the glass partition of the visitor's booth, kicking and screaming about horrible rich people, and how Ava was the worst kind, because she pretended to love her.

"But those were all lies, weren't they, Laz?"

"I never lied to you, I swear . . ."

"Dani wrote to the warden, did you know that?" Ava asked him, like a challenge. "She wrote to anyone who would listen. A rival gang was harassing her on the inside and she begged to be transferred out. She drafted petitions. I saw them all, every tear-stained letter. She never would have refused help, even from you."

"Well, she did. Maybe she changed her mind after, I don't know!"

"Enough! She wrote to her grandma, Laz. 'Please find Tom Lazaro, he promised me he'll help. He's Ava's friend, he's a good person.'" Ava's tears fell. "She feared for her life, and you fucking strung her along then left her hanging."

"Please, let me explain—"

"She didn't have to die in there. But you condemned her way before the jury did, and you killed her way before she got stabbed in the gut. And all this time I thought she hated me. Twenty-five years, thinking that she felt betrayed by me. That's a long fucking time to bear that guilt. But now I know."

"Ava, please, if you would just give me the chance—"

"You've had every chance." She unbuckled the carabiners of her tether. A warning signal flashed on both of their helmet screens. With all her strength, she pushed Laz away from her. He drifted away, flailing.

"Fuck, fuck, fuck!"

Faiza jetted toward them, and Ava commed her. "He needs help," she said curtly. She then took control of her jetpack and hovered back to the Altaire.

Chapter 18
Ashwin Khan's Final Days

The important part about Ashwin Khan's death was that by the time he was found on Sunday morning, it was impossible to know exactly when he had died. The extremes of desert weather and the chemical reactions of the salt flats could seriously complicate decomposition. Wednesday was not that far off, and if his friends hadn't seen Ashwin alive on Friday, Henry could have easily been suspected of murder. After all, the three of them almost could have killed him two days prior.

The fight was not Henry's idea, in a reversal of sorts. He was the one who formulated plans, while Laz pointed out the holes and weaknesses in said plans. That time was different. Ashwin had recently dislocated Ava's elbow and Laz decided enough was enough. Ashwin needed a strong enough message, and there was only one way to reach the likes of him.

Henry countered with a plan to level with the guy. Pay him off maybe, or find some way to appeal to his baser instincts. He feared what Laz might do as much as he feared how Ashwin might retaliate, and so Henry took great pains to dissuade Laz, who was determined to beat the crap out of Ashwin.

"He is chaos personified," Laz told his friends. "And there's no negotiating with chaos."

"You've had, what, one fistfight your entire life? And that was back in middle school. Ash does this every god-damn day. You will absolutely get clobbered," Henry asserted. "Do you wanna end up in the hospital like Ava?"

"Not if it's three against one." The other two startled at Sloane's words. He'd been quiet, and Henry had assumed he'd sided with him. "It's about time someone stood up to him."

On his own, Laz could be very persuasive, but what ultimately recruited Sloane to the cause was his own pain. Henry knew then that there was no sense arguing. All he could do was join his friends and make sure no one ended up too badly hurt.

The three of them cornered Ashwin behind the sports complex, in that secluded tract of unkempt woodland where junkies hung out. He splayed out by the foot of an elm tree, alone, with a manic look on his face brought on by the high he was on.

"What can I do for ya, boys?"

Laz stepped up to him. "You need to stay away from Ava."

"No can do. We're inseparable." Ashwin lifted himself off the ground and met Laz's stare. He held up a fist and wrapped it with his other hand. "We're joined to the core of our very beings."

"I mean it. It ends now. You never lay a finger on her ever again."

"Didn't she dump you already?" Ashwin laughed, teeth bared. "You know what she told me—" Here he began to giggle. "She said you creeped her out. 'He's so needy, Ash. Oh, he's so pathetic.' You're a fucking freak."

Henry took hold of Laz's arm but he was too late. Laz charged at Ashwin, slamming him into the ground. The two wrestled, kicking and flailing. Ashwin found his footing and taunted Laz, arms open, daring him to charge. He didn't care that he was outnumbered. Laz landed a punch squarely on Ashwin's jaw. Sloane rushed in too, hitting him on his side and his back. Henry, who had never been in a brawl his entire life, stood frozen.

Ashwin put up resistance, wrapping his arms around Laz's torso and taking him down with him. Sloane tried to pull Ashwin away, but before he could, Ashwin took out a switchblade from his jacket pocket.

"You done fucked up now, kid."

Ashwin menacingly waved the blade around Laz's chest. Pinned to the ground, Laz opened his fists in surrender.

"Are you willing to die for my li'l sis?"

Without a moment's thought, Henry came upon Ashwin from behind, grappling at his hand. He landed a knee to Ashwin's back and wrested the knife away, slicing Ashwin's palm. The blade glistened with blood.

"Enough!" Henry shouted, his lips trembling.

Ashwin got off his feet with no show of fear. "Do you even know how to use that thing?"

"You need to leave Ava alone."

"Are you threatening me, pretty boy? You really don't wanna do that."

"I'm not." Henry lowered the switchblade, and his voice. He gestured to his friends to get behind him. "I'm asking you. It can't go on like this."

"Tell you what," Ashwin replied. "Gimme that back, and we all walk away. I'll forget this ever happened."

Eyes trained on Ashwin, Henry handed the weapon to Sloane, who knew how to stow the blade away. Laz swiped it from him.

"No, you won't forget. You'll remember," Henry stated. "Or else it's a quick trip to the headmaster's office and then the sheriff's department."

"Like that'll stop me."

"If that won't, our families will. See what they'll do to you once they find out you almost tried to kill their kids."

Ashwin smirked, amused but somehow also impressed. "It's your funeral."

Henry never fully grasped the full import of those words until later. At that point, all he knew was that they'd all seriously fucked up, all four of them, with their machismo and misplaced passions. Things would get worse before they got better, if they would at all. The three friends silently walked back the way they came, the air between them charged with enmity.

By Friday, Ashwin had reached his boiling point. It had been two weeks of no drops, and he faced yet another weekend of no sales, not to mention rich, irate pricks who demanded their candy right fucking now. Top it off, now Dani was ghosting him. This was what he got for going into business with fucking Mexican gangs with their never-ending turf wars.

If he'd only kept his head down for a bit, maybe he wouldn't be in this mess. But now he was on his last strike. One slipup and he's expelled and Daddy's gonna kill him. He might actually do it this time. So nah, he can't just leave the grounds and storm into Dani's dumpster fire of an apartment to sort her out. He'll have to go to li'l sis.

He waited for Ava after Exogeology, dragged her by the arm into a courtyard so no one would see. He didn't care that her elbow still hurt. He was desperate and Dani needed to get the message.

"Look, she's shut me out. You gotta go talk to her."

"What do you want me to say?" his sister asked irritably. "There won't be any shipments until things cool down. That's not exactly up to her, is it?"

"Pfft—you think this turf war's real? Dani's just sweating me so she can jack up the prices." He lifted Ava's chin, peered into her eyes. "And you look like you're getting your fix just fine."

Ava swatted his hand and pushed him aside. "I'm on goddamn pain meds, you dumb fuck."

He liked it when she showed a little life. Made him think there was still the old Arvind in there somewhere. "All right, I'm sorry I got rough on you. This whole thing with Dani's got me on edge. The kids aren't happy, I'm not happy, nobody's happy."

"You have your rainy-day stash, and you definitely aren't hurting for money. Can't you wait it out?" she asked. "It's probably for the best too, unless you're really looking to get expelled."

"Damn it, I'm not gonna live like an imprisoned fucking monk, especially during my senior year," Ash yelled, seething. "And I don't like being fucked with. Which is what this whole situation is starting to feel like."

"Dani's for real, all right? She's scared shitless. The cartels mean serious business. They go after everyone, top to bottom, even the small players."

"Yeah, yeah, she fed me the same line. 'It'll blow over soon,' blah blah blah. She's a damn good actress, isn't she? You teach her all that?"

"She's serious, Ash. You do not want to mess with those people."

"We all had a good thing going here," he said. "And I seriously feel bad asking you to do more work. But I gotta talk to her so I can figure out my next moves. I know you two go fuck in the woods on weekends. You seeing her today?"

"Like I would tell you."

"I could just stalk you."

"Yeah, right. And then lemme call security, see how they feel about that."

"She's really gotten to you, hasn't she? How do I know this isn't all part of your plan, huh?" Ashwin gripped her bad arm and leaned in. "You're probably plotting against me when you go off to your fuckfests. Are you trying to cut me out?"

"Jesus Christ," she yelled, wincing. "I didn't even want to do this in the first place."

"Oh, but you do now, don't you? Now that you have her. Hah, or is she the one pulling the strings? Was this her idea?"

"You're paranoid."

"I keep telling you, sis—Dani's trouble." He softened his tone, trying to take the benevolent brother approach. "She's got her use, but she's not one of us. She will fuck you over. You gotta stop seeing her."

"You're dead inside so you'll never get it, but what we have is real."

"Don't forget where your loyalties lie, li'l sis." Ashwin sneered. "Tell your dyke that if she doesn't get me my delivery ASAP, I will burn down her shack with her inside it."

"Fuck you!"

Ashwin dug into Ava's arm and she yelped in pain.

"Let me go!" She tried pushing him off with her other arm, but he only squeezed tighter. Right then, urgent footsteps issued from the other side of the courtyard. At the far end of the colonnade, Laz and Sloane were fast on the approach.

"Well, look who it fucking is again," Ashwin said, annoyed. He let go of his twin. "Send Dani my message, or else."

"I swear to god, Ash, if anything happens to her . . ."

"And stop siccing your dogs on me," he added, laughing. "I don't think they're ready for another round."

Ashwin backed away from her, flipping off the boys with both hands as he left.

Fridays after class were for low-intensity climbs, and on those late afternoons, Sloane visited the farther reaches of the Rochford grounds. That was where his favorite crags were, and his favorite routes, ones that gave him a decent workout and a nice endorphin high from achieving a victory.

He often climbed alone on Fridays, choosing to boulder instead of doing ropes. He needed time away from the climbing team, from everyone really, and nothing gave him a deeper sense of solitude than soloing a rock face, the dry desert wind on his back and a peak right above him.

Windup Girl was a slabby V8, a flat problem drawn across the face of a huge limestone rock the shape of a sideways teardrop. When the sun hit it just right, as it did that afternoon, the rock's surface glowed with a rich amber hue. He'd flashed *Windup Girl* a ton of times before, and on his best days, he could complete it with his eyes closed. Twenty-five feet lay between the finish at the top and the ground where he stood, and though some would say it needed to be a roped climb, elite climbers like Sloane could do it without. He didn't even need his visor-scope; he knew every flake of rock and every crack that he could exploit. All he needed were his hands, his feet, and control.

Sloane crouched low, arms extended, his butt hanging a few inches off the ground. He launched himself up with a push of both feet, reaching a thin edge of rock with his right hand. The edge was short and shallow, giving little purchase to the pads of his fingertips, but it was more than enough. He lifted his left leg, his knee reaching up to his chest, landing his foot on a protrusion right below his hip. He pushed off that foot, arcing his left arm above his head to reach for his next hand hold, which he found without having to look.

He liked returning to these kinds of routes, ones that required less strategizing to complete. They allowed him the silence to ruminate. When his thoughts drifted toward the positive, the climb felt more enjoyable. When they were negative, those thoughts fueled him to finish. The climbing problem became a substitute for his actual problems, and if he could solve the climb, then he could solve his problems too.

In those days, the problem was his father. It had only been a month since he'd begun serving his life sentence after being convicted of large-scale embezzlement. His older brothers had been convicted too, and his mother had long sailed off to Gibraltar to flee the madness and potential fallout. She last spoke to Sloane in the middle of the trial, calling from one of the family yachts to say that she had no plans of returning to the country for the foreseeable future. The senior Sloane could thus only turn to his youngest son for support.

Even in his incarceration, Sloane's father had no compunction about abusing his privileges or bribing the guards. He called his son from prison every day, at different hours of the day, keeping Sloane on the line for as long as he could. Each time, Sloane picked up; he could have refused him, but he never once did.

Sloane jammed his hand into a small crack in the rock, a breadth barely wide enough for all his fingers. The rock scraped the side of his wrist, and a dull ache reminded him of an old fracture, one that he was sure had healed. He'd grown accustomed to climbing through the pain; after all, injuries were part of the sport. But his fortitude was shaped most by those times when his father's beatings compounded his scrapes and bumps. They felt so long ago now, those weekend nights when Sloane's father was placed on mandatory house arrest and would send for him as the trial raged on, or that last winter break when the only Sloanes in the mansion were the two of them. So long ago, and yet.

Sloane never told his mother, who couldn't be bothered, nor the school counselor, nor his friends. He learned how to mend himself with first aid training so he never had a reason to visit a clinic. When once he came to school with a swollen ankle, he passed it off as a climbing injury, and no one gave it more than a second's thought.

He pushed down on the small crack, lifting himself on the strength of a single palm. With his other hand, he flailed for his next move. One step followed a reach followed another step, left leg, right hand, right leg, left hand, until his fingertips felt the even surface of the peak. He launched off his legs for one final push. He clambered, mantling with both hands, pushing himself away from the edge and landing face down on the rock. He had reached the top.

Sloane lay there for a moment, legs dangling over the edge, trying to catch his breath. When he had, he rose to his feet. He walked to the zenith, then sat with his legs crossed as he looked out onto the desert horizon.

He thought about the days ahead, in part because his father had been badgering him about it. *You gotta make something of yourself. You're this family's future. There is a reason I gave my name to you and not your brothers.* The words felt good to hear, even through the staticky line of the Englewood Federal Correctional Institute, his father constantly repeating them in varying states of emotion. He wasn't always so magnanimous, especially when he had access to contraband rum. His father was a violent drunk, and he still found an outlet for violence, despite the hundreds of miles that separated the two of them. Yet Sloane stayed on for every second of these calls, taking the blows as he always had. He had to care for his father. Who else would? And what other way could he?

The family name was an unfair burden, one he did not want to carry. Perversely, his father's message still burrowed itself deep into Sloane. He did need to set himself up for the future, just in case their unseized assets dried up and his mother never came back. Graduation was close, and he had to think about college. Being a pro climber wouldn't pay his tuition, not to mention his living expenses. Climbing had brought him prestige, but it was nothing more than a hobby, one that he might not be able to afford soon enough.

He'd been trying to formulate a plan, but he kept coming up short. All he knew was that he needed to survive on his own terms. There was no one else he could rely on. He was on his own, and as he did when he bouldered on that late Friday afternoon, he would keep climbing alone, ever upward, until he reached the top.

The sun dipped lower into dusk, and the arid landscape smoldered in a fiery glow. Sloane savored the view, his enjoyment shortly interrupted by a dune buggy racing through the desert and trailing billows of dust behind it. The whir of its wheels was barely audible from the distance. He checked the time. He himself should be heading back before darkness fell. No one should be heading out, not this far out, and not toward the salt flats.

Sloane flipped on his visor and magnified the scope. It wasn't Rochford security. He zoomed in closer and thought he recognized the driver, but the image had blurred with the magnification. Night vision might have been useful if it were sundown, but the sky was still partially alight. Instead, he activated his visor's friend locator.

It blinked green and displayed a name.

Chapter 19
Marionettes

The spacewalkers spun and swerved and dived and flew, floating about like marionettes tied up in string. Cielo observed them through the viewing window, tracking each guest on her tablet. Some flailed wildly, grasping onto their tethers as a lifeline. Some tumbled and careened with balletic grace, while some stayed stationary, stiff as boards. Enthralled by the figures' dance, she allowed herself a rare genuine smile. She caught herself quickly enough.

"Please come see me by the fishbowl," she spoke into her comm. Charles Sloane had returned to the station too soon and she needed to know why.

"Coming, Ms. Cielo," Benita called out from the bottom of the stairs that led to the mezzanine platform. The fresh-faced midshipmate eagerly bounded up the steps like a Labrador summoned. The newer recruits were always so vivacious, and this one more than usual. It was that aim-to-please Filipinoness mixed with the exuberance of youth mixed with the woman's own general temperament. If she weren't already part of the deck crew, Benita would be a great fit for Guest Relations. The work would be no easier, but at least the pay would be better.

"Welcome back on board."

"Thanks. The flight had some hiccups, but I'm happy to be back." By the twinkle in her eye, Cielo could tell she meant it. Spending a few weeks planetside always did wonders for the spirit. No matter how bad things were down there, nothing beat being home.

"'Hiccups' is an understatement," Cielo replied sharply.

The younger woman ignored her tone and continued. "And I'm glad I got to hitch a ride on the Excelsior too. The last time on the service shuttle was miserable as fuck. We were all crammed in with barrels of hand soap and detergent. Felt like I was back to working on a cargo ship. Remember those days?"

Cielo recognized the deflection for what it was, but she indulged Benita in a reminiscence of their former lives, those dues-paying years when the prospect of working at a space orbital felt as distant as the stars themselves. Despite the backbreaking work in harsh conditions, Cielo recalled that time fondly, and Benita knew this all too well, for she was the one who'd made it bearable.

"What happened with Mr. Sloane?" she asked, after a while.

"The spins, I think. And a vicious hangover. He could barely keep it together."

"He's changing out of the suit now?" She got a nod in reply. "And then what, do you know? What's the rest of his day like?"

"Probably back to bed. If you ask me, I don't think we need to keep so close a watch over this one, Cielo. He's a drunk but he's harmless. And he's not—what was it you said . . . high value?"

"True, but he's connected. Everyone here is." Cielo turned back to her tablet, matching each figure to the beacons on her tablet display. Counting, observing. Benita peeked over her shoulder and pointed to one of them.

"How connected is this one?"

Cielo projected her tablet onto the viewing window, overlaying each spacewalker with labels. "That one is Akane Nishimura. Her companies make eighty percent of the microchips in the entire world . . ." Here she paused to wait as another guest floated into view. ". . . which are made of silicon from this one's mines." A popup indicated the name Huang Junyu, along with some vital stats.

"And that one?" the midshipmate asked.

"Number one manufacturer of solar panels. Also made from Huang's silicon mines."

"This one?"

"An ambassador. And that next to him is an investment banker, she owns part of the Altaire Group."

Benita whistled.

"The highest concentration of money, power, and fame you and I will ever see in one place."

"Oh, is she the one who they're saying killed her twin?" Benita asked, reading out Ava Khan's name. "That Aswin's Law kid?"

"Ashwin. Yes, that's her."

"Do you think she did it?"

"I think these people are capable of anything."

For a while the two women stood in silence, watching their wards watch a sunrise they'd seen hundreds of times before. Benita seemed at peace, blissful at the sight. It reminded Cielo of their times together, back in the early days, when all was simpler and they were younger. When they found in each other's arms what they thought was love. They still ended up in bed sometimes, seeking solace and comfort after a long day's work, and though they'd grown, Cielo still saw a trace of that bliss in Benita's face after each encounter. Benita never hardened, not quite like her. Cielo envied her that. Bliss never came to her these days, and repetition had robbed even the most majestic sunrises of their magic. The overview effect had no power over her. Whenever her schedule permitted a moment to peer out over the planet, what she felt was not awe but dread. All she could think of were the earthbound, and oh, how bound they all were.

"How's your family?" Cielo asked. "Must've been nice seeing them after over a year."

"They're getting by, despite everything. I have a new nephew." Her tone took on the stiff yet singsongy cadence of the Waray tongue as she gushed about the latest addition to the Sison clan. "I miss them already."

"They're all still in Samar?"

"Yup," Benita replied, resigned. "They're never moving to Manila. The city's too big, and too hot."

Cielo understood what that last part meant. It couldn't be easy running arms through the capital, even if that was where all the money flowed through.

Before working on the merchant ships, Benita had lived in Manila on her own, abandoning her family to make a life for herself. She'd always felt guilty for leaving so soon after the typhoon and the ensuing landslide devastated her family's corn plantation. The disaster shifted the topography and erased the land boundaries, which allowed corporate farm owners to swoop in like vultures. They didn't bother maintaining a respectful charade and offering to buy the Sisons' land at a deep discount, as they did during other natural calamities. This time, they just redrew the borders. The Sisons' meager tract got tied up in unending litigation filed by big-business landholders. Benita's father got fed up and took up arms, literally, trading ploughshares for swords. She fled the province then, aiming to distance herself from her family's new venture. She didn't know that years later she would have to come crawling back.

"Listen, I never got to apologize," she told Cielo. "I really tried to get it all loaded up."

"You never got to explain either. The Boss is livid."

"Yeah, well, let's see her try getting contraband past three international ports. I spent my entire month off getting this set up. Weeks of flying back and forth, spread fucking thin, running around like a headless chicken. I rode with those damn crates across the ocean. Samar to San Diego then to the launchpads—and our ground crew wasn't much help either. The number of times I could've gotten caught—" Benita shook her head, displeased. "Not to mention my shithead dad now owns my ass."

"And we all appreciate it," Cielo replied. "But it'll be tough to get our targets to comply without a show of force. Fighting off hostiles will be even tougher, not to mention commandeering a shuttle. Every stage of the plan relied on that other crate, and it's got our crew on edge, that's all."

"What matters is everyone got some, all right? We got ours, the other stations got theirs. Everyone got enough."

"You're right, we have enough." Cielo leaned in, stroking the younger woman's arm. "And you did a great job. Personally, I'm impressed. We can pull this off, even though we're short a few guns."

"You're sure?"

"Positive."

"I didn't sign up for a suicide mission, okay?"

"And this isn't. I've already made sure of that. Jin's taking care of Security, and our path to escape will be clear," Cielo explained. "We'll get everything we ever wanted and we'll make it back home in one piece. I promise you—we won't die up here."

"How do you know?"

"I'd sooner kill this plan myself if I didn't think we have excellent odds."

Benita had her reasons. They differed only slightly from Cielo's, or Dominque's or anyone else's on their crew, and Cielo knew that the reasons can only take you so far. In the face of great risk, of unexpected deviations from the plan, of one's own wavering resolve, it's the odds of success that could make you or break you. Cielo believed that they would succeed, and she needed everyone to keep the same faith. Benita nodded in response, her gaze steadfast, and Cielo knew that she'd done her job.

Then, the midshipmate grabbed her arm, pointing out of the porthole. "Those two are untethered," Benita exclaimed. "That wasn't in the assignment list."

"It's not, but Pio has it handled. A last-minute request. You gotta give in to these people's whims, you know."

"Rules be damned, even the ones for their own safety. Goes to show, money doesn't make you smart."

"It's not about smarts. It's about power. They think they're untouchable. Insulated from harm and the consequences of their actions. They're convinced that they're in total control, even when the universe with all its wonders and horrors reminds them that they have no control at all. And that kind of thinking," Cielo said. "That is why I'm sure we'll succeed."

Cielo counted down the minutes, the slow and steady march to the point where everything changes for them. She straightened her back, wrapped an arm over Benita's shoulder and pulled her closer. Together they looked out at their guests. She smiled. They'll never see it coming.

Chapter 20
Beggars, Whores, and
Ne'er-do-wells

Sloane waved his hand over the reader a couple of times before the gate admitted him into the theater lobby. The bangles and cuffs that were stacked on his wrist, if not the embroidered capelet that obscured his forearm, blocked the signal from his chip implant. The capelet, held by a baroque chain that hung neatly across his chest, fluttered as he flounced toward the lobby bar. An array of pheasant feathers adorned his right shoulder like a striped and spiky pauldron, sure to rival any opera costume.

For good reason, most people assumed that he held an affinity for the dramatic arts, but Sloane didn't care much for the theater. He found plays tedious, and he preferred his music lyricless, allowing the notes and melodies to tell their stories. Still, one needs show up to these things. One never knows what might happen at the matinee.

His fingers, heavy with jeweled rings, clinked on the marble as he waited for a scruffy, old bartender to attend to him. He observed the man languidly pour wine for other patrons, failing to notice Ava's arrival.

She sidled up next to Sloane, slipping onto a stool with a fluidity that defied her appearance: an organza jumpsuit in bronze, her hair straightened and tied in a tight ponytail. He thought it too severe and contemporary for the occasion and almost said so himself, but her mood seemed unreceptive to barbs.

"I just spoke to Laz," Ava said without preamble. "About the day Ashwin died."

Sloane signaled to the bartender, who was still busy at the far end of the bar. "What about it?"

"No one told me that the three of you found the body. Only learned it two months ago, after I got the court to release the records."

"What records?"

"All of them. Why didn't you tell me?"

"Well, you were quite hard to find those days," Sloane replied bluntly, forgetting himself. Despite what everyone else thought, he understood that Ava's disappearance was only partly due to her family's attempt at fleeing potential consequences. She'd been placed in a facility following numerous mental breakdowns, and after what happened, Sloane couldn't blame her. "But we would have told you everything at some point."

"Even the fight?"

"What fight?" he asked, unfazed.

"I know, Sloane." He blanched, and Ava's lips thinned into a taut smile. "The three of you got into a fight with Ashwin shortly before he died. The autopsy report mentioned unexplained bruising on his sides and arms, plus a knife cut on his hand. Because of the condition his corpse was in, the ME couldn't be sure if they were older or were inflicted at the time that he was killed. Besides, given the way he lived, a few scrapes didn't seem unusual to anyone. Then I remembered the last thing he ever said to me."

"What did he say?"

"He said, 'Stop sending your dogs after me, I don't think they're ready for another round.' I never understood what that meant, but it stayed with me. Then I remembered Laz having a bruise on his jaw that week."

Sloane pulled her aside, away from prying eyes and ears. More guests had filed into the lobby, and there were few quiet corners. They found one behind the coat check.

"So who was it?" she asked, like a dare. "Must have been all three of you, right?"

"Ava, we couldn't stand it anymore. It happened a few days after he broke your elbow. We picked you up from the infirmary and brought you to your suite, remember? The three of us finally decided to do something. Ashwin was a raging psychopath. Depending on his mood, you were his pawn or plaything or punching bag. He would've killed you, or us, and it was only a matter of time."

"You all keep saying that, but it's just not true," she answered. "My brother wasn't a psychopath. He wasn't sick. He had another side to him, one you never got to see."

"The side of him I saw was enough."

"He's not the saint that everyone made him out to be after he died, but he wasn't this uncontrollable monster either."

"You're right," Sloane replied. "He wasn't out of control; in fact, he was fully in control of his actions, and he chose to hurt you and everybody else. Doesn't that make it worse?"

"He was seventeen. He was just a kid."

"Old enough to know better."

Ava's eyes threatened to well up at her friend's callousness. She'd never gone so far as to forgive Ashwin, but she always believed that, had he lived, he could have had a chance at redemption.

"He had this . . . switchblade," she continued, steeling herself. "He carried it everywhere, said it was a necessity. The cops never found one on his body."

"Yes, and he almost used it on us before we pried it off him. He could have killed us, you know."

"And none of you told the cops about any of this, did you?"

"We were scared," Sloane answered, his head hung low. "It happened Wednesday and he died two days later. To top it off, we were the same ones who found his body. You know how that would have looked."

"So you all covered it up—Sloane, this is not how innocent people act."

"What are you trying to say?"

Ava leaned in closer, jabbing a finger at him. "I think the three of you killed Ashwin. Together."

Sloane's face darkened. He'd long feared the day would come when someone would say those words. He had lived with that fear since that day on the salt flats, and hearing them now, from Ava no less, brought him immeasurable despair.

"You don't mean that, Ava. You can't possibly." His tone was plaintive, like a man facing the gallows.

"Dani was with me when he died, and I don't know where the fuck you all were," she continued, on a roll. "Laz had debate practice, or so he told the cops. You said you were out climbing, Henry said he was at the

EVA prep room doing volunteer cleanup. All three of you were conveniently busy with extracurriculars for a Friday night."

"And I was," Sloane insisted. "We were."

"Can anyone vouch for it? For any of you, aside from the three of you covering each other?"

"I—I was alone, but I swear to you, I never saw Ashwin that night."

"Do you know how that would have changed things?" she asked. "If the cops knew what I know now, and asked the questions I'm asking?"

"I've never doubted your innocence, nor Daniela's. But we didn't kill Ashwin either."

"Really? Then who did?"

Sloane struggled for a response. "Look around you . . ." He gestured at the crowded theater lobby, the well-heeled patrons of the arts, the women in their gowns with their elbow-length gloves, the men in their tuxes, flourishing their opera glasses. "How many of these people did Ashwin victimize? Any one of them could have had a reason."

"Yes, but no one pointed the finger at them, or at you. No one made even a passing glance at the three boys who discovered the body. And why would they? We stand by our own, right?" she replied. "But everyone jumped at the chance to accuse Dani. One look at her and everyone found no other conclusion. You all saw a murderer, but I knew her for who she truly was."

"Ava, please . . ."

"Dani might have done bad things to survive, but she wasn't a killer. And she was a far better person than anyone else on this station."

The lobby lights dimmed and brightened intermittently, casting their alcove into darkness. Sloane's chest tightened, an involuntary response following yesterday's debris impact. An announcement beckoned the guests into the hall.

"And you," she told Sloane. "I see you for who you are. Henry and Laz too. You can protest all you want and say you didn't kill Ashwin, but you still have blood on your hands. You're cowards, and your cowardice condemned Dani to her death."

Sloane reflected on the thought, the same way he had in the years since. Of course, he had imagined how things might have ended differently if he had told what he knew. He'd imagined every possibility, and he understood that the truth would have only made everything worse for him and his friends.

"We all have things we have to reckon with from those days," he replied, treading carefully. "But I won't have Dani's death on me. I've punished myself for enough."

"Dani was the only true and good thing in my life, Sloane. And she died because of my brother, my friends, my parents and their lawyers. She died alone, thinking I sacrificed her to save my own skin. She's the only person I ever loved. The only one I could ever love. So don't talk to me about punishment. You have no idea what that means."

Ava made her way up the grand staircase, ready to catch the polished mahogany railing if the need arose. The force of gravity was more palpable here, and as she ascended to the theater's upper tiers, each step felt heavier than the last. Still, she carried on, energized by her recent conversations. She may have unearthed as many questions as answers, but she felt tantalizingly closer to the truth.

Isobel Lonsdale stood at the top of the stairs, leaning over the balustrade like an expectant Juliet. She wore her hair long for the matinee, eschewing her severe bob in favor of strawberry-blonde extensions that flowed seamlessly into a shimmering backless gown of blush silk chiffon. Ava caught her eye and smiled warmly, swiftly slipping on the mask of politesse.

"There you are. Julian should be here soon."

Ava leaned in for an air kiss. The women complimented each other's outfits before moving on to small talk. Updates about Isobel's conservationist efforts, complaints about the room service. The two of them had never been friends, not even back in high school when both of them were outcasts of a sort, and they struggled to fill the silence. They resorted to gossiping about the Rochford folk making their way up the stairs to their boxes. Isobel tilted her head at Captain Edmonia Williams as she entered the lobby below. She still had her standard uniform on, the stiff white number piped with Altaire red. Ava wondered whether upper management had dress uniforms. Certainly an afternoon at the opera warranted it.

"She runs a tight ship," Isobel said.

"Yes, she's very capable."

"She might be moving on up soon," whispered Isobel. "Lonsdale Aerospace is trying to pirate her from the Altaire Group. But you didn't hear it from me."

"Oh? To do what?" Ava asked, though she could guess the answer.

"To help them run the Mars bases. She has so much technical experience, and her training's wasted on this floating hotel."

"It's not a complete waste. Folks would kill to run the Altaire."

"It's a means to an end. A rung on the ladder."

Ava pursed her lips. She could tell where this was going, and she didn't have the time for it.

"You have to admit, the Altaire Group is nothing more than a tourism company," Isobel continued. "They have the technology, but this isn't aerospace, not really. It's interested in the status quo, not the future."

Ava suddenly felt Julian's presence through his wife's words. She'd heard this pitch before, in the board room of Khan-Powell Financial, and once more Ava found herself with someone who presumed to know what she needed. What was good for her. Pawn, plaything, punching bag. To Lonsdale Aerospace, she was a purse, and a direct line to the US delegate to the Mars Settlement Agency.

"All right, my love. This weekend is supposed to be about the past—not the future," Julian said as he approached. He slid an arm around Isobel's waist and kissed her on the cheek.

"This is a new dress," he remarked. "Picked something pretty from the shops, I see."

"Wrapping paper. Only bought it so you can take it off," Isobel answered, doing a playful twirl for full effect. "They just made the announcement; we should get to our seats."

Julian turned to Ava and kissed her hand. "You look exquisite."

"Thank you, and thanks for the invitation. I had too much on my mind, I forgot to ask my liaison to book a seat."

"Well, at least this allows me to do something nice for you, for a change. It's not every day I get to show my gratitude to one of my company's largest investors."

Arms held out like a steward, Julian escorted the two women to the Lonsdale box, second tier, center. As they walked the damask-carpeted hallways, Ava peeped a view of the stage, its velvet curtain drawn back to reveal the show's milieu: ramshackle tenements, dilapidated fences, clotheslines strung with tattered sheets and clothing. Boxes and barrels stacked haphazardly on top of each other, and a couple of upturned boats resting on what appeared to be the edge of a breakwater. A sign hanging by stage right read *Catfish Row.*

She saw more of the elaborate staging as an usher welcomed them to the box, but by then the full view of the theater took over her attention. The hall was styled with ornate resplendence copied directly from La Scala. Though it was smaller, with a quarter of the capacity of the actual Milanese opera house, the same gilded sconces and Italianate moldings, the same plush seats of red velvet, the same domed ceiling with a massive crystal chandelier. The chamber had three tiers of private boxes, each appointed with mid-nineteenth-century furniture.

"So tell me about this show again," Isobel asked her husband. "It's a musical?"

"It's an opera."

"It's kind of both," Ava corrected. "*Porgy and Bess* defies categorization."

"You sound like a fan," Julian said.

"It's quite special. I've seen the West End staging, but I'm looking forward to this one. I heard they got the North American tour cast."

"And last minute too," Isobel added. "I seem to recall them riding up with us on the Excelsior below decks."

"Yeah, well, that's the Altaire Group for you," Julian said, on the verge of being complimentary. "But if you ask me, this whole show is a diversity push more than anything."

"Because it's an all-Black cast?" Isobel asked.

"The Altaire was getting flak for hiring non-American staff and crew. Foreigners are cheaper after all, and not bound by strict labor laws. But even with upper management, it's predominantly white."

"The captain's Black," Isobel said.

"The exception that proves the rule," Julian replied.

Ava bristled. She suspected as much but didn't dare to say it out loud. It was an insult to the show's cast and crew to say that they only made it to the grandest stage in space to fulfill a race quota. Ava now doubted whether this show deserved this audience. The rest of the Rochford crowd probably thought the same as Julian: This show was meant to be nothing more than good PR for the Altaire. After all, why would any of them care about the lives of Black fisherfolk in 1920s South Carolina?

"In any case, I've read up on it, and I think it is an important story," Julian said after a pause, sensing Ava's discomfort. An usher bowed politely as they reached the Lonsdales' box, guiding the party to their seats. "Besides, it'll be good to remind ourselves of our privilege."

"You don't say?" his wife teased.

"Yes, remembering our privilege makes it easier to remember our purpose."

"Which is what, exactly?" Ava asked.

"For me, personally? To bring everyone to Mars. And I mean everyone, regardless of race or background."

Ava stifled a laugh. Surely, Julian hadn't seriously de-luded himself with these platitudes? People like them might say it over and over, and a lie repeated enough becomes the truth, but they all knew better. The people in the upper echelons of the Mars project picked and chose who got to have a future, and it certainly wasn't everyone.

"You still haven't answered my question," Isobel complained as the usher left and drew the box curtain behind them. "What's this show about?"

Ava leaned over to answer, but Julian beat her to it.

"It's about beggars, whores, and ne'er-do-wells."

Chapter 21
With A Little Hard Work

Cielo found an odd sort of tranquility in the newly emptied theater lobby, in the quiet opulence of its drapery, its filigreed banisters and velvet divans. A grim stillness, like the calm before a storm, or the hush at the sight of a passing hearse. The long wait had commenced. They'd done all they can. Prepared for every contingency, made key partnerships with the right people. The only thing left was to hope for the best.

She leaned back on the lobby bar and clutched her gin and tonic. The old bartender wiped down the marble top and Cielo tipped her glass toward him. It helped to be in the good graces of the Beverage staff in general, but especially now. The more allies the better.

"What's this I hear about a list?" he asked her. His gravelly voice made the question sound like a rebuke.

"You really do catch wind of everything, don't you? Who told?"

"People talk to me," Konstantine replied, shrugging. He braced himself on the bar. "You going to tell me or no?"

"I thought you didn't want to get involved."

"I don't take sides. Still, I'm curious. This is because of yesterday?"

Cielo nodded. The bartender heaved a sigh, the bristles of his silver beard stirring. He drew a flask from his vest pocket and poured its piss-yellow contents onto a tumbler. The scent stung her nose.

"Chacha?"

"Chacha." The barkeep sipped, not bothering with the customary raise of a glass.

Cielo never got a taste for the Georgian grappa. If Konstantine was breaking out the strong stuff from his secret stash, then all might not be copacetic. She took a long sip of her own drink to calm her nerves.

"I don't like this plan you have. Never did. More, more, everybody wants more. We learn to be happy, we cope. That is the way." The barkeep's every word took effort, because of the drink or the conversation, Cielo couldn't tell. "But I am old, and you children never listen."

"It's not about having more, it's about having what should be ours by right," she answered. "Kote, we deserve a future just as much as these bastards."

"And you think that makes all of this justifiable?"

"That makes all of this inevitable."

Konstantine nodded slightly, the only sort of concession Cielo might ever get from him. He'd never join them, weary from the violence of his life as a soldier, but the old man knew how it was to live in a world that didn't have good choices. That didn't have choices at all. Government intervention, diplomacy, international aid, the rule of law, and ethics itself all crumble to dust when your entire country is trapped in a nuclear winter for decades. You do what you can to survive.

After a while, he asked her, "There will be a place for me, when this is all done?"

"Yes."

"And all I have to do is hang back?"

She nodded. "We have enough people." The veteran's skills would have proven useful, but Cielo understood his reasons, and she never let them stop her from trying to save him. Whether she'd succeed in doing so was another matter altogether.

"I don't know if I'll do well in Greenland. My blood runs hot."

"Could have fooled me," she said sarcastically.

"I'm serious. This safe haven . . ."

". . . is temporary. At some point, we'll all need to move on from there, go back home."

"But there is no home for me," Konstantine replied. He took a big swig of his drink, punctuating it with a wince. His brow, lined and weathered by time, riddled with liver spots, glistened with sweat.

"Yes, there is, Kote. There will always be a home for you," Cielo assured him. It may not be in the shining city they were building on Mars, but it will be a place where everyone got a fair shot at a decent future. "We'll make sure of it."

Right then, the harried patter of footsteps echoed in the lobby. A guest swiped his wrist past the admission portal. From afar, Cielo recognized her ward. Ambassador Tom Lazaro paced to and fro, unsure which hallway led to his theater seat. She had wondered when he would arrive. She straightened herself as he approached.

"I think I'm late," he said with a crooked smile.

"Good thing the show just started. If you go through those doors, the ushers should let you in between songs."

"Oh, good. I was afraid I'd have to wait until intermission."

The ambassador noticed the glass set before his liaison and the barkeep, and his face assumed the look of confused dismay. Cielo hoped he took her drink to be nonalcoholic, though the smell of Konstantine's golden chacha would be harder to explain.

The ambassador saved her the chance to lie. "Ah, who cares if I miss a number or two?" he said casually. He took a stool and asked Konstantine for a double Macallan 50. He downed it with haste, not taking a moment to savor the drink. He then signaled the bartender for another.

He reminded Cielo of something her papa liked to say: If a man drinks too fast, he'll drown himself before he gets to drown his sorrows. Beneath the apparent joviality, Tom Lazaro seemed to be attempting both.

Cielo had half a mind to leave, make up an excuse. Yet she couldn't help herself. She thought she'd made up her mind about this guest. He's Filipino, but he's one of *those*. She'd decided to dislike him, actively abhor him, even. Yet now, she felt an unnatural desire to connect with him. Despite herself, she yearned for this man's favor.

"You know, I never got to ask," Lazaro said to her. "Taga sa'n ka sa 'tin?"

His accent was neutral, not Americanized with the long A's and the soft T's. Good use of the informal tone too, not stilted as Cielo would have expected from a Fil-Am. Her surprise must have been evident, as the ambassador flashed a smug grin. They'd had many interactions since he boarded the station, but he'd never tried talking to her in Filipino.

"Cebu, sir."

"Ah, the Queen City of the South," the ambassador replied, switching back to his English. "Been there once. Lovely place."

Cielo almost grimaced. No one called it that anymore. She also doubted that the man was aware Cebu was both a province and a city. She debated specifying where exactly she was from, but Tom Lazaro wouldn't know her hometown, that backwater sitio slowly being swallowed up by the Cebu Strait. As far as she knew, San Sebastian was still on the map, though she hadn't checked in a while. Island borders had been redrawn enough times in her lifetime that she wouldn't be surprised if the town was now beneath the narrow channel that separated the province from the island of Bohol.

Cielo still called San Sebastian home, and she held the place in her heart with a painful longing. Before the water crept closer to the inland, it had been a fishing village. She still had vague memories of going out to sea as a little girl, playing among the nets on her grandfather's bangka that smelled of brine and kelp and fish guts. Her father, too, was in the family business, though not as a fisher himself; he built and repaired boats, had done so as soon as he could pick up a wrench—that is, until the server farms started cropping up along their shores. Since then and for most of her life, Cielo's papa had supported the family with the paltry sum he earned as a maintenance man on those floating data centers. For her part, Cielo's mama worked as a housekeeper for one of the American expats who oversaw the same data centers. Six days a week, she lived in the maid's quarters of a fancy penthouse suite in Cebu City, coming home only on Sundays to take her children to church and to make up for the mothering she'd been unable to provide them.

With her job now, one could say Cielo had gone into the family business too. Her mama wanted her to become a doctor, but Cielo wanted to travel the world. Besides, they couldn't afford it. "But if they want to, maybe Delfin could become a doctor instead, after I graduate and earn a bit of money," she told her mother. "Between you, me, and papa, we could scrape up enough to send them to med school."

She was in Manila, finishing the final year of her Hospitality Management degree, when the flood banks and levees were built. The walls were meant to protect the town from being swallowed by the sea, but they'd been built using substandard cement, a common tactic when a half-hearted attempt at an infrastructure solution meets good old-fashioned government corruption. Before the year was over, the walls crumbled, powerless against the storm surges at the height of typhoon season. The levees were breached, drowning the whole of San Sebastian. Forty-four people perished. That Delfin survived was a miracle, but their mama and papa hadn't been so blessed.

"And look at you now, from Cebu to the best space orbital in the system," the ambassador said with no trace of condescension. "Your family must be so proud of you."

"They are." She bowed her head reflexively even as she dissembled.

"Just goes to show, with a little hard work, anyone can make it."

Cielo didn't know where to start, the notion that she'd "made it," or that hard work was all it took. She'd worked hard, yes. But she hadn't made it, not by the ambassador's definition, and they both knew it. What the ambassador really meant to say was that she *made it out of the old country.*

"I don't think I've made it," she replied with an affected smile. "Not yet anyway."

"Don't sell yourself short. You're a staff officer in charge of an entire department, for god's sake. Not everyone gets to be where you are."

And why is that, she wanted to ask. Why doesn't everyone get to achieve even the little she has?

"Yeah, hard work," she instead replied, aping the ambassador.

"That's right. Sipag at tiyaga. That's the key."

It was a common enough mantra back where they were from, a catchphrase passed on from parent to child, from teacher to pupil. That false promise, a mirage in the desert as a national ethos. Success as a function of nothing more than self-application. Cielo couldn't think of a more perverse concept.

Tom was born into a political dynasty, his father a congressman, his grandfather a senator, his forebears rich and powerful people in both the old country and the new. Cielo was born into a dynasty too, of a sort. She did the whole sipag at tiyaga routine like her parents before her, and their parents before them, generations of people keeping their head down and doing the right thing, the promise of a better life as their sole reward. The difference was, his dynasty inevitably led to greater heights, as high as an entirely new planet.

Her dynasty, lifetimes of sipag at tiyaga, led only to misery.

"Is that how you got where you are?" Cielo asked bluntly.

The ambassador paused and cleared his throat. "I'd like to think so."

"And to think, with all that sipag at tiyaga, I could have been a diplomat instead."

"Well, I think our paths may have diverged a bit farther back," he replied awkwardly, drawing out his words. "But . . . yes, sure, anyone can be whatever they want to be if they strive for it."

"That's a really nice thought, sir." Cielo raised her glass, staring fixedly at the ambassador. He hesitantly clinked back and downed his second double of the last few minutes. He drew a bill from his tuxedo jacket and slid it under his empty tumbler. With a nod, he bid her adieu.

Cielo wondered how well she'd hidden her disdain. Whether the ambassador could tell, whether he might cause a problem. As her countryman went up the marble staircase toward his private opera box, Cielo kept her sight trained on him, but Tom Lazaro never looked back.

Chapter 22
Summertime

Henry's husband tugged at his tuxedo sleeve as they rode the elevator up to the theater. Nick preened him again, making sure that his crisp white shirt exposed the right amount of cuff. Every millimeter needed to fall in the right place. Henry secretly savored these moments, one of the few times that Nick lavished his attention on him the way he did his celebrity clients. Whenever Nick checked his hair or realigned his waistcoat just so, Henry felt like a movie star. To be sure, each adjustment also carried a signal, an unspoken warning. *Everything must go perfectly. Don't fuck it up.* Henry was the king, and Nick was an exacting kingmaker.

"You've seen this show before, yes?" Henry asked.

"Too many times. Xiomara didn't just invest in the production, she actually cares about this shit. And whatever she likes, I have to like too."

"Well, I've never been big on Gershwin, but I think it's great that she decided to bring the show up here."

"The Altaire Group thought it was good optics," Nick answered wearily. "All-Black cast and all that. Like it's not enough that Xiomara is the face of the company."

"Well, they could definitely do more," Henry asserted. "And I doubt that *Porgy and Bess* is the right move, given this crowd."

"It's the opera, love. No one's here to watch the show; they're here to watch each other."

Box 215 was situated stage left, at a comfortable angle that gave the Gallaghers a clear view of the stage, the pit, and most importantly, the audience. Guests shuffled into their seats on the orchestra level, and in the boxes too. Nick surveyed the scene, standing by the edge of the parapet with his opera visor.

"You could join us," Henry told their valet Pio, who had tailed them since they entered the theater. "I'd hate to see these extra seats go to waste."

Nick lowered his visor, appalled. "Love, I'm sure he has other duties to attend to. Isn't that right?" The valet nodded weakly. "Besides, he might not even want to watch an opera."

The couple looked to Pio, who replied, "We're not allowed in private boxes. But you can reach me by earcuff any time, in case you need anything. I'm always close by."

Nick turned to Henry as soon as the valet left their box. "He should be next door by now. Are you ready to pop in and say hello?"

Henry sighed somberly. He took his husband's hand and led him through the curtain, back out onto the hallway, and into the box adjacent to theirs. Inside was Tobias Coen, alone, settled into a Savonarola chair that appeared to strain under his heft.

"It's promising to be quite the show, Tobias. You must be excited," Henry said effusively.

"Ah, the Gallaghers, once again," the old man said without turning. "It's been half a day since I saw you last, I was beginning to miss you."

"We've been exploring your station," Nick answered. "So many things to see and do, we've barely had time to sleep. I'm sure you can relate."

"No rest for the wicked."

Henry took a chair beside the Architect. With benign interest they watched the orchestra players trickle into the pit, tuning their instruments and reviewing their sheet music. An usher entered their box to ask the old man if he wanted refreshments. Coen waved him off. Nick escorted the attendant out into the hallway, drawing the curtains closed as they left.

"I feel like we've gotten off on the wrong foot," Henry told Coen once they were alone.

"That's an understatement."

"Passion is one of my better qualities, though I admit that sometimes courtesy falls by the wayside," Henry said. "But it's all with this opportunity in mind."

"Have you a new offer, or is it still internal organs for a spot on the new settlements?"

"I wouldn't put it in such stark terms, Tobias."

The old man laughed wryly. "And you still won't tell me why you need me to make his happen. Come, Henry, let's drop the pretenses." He leaned in closer with eager expectation. "Of course I hold special privileges. Of course I can get the MSA to give me whatever I want. I could ask for an entire sector if I wanted to. Now what's *your* deal?"

Henry had decided that he would eschew the politics of the MERIT system when it came to it. The system was unfair, yes, but it always had been. Life's not fair.

Insinuating that the Architect was complicit in genetic discrimination, eugenics even, wouldn't advance his cause. Instead Henry chose to appeal to his empathy.

"I'm sick. Like your son. But unlike Leighton, my condition isn't treatable and no transplant can fix it."

"Is it genetic?"

Henry nodded. "We found out when I was seven. It's quite rare, but it's not communicable, and it never held me back in any way." A flood of relief washed over him as he spoke of things he'd kept hidden for so long. "It's not one of the big ones, but it doesn't matter what it is—I won't pass the MSA's medical screening. Not without some help."

"But there must be records of you having it?"

"It's all been taken care of, for the most part," Henry replied. "But the MSA is far beyond my reach, and I need someone with clout there."

"I see."

"Tobias, you know I'm a good candidate. It's as you said, I could get to Mars on my points alone, but my score means nothing if I'm screened out. And I'm not planning on having children, so whatever I have won't enter the gene pool up there anyway."

"I'm sorry, I didn't know." The old man patted Henry's hand. His papery thin skin felt rough, and it surprised Henry to know the man had worker's hands. Coen stood from his seat. "But the answer is still no."

"You said you wanted to know the truth," Henry said, as self-righteous as he could muster. Deep down, he wanted to fling himself at the Architect's feet and plead.

"And now I do."

"Is this some sort of game to you?"

Coen grinned. "Oh, now, don't begrudge an old man his amusement."

"Then why make me go through all this?"

"When you first approached me with your offer, I was merely intrigued. But then you became tedious, you and your husband hounding me, patronizing me. It irked me. When the veiled threats came, that's when I made my decision. I will not tolerate impertinence, Henry, and I will not be intimidated into anything."

"And so you decide to string me along? This is my life we're talking about," Henry replied, fuming. "And your son's."

"That's the worst of it," Coen snapped. "You've reduced Leighton to a token to be traded. Each time his name left your lips, it felt like a slap in the face."

"I had every intention of helping Leighton if we worked something out. I'm a man of my word, unlike you."

"Is that so? And what is that word worth?"

"I could have been an ally, Tobias. Instead you've made an enemy. Good luck getting Leighton a kidney." Henry's face darkened. He rose from his seat. "I'm going to get him off the waiting list, and just for fun, I'll make sure all his records make him ineligible. He'll have every complication and comorbidity known to man, and no doctor would even think about giving him a transplant. You don't know what I can do, Coen. What I've gotten away with for decades."

"Oh, I can imagine," the old man replied. "Hospitals, insurance carriers, your family either owns them or has them in their pocket. Making a genetic mutation disappear from a person's medical history isn't a tall task for GDX Pharmaceuticals. What's a donor registry?"

"So you know I can deliver on my threat."

"But you've miscalculated, Henry. Owing to your youth or to some false sense of power, you believed you had something to bargain with. Now you believe you have the alternative of coercion. You never had either."

"We'll see about that."

"Yes, we shall. You do your best, and I'll do mine." The Architect glared, rising from his seat to meet Henry. "Whatever influence I have over the MSA, whatever leverage my name affords me, I'll use them to crush you and your entire family. You believe I have that much power. Well, let me show you just how much."

The house lights began to dim.

"You fucking bastard," Henry said through gritted teeth. He grabbed the lapels of Coen's coat, dragging the old man toward the shadows in the back of the opera box. He pushed him against the wall. "I won't let you ruin me."

Henry's hands moved from Coen's lapels to his neck.

"Stop it. You're hurting me," the old man gasped.

Applause filled the theater as the conductor took his podium. A moment's hush was soon followed by a jazzy overture of brisk violin strains and rousing trumpet blares.

"This could've been good for both of us, Coen. It didn't have to go this way."

Coen swung his weight around, his hands flailing for freedom, but Henry's grasp was tight and unyielding.

"I know your medical history," Henry threatened. He pressed a forearm against Coen's neck, and with the other hand covered his mouth and nose. "I can claim cardiac arrest and no one would question it." The old man's eyes fluttered frantically, tears collecting in their corners. Henry pressed down harder.

Before long, the man's body went limp. His legs buckled, and Henry almost failed to catch him as he collapsed to the floor.

A single spotlight landed on the center of the stage. A smooth soprano voice belted the opening words to a soulful lullaby.

Summertime.

"Fuck," Henry said under his breath. Beads of sweat dripped from his temples. His hands shook as he loosened the man's tie and undid his collar button, feeling for a pulse. The thick folds of Coen's neck made it difficult, and so he leaned in to check for breathing. It was faint, but it was there.

Henry saw under the curtain door that Nick stood guard right outside the box. He knelt over Coen, placing his hands over the old man's chest, and started compressions. No response. He pushed hard and fast, one, two, three, four, and then a rescue breath. Still nothing.

Henry crawled toward the hallway, calling out to Nick in a whisper. A look of horror crossed his husband's face when he reentered the box.

"What the fuck happened?" He bent down next to Coen's body.

"Things got out of hand," Henry replied, grunting through his compressions. "I told him—and he said no—and I—and he said he'd get us disqualified—and I snapped."

"Fuck! I told you to finesse it. What do we do now?"

"We save the fucking man's life is what we do. Go get help, but keep it quiet."

The soprano's voice, now joined in duet by a deep baritone, calmed the tremble in Henry's hands as he continued resuscitating Coen. He hadn't noticed that Nick remained frozen in his place, heedless to his command.

"Why the hell are you just standing there?"

"What if . . . we just wait?" Nick said.

"Fuck, Nick. We don't have time for this. Go. Now."

"This might be a good thing. Who knows what he'll say when they revive him? Think about it."

Henry's eyes widened, finally understanding the lengths Nick was willing to go to. All at once he saw his husband anew, for the first time, and as he had always been. Unable to bear looking at him, Henry ran out of the box and sped down the hallway to call for aid.

Chapter 23
The Banquet

The Astrarium lived up to its name: the ballroom had a clear dome with an unobstructed view of the stars. The seams of the glass enclosure were imperceptible, and one could wonder, with some worry, how the dome supported its own weight. The walls of the circular hall rose into a delicate curve that from the outside must appear to form a snow globe.

Holographic meteors gently fell from the ceiling, disappearing into thin air in a diffusion of soft light. Mystified guests tried to catch the falling stars in their hands, shrieking in glee as they vanished from their clutches. Laz searched for the projectors but couldn't spot any. The Astrarium was a fantasy, and though he knew they existed, the builders of the Altaire would never let the puppet strings show.

In the front end of the hall (as much as a front could be designated in this circular chamber) a stage had been set. A sleek podium bore the Rochford crest, a shield of navy that matched the drapes hanging across massive horns of gold that formed two converging arches. On their apex was projected a hologram of the same crest.

An Altaire staffer greeted Laz as he came in, leading him to a display that listed the table assignments. He was early, and only a handful of his classmates had arrived, none of them people he was particularly excited to meet.

He saw Paloma Phillips, the former captain of the Rochford chess club who, much to everyone's surprise, ended up being a mixed-media sculptor of some renown. She wore a flouncy dress of fluorescent green, a sharp contrast to her wife's dour beige pantsuit. Laz heard that she was an auto exec. The women chatted with Foster Jennings, the former mathlete who ended up quite where everyone expected: he took over his mother's cryptocurrency exchange, still living his life in numbers. Laz didn't bear any sort of ill will toward Phillips or Jennings, or anyone else then present with whom he could have shared a quick chat. They were perfectly pleasant people, and wasn't this the occasion for exactly the kind of conversation he avoided? Laz had done the routine plenty since arriving at the Altaire: asking old classmates how they've been, what's changed in the last two decades. He fielded these kinds of questions and delivered his stock replies, but with every repetitive conversation, his energy dwindled. After all, how many more times could he talk about the best spa resorts to visit, the diplomat's life, or worse, the uprisings in Santiago?

He'd been assigned to table 17, along with eight other vaguely familiar names, and one that stood out. Just as he thought, they'd been sorted alphabetically, and he'd been placed at the same table as Ava. He searched the hall for his table, a knot rising in his throat.

"Tom Lazaro, punctual as ever," someone greeted. "How have you been?"

Laz turned to find a petite woman, dressed in a full-sequined peach gown with a matching mantle of wispy ostrich feathers. He tried to place her, stalling with a handshake and a compliment about her hair, but a name eluded him.

"Great. And how about you . . . Marisa?" he replied, remembering her name just in time. "How are the kids?"

"They're doing very well," she said, then rattled off her daughter's ages and the prep schools she'd placed them in. The way she inhabited the suburban mom role, one would forget that she owned enough heads of cattle to feed the world many times over. "Mike and I are very proud of them."

"Where is Governor Speier, by the way?"

"He's around here somewhere," she said. "Shaking hands and kissing babies, I'm sure."

"He hasn't changed at all, has he?" Laz replied. Mike Speier was Henry's student council VP, and everyone could tell that he was bitter about not being president. "I heard some rumors that he's running."

"Oh, don't tease. You very well know that he is. We both are. I'm to take over the governor's mansion when he moves on up to the Senate."

"Well, the Commonwealth of Virginia is lucky to have you both."

"Don't think I haven't noticed you've been avoiding our calls," she replied, wagging a finger dramatically. "Our campaigns could use a final boost to get us through to November."

"I haven't been avoiding you," Laz said with a laugh. "You know I'm a big supporter, even though I'm not a constituent."

"Then you better put your money where your mouth is," she said. "And of course, *when* Mike wins, he'll be a useful ally for your dad in Congress."

"Of course," Laz answered, despite his disapproval. He never got used to the brazenness of electoral politics; the flouting of ethics rules wouldn't have been so openly acknowledged in diplomatic circles. "I'll be in touch as soon as we're back planetside."

The banquet hadn't yet begun and already his vigor had begun leeching out of him. The repetitive conversations enervated him. There was always a deal to be made, an alliance to be forged, an exchange to be facilitated. Favors to be traded, opportunities seized, information obtained, services bought and sold. They put on the fancy clothes and put up a front, pretended that this weekend was a much-needed vacation and a time to reminisce, but in reality, this was work.

Laz excused himself and soon found his seat. All the tables were laid out in two concentric circles, and table 17 was more centrally located that Laz would have thought given the number. He had a clear view of the hall and the stage, right by the anti-gravity dance floor. As more guests settled into their seats, Laz searched for his friends. Sloane and Henry were nowhere to be seen, and neither was Ava. Her seat was the only empty spot at their table. Was she even coming at all? She'd almost skipped the opening night reception, and he hadn't seen her at the opera. Laz now worried that she might skip the banquet altogether, if only to avoid him.

Next to him sat Elise Lafontaine, who was on the equestrian team. She gave Laz a shy smile. The two never spoke a word to each other back in high school. He leaned in with a handshake, and after establishing some rapport, he asked if she would be so nice as to trade seats so that he might sit next to Ava. She agreed, much to his relief.

Like ballerinas making their entry into a scene, servers glided into the hall in ordered files, balancing trays on their hands. Before each diner they flourished a small plate atop which lay a pearlescent oval case. A jewel box. The guests around the table giggled and tapped it with their spoons, unsure whether it was an elaborate amuse-bouche or an actual box.

The thing felt solid in his fingers, and as Laz lifted the lid, he found in its center a tiny purple flower bud. He turned to Elise, who sniffed the box and the flower, unsure what to do with it. Following others' lead, Laz took the bud between his fingers and popped it into his mouth. A sudden surge of euphoria rushed to his head. It wasn't narcotic, not really, not hallucinogenic either. It felt like taking a sip of the sweetest nectar, a flavor he'd never tasted before and doubted he ever would.

"You're supposed to chew it," Ava said, plopping down on the empty seat next to him. She wore a bronze jumpsuit; her hair pulled back high and tight. Laz guessed that the attire was to minimize any mishaps while dancing at low-g. He cleared his throat, struggling for a witty comeback, but one never came.

He turned the box over and sniffed its now hollow inside. "What was this, anyway?" he asked Ava, trying to keep his cool. She was at least talking to him. Ava ignored the question, as well as the jewel box in front of her, instead asking a server for champagne. She took a gulp with a grimace on her face, dashing any hope that Laz had. Of course, she was still upset.

"Some lab-grown thing," Lafontaine answered instead.

In short order, the band began to play a pop-tune version of the Rochford anthem. The orchestration was oddly infectious, though some guests groaned in pained recognition.

A voice-over welcomed to the stage Bryce Cho, the reunion's master of ceremonies. The crowd cheered and clapped as Cho waltzed onto the stage in a funereal all-black tuxedo, an odd sight in the sea of glitter and color. He welcomed the Class of 2064 with some pithy jokes, teasing an audience member or two and making naughty references to old teachers and the headmaster, much to the guests' amusement.

"And now that I've warmed you all up," Cho announced, "let me turn it over to our student council president, homecoming king, voted 'Most Likely to Succeed' at the Rochford senior prom, and on a personal note, the most upstanding guy I've ever known . . . Henry Gallagher."

The Astrarium erupted in applause that matched the band's swelling music. Laz lifted himself from his seat to see his friend walk up to the podium; Henry didn't mention he was giving a speech.

Seconds passed with no Henry in sight, and the clapping ebbed as Bryce Cho reclaimed the stage. "It seems like Henry isn't quite ready for his close-up," he announced with a chuckle. "Is this the first time he's ever been late to anything?" The crowd laughed politely.

Laz and Ava looked at each other with worried confusion. He turned toward the other tables and found two empty seats where the Gallaghers should have been.

"Well, the show must go on," Cho said. "For now, let's all take a moment to commemorate the members of the Rochford family who unfortunately could not be with us today."

The lights dimmed, the ballroom illuminated only by the falling stars above them. Then, a sharp beam of holoprojector light shone onto the stage. The words *In Memoriam* materialized out of thin air. A black-and-white video played, showing the smiling faces of teachers, staff members, a couple of librarians, Rochford's dearly departed. Laz recalled some of them, knew them at least by face. He felt a twinge of sadness when he saw that his favorite teacher, Mr. Saviano, who taught Advanced Calculus, had died three years ago.

He tensed as a familiar face appeared on the stage, his thick head of hair and strong brow rendered in striking detail. It shouldn't have surprised him that Ashwin Khan would be part of this presentation, yet it did, and bile rose in his throat at the sight. Video clips showed Ashwin in various poses: walking down Rochford's stone halls, suiting up for the buoyancy lab, brooding in a corner unaware that he was being observed. All Laz could think about was the final image of Ashwin he had in his mind: the desiccated cadaver in the whiteness of the salt flats.

He scanned the room and the guests' wistful faces illuminated by the light show. Was it all a front, he wondered, or did they truly think back on Ashwin with kindness? Death did have a peculiar way of making people forget one's sins. Or was that pity written on their faces, a mournful regret at a life lost before it reached its peak? He turned to Ava, who looked nauseated. She excused herself from the table and left the Astrarium in haste.

"Are you all right?" Laz asked as he caught up to her beyond the doors.

"Leave me alone," she snapped. The corridor wasn't empty, and a couple of crew members discreetly tried to avert their attention from the scene. "You're the last person I want to see right now."

"Ava, please. You have to believe me. I never meant for Daniela—"

"Don't say her name."

"I've carried that guilt with me forever," he continued. "And as much as you might think you can never forgive me, trust me, I will never be able to forgive myself."

"I don't care about how you feel. You've all been lying to me. And you—you're the worst of them because you claim to do it out of love," she continued. "This sick, twisted, pathetic fantasy love you have in your head. I can't love you, Laz. And honestly, I never did. So just leave me the fuck alone."

Each word pierced Laz like a knife to the gut. He made to respond but what else was there to say?

To save his dignity, and to spare Ava any more pain, he turned his back and left. Yet before he could reenter the ballroom, Laz heard Nick call out to them both. He paced rapidly, panting and panicked.

"Henry is missing."

"What do you mean?" Ava asked. "Missing how?"

"Station security said his tracker implant has been offline since this afternoon."

"Off? They can't be turned off," Laz argued.

"It's not pinging, which means that Henry isn't on the station. And he hasn't been for the last three hours."

Chapter 24
Search and Rescue

Cielo marched to the infirmary as she had been instructed. She needed to ensure the Medical staff understood what was coming. She reminded her team of the timetable, and before leaving, she checked on the status of Tobias Coen.

"Still dead," one of the medics said. He stood by the sheet-covered corpse as it lay on a stretcher. "We're about to move it to cold storage."

"Or we could just chuck it out of the airlock," a nurse suggested, only half-joking.

The medic took in a sharp breath, aghast. He looked to Cielo for support, but only got an uninterested shrug that seemed to say, *Do whatever you want with it.* He then told the nurse, "It's protocol. We don't disrespect the dead."

"Even if they were unworthy of respect in life," the nurse replied.

Cielo was less concerned with what to do with the late Architect's body than what brought him to his end. It may well be that Coen's ill-timed heart attack had nothing do with Henry Gallagher, but Nick Gallagher reporting the death right around the time his husband took his unscheduled spacewalk—that seemed more than mere coincidence. And tonight was not the night for coincidences.

"What did Gallagher say, exactly?" she asked the medic.

"Said he and his husband were in the theater and then heard something fall over in the next opera box. Then they found Coen on the floor, unconscious. They tried to get help, but by the time I got there, the man was dead."

"He wasn't too healthy to begin with," added the nurse. She poked at the dead man's rotund belly with a gloved finger. "These old-timers really should be screened from coming up here. They're too high-risk."

"Good job keeping it quiet, by the way," Cielo said to the whole room. "None of the guests seem to be aware. I know it couldn't have been easy to pull off in the middle of a show."

"Well, it's not completely contained. The Gallaghers obviously know," the nurse replied. "Are we sure they haven't told anyone?"

The medic replied, "Nick might. He was shaky when I asked him questions, and he seems like the kind of guy who would talk."

"Henry wasn't there, was he?" Cielo asked.

Everyone shook their heads. The medic added, "Nick was the one who called it in, and he was alone when we got there."

"Yeah, that's what I thought," she replied. "The other Gallagher's missing. Security just told me. They think he might have gone overboard. Nick might be the kind to talk, but he's got other things to worry about right now."

"Overboard how?" the medic asked, his concern mirrored on everyone's faces. "That wasn't part of the plan, was it?"

"Don't worry about it. Just make sure to be at your posts at the appointed time."

"You need to give us something, Miss Cielo. We need to know," the nurse said tersely. "Is this missing person going to be a problem?"

Cielo received a message on her earcuff from Jin. The shuttles were minutes away from being deployed. She confirmed the information and told him that she was on the way. She turned to the medbay staff anxiously awaiting her reply.

"Definitely not a problem. More of a solution. There'll be a search-and-rescue operation, which should keep Security out of our hair for a while."

After the infirmary, Cielo then headed to the hub to ensure exactly that. She reached the hangars right on time. By the portholes that overlooked the docking bays, she watched the shuttles coast past, engines roaring. The utility vessels Castor and Pollux flew side by side, trailed by the larger cargo vessel Demeter. The light shuttles typically did exterior maintenance on the Altaire, and both had never been in use at the same time since the habitat opened. Now the twins had been deployed, the second time in less than a day, with the Demeter joining their ranks to accomplish a task it wasn't designed for.

The vessels receded from view and went toward their separate sectors. Cielo felt a rush of trepidation. This is a good thing, she assured herself. No promise or payday would be big enough to make those men abandon their deluded self-image of being space soldiers.

Well, at least now they were out there playacting a military operation. They must be as pleased as pigs in muck.

"They're off," she said into her earcuff.

"Perfect," Pio replied. "Did you talk to Jin?"

"Yes. Dominique gave him the list. He got it handled."

"How long do we have?"

"Ninety minutes, max."

"Plenty of time," he said. "And our people know to secure the hangars before then?"

"It'll be a fight, but yes."

"All right. I'll let the Boss know. Good luck with your end of things."

Cielo wended through the station's halls to her next stop, the Altaire's Security Command Center. Though it now contained fewer crewmembers than usual, the place buzzed with activity. Monitors displayed the shuttles, with graphs and maps of the surrounding space, tracing the Altaire's orbit and projecting its route backward and forward. Two officers manned the comm links, guiding the shuttles to where they needed to search.

Security Chief Pete Drummond leapt off his seat as soon as Cielo entered his office. His gaunt face looked more hollow than usual. "Sorry for the rush," he said sternly. "The captain wants you and me to report to the Gallagher husband."

"I'm a bit swamped myself," Cielo replied, mustering as much warmth as she could. She didn't have time for this, and shaking off Drummond might prove complicated. "Besides, didn't you brief him already? What else is there to report?"

"Updates, I suppose. I'll make it up as I go along," he said, escorting her out the way she came. "I think she just wants us to reassure the guy."

"Wouldn't it be better for him to hear from the captain herself?"

"Copy that, but apparently she's got bigger fish to fry. You know, with the dead Architect and all. It's been one bitch of a day, I tell ya."

Cielo winced. "Maybe you should let me take charge of the conversation," she said. "I know how to handle these guests. I'll give Gallagher the updates, and you can . . . just stand there."

"Lot of use I'll be."

"You're there to provide an authoritative presence and make him feel that things are being handled," Cielo answered. "I'm the good cop, you're the strong, silent cop. Now tell me everything you know about the rescue mission."

Drummond briefed Cielo on the status of each shuttle and the risk projections, stopping at a couple of desks to pick up the latest data. A uniformed supervisor paced the command center floor, checking on the monitors and fielding officers' questions. He gave Cielo a respectful nod as she and Drummond walked past.

"I'm off to do some babysitting," Drummond shouted at the supervisor as he and Cielo made to leave the room. "You're in charge. Make sure nothing burns down while I'm gone."

"Copy that."

Cielo nodded at the officer, sneaking him a quick wink.

Everyone thought Yang Jin was one of the Pinoy staff, but he was Malaysian-American, and the American part might have been the reason that he got second-in-command in such a critical subdivision of the station's hierarchy. If the Altaire didn't have such an obvious bias toward certain types of people in its upper management, he would be farther up the ladder and Cielo's life would be a lot easier. Still, she owed it to his resentment that Jin decided to cast his lot with their plan.

Cielo and Drummond ascended to the upper torus, where they'd tracked Nick Gallagher's implant by the Astrarium. Cielo worried about damage control. She wouldn't want to pull him out of the party and attract unwanted attention, and she definitely hoped Nick hadn't already made a scene. The guests must never know that one of their own was missing.

She was relieved to spot Nick alone in an empty hallway outside the ballroom, but her relief was short-lived as Ava Khan and Tom Lazaro came into view. By the looks of it, Nick had already told his friends. She reminded Drummond to let her do the talking.

"Mr. Gallagher," she said, extending a hand. "This is Security Chief Peter Drummond. I know you've been waiting for updates, and we were hoping to have a word in private."

"Have you found him?" Nick asked, trembling.

"Like she said, it's better to do this in private," Drummond said. Cielo shot him a look.

"Just tell me, goddamn it."

"We've analyzed the latest location data," Cielo said. "Unfortunately, we now can confirm that your husband is not aboard the station. As of ten minutes ago, we've deployed all our available shuttles to find him."

"Is he still alive?"

"We strongly believe so."

"How the fuck did this happen?" Ava asked.

"The tracking data shows that Mr. Gallagher left by the spacewalk port," Cielo explained. "We also found that one of our EVA suits had been taken out. We believe that he might have gone on an unauthorized spacewalk. He was likely untethered."

Laz asked, "Aren't you supposed to have security measures against that?"

"We do. It's against protocol for someone to leave the station unattended and without permission, and we're looking into how this happened."

"And what about surveillance video?" Ava added.

"Our Security team is reviewing them as we speak, but for now our top priority is finding Mr. Gallagher and bringing him back safely," Cielo answered. "Our shuttles carry every crew member we can spare."

"How many shuttles?"

"Three."

"What about the lifeboats?" Ava asked, turning to Drummond.

"Those vessels don't have location and navigational capabilities for what we're trying to do, nor are they equipped with retrieval mechanisms." Drummond's brow grew damp with sweat. "Trust us, ma'am, we got more than enough shuttles out there. And our boys know what they're doing. They'll bring him back."

"How the hell are they even going to find him?" Nick asked, tears streaming down his face. "We're talking about the whole of fucking space."

"We know what time he went out of range, which gives us a confident estimate on when he left the station," Cielo said. "Without any means to propel himself but a jetpack, he'd still be in or near our orbit. We've narrowed down the sectors where he might be, and with enough coverage, we're going to find him."

"Won't he run out of oxygen?"

"The suits have five hours' worth of oxygen, and are pretty self-sustaining for that length of time," Cielo answered him. "As for his jetpack, he theoretically could have used it to navigate his way back toward the station, but since it's been hours, we believe he might have run out of propellant."

"But that's a good thing," Drummond interrupted. "That means he's probably not maneuvering himself blind out there. If he's in a relatively fixed orbit, he'll be easier to find."

"What time did he . . . leave?" Laz asked.

"About four p.m. ship time, which gives us about two hours to find him."

Drummond said, "It's good that you reported him missing when you did, Mr. Gallagher. Any later and the situation would've been a lot worse."

"But not to worry, two hours is more than enough time," Cielo quickly added. She finished the briefing with a promise of updates every fifteen minutes, and a suggestion that Nick retire to their suite so they could reach him more easily.

"I can't believe this is fucking happening," Ava said. Her face was indignant, livid. She could cause trouble. Cielo hoped that her assurances would calm her down, at least for the next hour. She checked her watch as the three guests walked away. Soon, none of them—not Ava, Laz, or the Gallaghers—were ever going to matter again. The moment couldn't come soon enough.

Chapter 25
"Mayday, Mayday"

From where he was, the nighttime world looked like a network of neurons. Henry floated over the Western seaboard, upside down, and it took him a while to identify the slice of Baja California as it grew out of Los Angeles, that bright bundle of nerves with their axons stretching out from the ocean and across the continent. The lights brought Henry some solace in the dark loneliness of space. Neurons he knew, brains he could handle, and with enough grit, he'd handle this predicament too.

It had been an hour since he'd regained consciousness, adrift and bruised. An hour, too, since he'd burned up, his skin reddening and his blood boiling him from the inside. He screamed, fraying his vocal chords in fits of agony, but the ordeal mercifully ended fast. He regretted using up his limited water supply to ease the pain, but he was in no position for measured responses.

"It is 7:02 p.m. station time. Orbital decay has been minimal; despite the last few hours I'm still around fourteen hundred kilometers from the surface," he said into the suit's recorder. After his pain subsided, he had decided to memorialize his efforts at getting rescued. "At this time, the Altaire has left my field of vision."

His heart sank at the words, watching the station disappear into the next morning while he stayed in the dead of night. He'd been willing it to slow down, or for himself to float faster toward it. He knew it was futile—without any means of propulsion, he'd have no way to move upward into the same orbit as the Altaire—but he still held the station as a beacon. A destination to aim for.

"The goal remains the same." He spoke with the clinical tone he used whenever he was in an operating theater. "I am waiting to drift into comms range of a nearby satellite. The closest one has an orbit one hundred eighty-four kilometers above me. It appears to be a spysat. Computer estimates it'll be another half hour before it hovers by my location, at which time I should be within comm range."

The spy satellite gave him hope and a purpose, a viable plan that did not involve waiting for a space station that orbited away far too swiftly. That plan also brought him clarity. He recalled more of the events of this afternoon. Why he wore a tux underneath this EVA suit, the ride up the elevator to see the opera. Fragments of what had happened surfaced, and he recorded them, too, as they returned to him.

"We were headed to our box, Nick and I," he said. "That would have been a half hour before the show." He recalled Nick too, how dapper he looked, his wry smile. The way the sight of him still made Henry giddy, even after all these years. Henry chose not to record that. Those details were for him alone, and this recording was for evidence.

For when he got rescued.

Soon, the satellite came closer. His helmet beeped.

"Mayday, mayday," Henry said abruptly as his on-screen display showed him the Noboru, its name emblazoned on its side in hiragana and in Latin script, right next to the Japanese flag. Judging from its design, this one was made for surveillance. It had a single module, enough to give Henry hope that someone was inside.

"This is Henry Gallagher of the United States. Requesting assistance. I went overboard from Space Habitat Altaire and need rescue. I am untethered and injured."

He repeated these words, then looped the recording into a distress call.

He drifted near the underbelly of the satellite, well within comm range and close enough to identify its instruments and specifications. Its sensors should have detected him by now, and yet he received no response.

"Please someone be there."

Silence. He kept the distress call on, his frustration growing with each unanswered loop. When he got out of range, he ended the transmission.

"No response from the Noboru. Likely uncrewed. Moving on to plan B and trying for another satellite," he said, resuming his recording. "Defense array, from the looks of it. Will definitely have crew."

His display told him that plan B's orbit lay 215 kilometers below him, sixty-eight degrees off.

His pulse rate increased as he committed himself to his backup plan, after which there was no other. By the time he traveled to the defense sat, he wouldn't have enough air to travel to yet another satellite for a third try. He only had one shot at barreling down toward

Earth and closer to the satellite, and he needed to make it count.

He checked his levels. Enough O_2 for another couple of hours, and CO_2 buildup wasn't alarming. He just needed to breathe slower. He also checked the jetpack numbers again. It displayed the same thing it had since he gained unconsciousness: the tanks were thoroughly depleted. The only thrust he could ever hope to get wouldn't come from the jetpack's propellants, but from its casing.

Below him lay a debris field. The scattering of metal parts both big and small floated steadily along an orbit between him and his destination.

His helmet display identified a piece of debris large enough to grab onto: a shiny metal fragment that looked like a torn-off cowl flap, or possibly shielding from a decommissioned satellite. Rough on its edges, mostly rectangular, with a gradual concavity. The fragment was maybe half an armspan wide, and thick too. More than enough mass and area to use as a second jumping-off point.

Henry recalculated the speed and angle that he needed, comparing it with the fragment's speed and trajectory relative to the defense satellite. When he determined that the math checked out, close enough at least, he readied himself.

Two moving targets, one shot. Here goes nothing.

Henry unbuckled the jetpack, undoing the closures that attached the casing to his EVA suit. He detached it, slid it from his back and off of both arms. He held the jetpack by its straps and brought his knees up to his chest, carefully moving into a fetal position. He then swung the pack beneath him, planting both feet on the pack's flat side. He strained to contract himself into position, then, with both feet firmly on the pack and each hand holding a strap on his side, he waited for the signal.

He aimed himself, his head pointing directly toward the empty space where the fragment would float past.

His helmet blinked green as the hunk of debris drifted into position. With all his might, he pushed down with his legs before releasing his hold of the straps, kicking off his makeshift platform and launching himself forward like an arrow.

Henry drifted headfirst into the fragment, crashing his helmet into its width. It bumped off to his side, and for a split second, it seemed to fly away completely. Henry reached his arm out and extended a foot to prevent its drift. He scrambled to grab it by its edge, barely and only by the tips of his gloves.

He gripped the hunk of metal, drawing profound relief in its heft and solidity. It was a drastic sensory change that he didn't know his body craved until then. He wished he didn't have to let it go, but he had no time for even a moment's solace. His display recalculated, showing his final destination's fast approach.

The defense satellite moved closer into position. He pushed the shielding into position and moved in front of it, angling both the fragment and his body according to his calculations. He held the top edge behind him, then raised his legs. He placed his feet against its broad side, and, as a swimmer would, he positioned himself to kick off the shielding.

He counted himself down, waited for his helmet's signal, and when the green light blinked again, he let go of the edge and propelled himself.

Slow and steady, he glided toward the satellite, and though his maneuvers had caused a tilt when he pushed off, his display showed him coming very close to his destination. With his current speed and trajectory, he should be within range in twenty minutes.

For the first time in this whole ordeal, Henry allowed himself to smile, and when he did, he found himself unable to resist. He screamed in triumph, filling his helmet with the roar of his laughter.

Soon, Defense Satellite Khafir-5 moved into view, a few degrees northwest of his downward path. His calculations had been sound; he timed the flyby perfectly. The Khafir moved fast, but not fast enough for him to miss. Salvation was close at hand. He saw the Saudi colors, the satellite's name painted along its side in both Latin and Arabic script. Khafir apparently meant "the sentry." The seal of the League of Arab Nations shone in the sunlight, and Henry beamed as he approached his rescuers.

Henry sent a live transmission. "Mayday, mayday. This is Henry Gallagher of the United States of America. Requesting aid under the Global Defense Alliance treaties."

Seconds passed with no response.

Henry knew that the satellite was crewed—all defense arrays were. He also knew he was only eighty kilometers away from it, within visual range and not just comm range. Yet the satellite hadn't acknowledged his hail. It hadn't initiated any maneuvers either, speeding along its orbit as though there wasn't a live human being that called for help right next to it.

"Khafir-5, I know you can hear me, and I know you can see me. You're under obligation to aid citizens of all Alliance signatories. Mayday, mayday."

He drew closer and closer to the satellite. It continued to ignore him.

"Please, I'm untethered and I'm in need of medical assistance. I've been thrown overboard Space Habitat Altaire. Please answer me, for the love of god."

The gap between him and the Khafir widened. Soon, he would leave its range and once it passes, he would never intersect with the satellite again. He would run out of air before it circled back around the globe.

"Khafir, please," Henry said, crying, mindless of whoever heard, as long as they did. "Don't let me die out here."

Just then, the satellite rotated, unfolding two modules from its sides. Turrets extended from the module's articulated arms, exposing eight space-to-ground missiles. The tips of their warheads gleamed red. The turrets tilted and searched for their angles. Henry struggled to understand. He yelled into his comm with agitated urgency.

"Khafir, do you read me? Do you copy? My name is . . ."

Missiles blazed down to the surface of the Earth with jarring speed. The pressure around Henry shifted, displacing him farther away from the Khafir.

"What the fuck?" he screamed, hot tears in his eyes.

He kept screaming and cursing, by turns perplexed and enraged and horrified. Henry didn't even care to watch where the Saudis aimed. All he knew was that the satellite was too busy bombarding some place planetside, and now it had transited too far to save him.

Chapter 26
Impact Play

Sloane hurried around his suite wearing a satin robe that he didn't bother to cinch. The robe was merely an afterthought, thrown across his back to shield him from the transitional chill from the shower to his bedroom. He was already running late. He searched his closet and pulled out a suit, a cream-colored number with the texture of crumpled crepe, and the blush tunic that went with it. Still on their hangers, he placed them over his body and checked how he looked in the mirror. He needed something more, something bolder. It was simply too conservative for the Saturday night banquet.

A buzz announced Julian's arrival, right on schedule. Sloane worried there wasn't enough time for this meeting and then to get dressed, but he'd rather get this out of the way now. Sloane belted his robe before ushering his guest into the den.

"Let's talk about the terms of engagement," Sloane told him firmly.

Tonight needed to be controlled, he kept reminding himself as they negotiated. Rules needed to be clarified, safe words established, limits heavily enforced. Julian liked pushing limits on a whim, and Sloane needed to hold them steady. Only after he felt assured that the terms were clear did Sloane move things to the bedroom.

Julian carried with him a long briefcase, and Sloane ordered him to place it on the bed. He stood mutely as Sloane inspected its contents: A couple of paddles, a flogger, a wide leather belt with no buckle. An assortment of silk scarves too. All of them pristine. New.

Julian had brought them onto the station specifically for Sloane. He had planned this, intending to upgrade Sloane from being just a financial dominant, well before he boarded the Altaire. The fucking bastard.

Sloane took a deep breath and stretched his fingers. Then, with his pent-up anger, he swept the back of his hand across Julian's face. The slap made the man stagger onto the bed. Julian held his reddened cheek. Sloane swatted the hand aside, taking Julian by the wrist. He dragged him onto the floor and ordered him to kneel.

"You fucking pig. You filthy fucking pig." He lifted Julian's head by his hair, leaned into his face, then spat on it. "Now strip."

Julian unbuttoned his shirt and slinked off his pants, revealing a black trunk and an erection that strained its fabric. Sloane recoiled.

"What the fuck is that, worm?" he said, taking a paddle and aiming it at Julian's cock.

Julian knew the rules and kept silent. Sloane circled him, taking in his body.

"All fours, on the bed."

Julian eased into position, and as soon as he did, Sloane brought down the paddle with a loud thwack.

"What are you?" Sloane barked.

"An animal."

Another thwack. "What kind of animal?"

"A filthy, disgusting animal."

Another thwack, then another, each harder than the last. Through the slaps, Sloane thought he heard Julian mumble.

"What was that, worm?"

"Nothing, sir."

"You fucking said something," Sloane said, emphasizing his words with a harder slap. "What the fuck was it?"

"I said, harder. Please."

"Don't—tell me—what to do—pig." Sloane said, in between paddle slaps. "No one tells me what to do."

His paddle landed harder, swiftly and erratically. His rage grew and ebbed with every swing. Each thwack was a thwack that he himself received in the past, and he relished the power in finally being able to deliver them.

Sloane felt himself becoming his father and fighting back at his father, both at the same time. It drove him mad.

"Arrowhead," Julian said, out of breath.

"Are you all right?" Sloane asked, unsure whether he'd heard the safe word.

"I'm fine. It's really good."

"Then what is it?"

"I want you to get on top of me," Julian answered. "I want you to choke me, punch me with your bare hands. I want you to break skin."

"No fucking way. We already discussed this. I'll use the paddle but I won't do all that."

"Why do you bother with this? We know how this is going to end," Julian replied with a smirk. "I say yes, you say no, I dangle a carrot, and you ask how high. What was it Churchill once said? 'We've already established what you are,'" he continued. "'Now, we're just haggling over the price.' And you know there's no price I can't afford."

Julian turned over and crawled toward Sloane. He slowly ran his fingertip along Sloane's neck, ending with a playful flick on his chin.

"C'mon, Sloane. I meant what I said. I will get you to Mars. I promise."

It had been gnawing at him, how quickly he'd submitted to Julian's enticement. What did it say about his willpower, his capacity for protective self-deception, that it had withered at the first hint of possibility? To be reminded of his weakness only brought Sloane further into submission.

He grabbed Julian by the arms and pushed him onto the bed. He clambered over him, pinning down his forearms. Julian squirmed, though an expectant smile cut through his face as Sloane towered over him.

He placed a hand over Julian's mouth.

"Is this what you want?" he asked. He slapped Julian's face with the other hand without waiting for a reply. Julian shook his head. Sloane slapped again, and again, repeating the same question.

Julian's eyes watered. His face reddened with each slap. He continued to feign resistance, moaning through Sloane's assault.

"Is this what you want, you disgusting piece of shit?"

Sloane clenched his fist and rammed it into Julian's face. The crack of his knuckle startled him, and for a moment he worried he'd overdone it. A cut on Julian's cheekbone began to bleed. Julian touched the spot gently, then licked the blood off his finger. He laughed in that triumphant way that he always did, the way Sloane's father did. It was the kind of laugh that echoed in the hollows of one's bones.

Sloane lifted his fist once more and landed it on Julian's chest.

Julian kept up his slow, low laugh, eyes rolled back in ecstasy. "Choke me."

Without hesitation, Sloane took his hands and wrapped them around Julian's neck. He searched for the larynx with his thumbs, and he felt a thrill when he found it. He pressed down on it. Julian gasped and convulsed under the weight. Sloane's pulse raced. A tear started to roll down his cheek.

"Is this what you want, you puny little bitch?"

Sloane sauntered into the bathroom smelling of sex and Julian's fleur d'oranger. His skin had gained an unwanted slickness. He jumped into the shower, scrubbing himself vigorously. He scraped a loofah all over his body until he was red and sore, as though that changed anything. He'd been at this game for a while, but never before had any of it felt dirty. The worst of it was knowing that, even with all the oils and lathers in the world, the muck would be impossible to clean. It was in the pit of his groin. It was in his blood. Unlike the last time he'd hit someone for their pleasure, Sloane didn't end up a sobbing wreck. This time he let himself become the kind of person he'd always hated, and he loved it.

Such was a life lived in ever-escalating stakes and never-ending compromise, he assured himself. He'd always done unsavory things to survive, and surely no one could fault him for that. When he got his reward, this, too, would be forgotten. The path he'd chosen was always going to be littered with regrets, each one easier to forget than the last, and much, much easier to forget than the first.

Not long after he discovered Henry's secret, Sloane tried to convince him to come clean himself. See, that's who Sloane used to be. He was a good guy. "People will understand," he'd told Henry. "And it's not fair. You're better than this."

"No, they won't. You can't tell anyone," Henry begged, citing their friendship, the years they'd shared, the closeness of their families. "If anyone finds out, it will destroy my life. My future, and my family . . . I'm your oldest friend, man, and you fucking promised! I trusted you!"

"And I kept that promise, even though I know it's wrong."

"So, what, now you want me to pay for your guilt?"

"They took the house, Henry. They took everything. My mom's off living on a yacht on international waters trying to escape the feds and I have no fucking clue where she is. I have no home to go back to, no bank account. After we graduate, I'll have to live with my aunt in bumblefuck Wisconsin. And forget about college. Please, man, I am desperate."

Sloane wished now that either one of them could have been the type of person who valued the truth over security. Since that day, he'd convinced himself that he was just a child, scared and alone, left to fend for himself. What else was he supposed to do? The circumstances eased his guilt only somewhat, and only for some time. From then on, every compromise had been made for himself and in the service of his endless, empty pursuits. The difference now was that Sloane didn't have the comfort of his old excuses.

A groan issued from the bedroom as Sloane stepped out of the shower.

"That was sublime," Julian said, his voice muffled.

What was he still doing here? "We'll be late to the banquet."

"Oh, who the fuck cares? These things never start on time."

Sloane chose not to engage further, hoping that silence would prompt his client to leave. He didn't want to see him again after the things he'd done, at least not until he'd had a few cocktails to drown his disgust.

"I hope you enjoyed that as much as I did," Julian said, leaning on the bathroom doorway. Sloane continued to pretend he wasn't there. "We should do it again tomorrow."

Sloane unhangered his clothes and began dressing himself. Julian stood there, still in his underwear, blocking the path. Sloane nudged him out of the way. "I'll think about it."

"That's my fault for phrasing it as a suggestion—we *will* do it again tomorrow, before the flight down."

Sloane ignored him and proceeded to the bedroom. Julian grabbed his wrist.

"Let me go," he said through gritted teeth.

The two of them suddenly jolted at the sound of a high, piercing scream coming from next door.

"What the fuck was that?" Julian asked.

More screams followed, louder and more frantic. Sloane worried, recalling that Zofia Luksus occupied the neighboring suite. He always found her to be sweet, if a little too demure to be the heir of a notoriously warlike Baltic principality.

"I'm gonna go see."

"Don't be daft," Julian told him. "We should stay out of it."

Sloane placed an ear against the suites' adjoining wall and heard nothing. He did the same against the front door of his suite and, finding silence, creaked it open as he peeked out into the hallway.

"Stay here and call security," Sloane told Julian, shushing his protests as he slipped out.

He silently walked toward Zofia's suite, trying to catch any sounds from within. He planted himself a few paces away from the door and leaned into the wall but heard nothing. Further down the hall, another door opened. Sloane ran toward an emergency stairwell and hid.

The door to Zofia's suite opened.

"Walk," a gruff male voice said. "And no sudden movements."

"Please don't hurt me," she replied shakily. "I'll give you whatever you want. Please, I beg you."

The man ignored her and instead issued a command. "Check the other rooms." Another person made noises of assent.

Footsteps receded and once convinced that the group was farther away, Sloane slid the stairwell door open. He caught glimpse of an Altaire crewmember as he rounded a corner. The man held a gun.

Sloane dashed back into his suite, locking the door behind him.

"My comms are down and I can't get a hold of security," Julian told him in a hushed tone. "Or anyone for that matter."

"We're in trouble," Sloane answered, describing all that he'd seen and heard.

"The crew's robbing the guests?"

Sloane shook his head. "They took Zofia, and they're searching other rooms. This isn't just a stickup job."

"They're taking hostages."

Sloane tried his earcuff. No signal. Same with his phone. "We can't stay here. We might be next."

"Well, they might not be after me," Julian replied. "Or us, I mean."

"Are you fucking serious? You're one of the richest people on board. Of course they'll want you. Why else do you think your comms are down?"

"I need to get to Isobel, make sure she's safe."

"She's safer in that ballroom than we are here," Sloane replied. "Everyone's there right now."

"Let's go there then," Julian argued.

The lobby, the promenade, and three orbital spokes separated the suite from the Astrarium. Sloane doubted they'd get off their floor safely, let alone all the way to the banquet. He didn't want to risk chancing upon the hostage takers, especially not so Julian could reunite with his wife.

"Have you forgotten about our implants?" Sloane asked. "They'll know where we are."

"Fuck me!" Julian said, flailing his arms in frustration. "Fine, let's go to station security then."

"Or we could find someplace safe to hide. If those bastards managed to hijack guest comms, then Security might be in on it. We'd be better off hiding, and somewhere that'll give us a quick escape in case they close in on us."

"And how the hell are we going to do that?"

"The service shuttles."

"My piloting's a little rusty," Julian replied sarcastically.

"And I don't intend on burning to death on reentry," Sloane snapped back. "But those shuttles have private comms and we can try to reach Isobel that way. We get her to come to us, and we all hide out there. And if they track us down, we can eject the fuck off this station."

"Do you really think that'll work?"

Sloane knew there were holes in this plan, but it was the best he could do with the little that they knew. Of course, this could very well go to shit. But Julian was his meal ticket, the latest and greatest in his long line of human ATMs. He'd let nothing touch so much as a hair on Julian's precious head.

"Don't worry," Sloane said, lifting the man's chin. "I got you."

"We're not leaving without her."

"Absolutely. You have my word."

One after the other, they snuck out of Sloane's suite and sped toward the stairwell, hoping to find safe harbor in the belly of the Altaire.

Chapter 27
A Friend In Need

To Ava's endless chagrin, Laz proved difficult to send back into the reunion banquet. Fortunately, Nick took little convincing to let her keep him company in his suite. He needed to be somewhere quiet, with someone to listen to his worries and fears. At the very least, the man needed someone to fix him a drink. Ava rifled through the jars and bottles, searching for something she could use to polish off the martinis. Her stomach grumbled. The garnishes might be the only food she'd get tonight. She found a jar of olives and popped one in her mouth.

Nick stared into the massive faux fireplace before him. He splayed on the leather chaise like a man who'd lost the will to live.

"This should be strong enough," she said, handing him his coupe.

"I don't think anything can be." He exhaled, taking a gulp of his drink. It failed to calm him. He shot up and paced around the room, studiously avoiding the windows. The vastness of space seemed to suck all the light out of the room. "Ava, what am I going to do?"

"The best thing for now is to just wait."

"Should we call someone?"

"They'll update us soon," she replied. "Likely with some good news."

Nick fumbled as he undid his bow tie, then took his jacket off. His shirt was soaked in sweat. Ava knew this wasn't the right time, but Henry's disappearance meant that she had to handle this now, regardless of how much Nick knew.

"Would it help to talk it out?" she asked in a measured tone.

Nick nodded. "I don't understand. Why would he go on a fucking spacewalk?"

"He didn't say anything about doing that?"

"No," he whined. "We had just gone on one this morning. And we were in the middle of a show! It doesn't make sense."

"Is that where you saw him last?" she asked. A perfectly normal question under the circumstances.

He nodded again. "We were in our box. He said he felt lightheaded, so he stepped out to get some air. Then he never returned."

To his face and behind his back, people called him Slick Nick for a reason. He told his story without a tell—no fluttering eyelids, no pauses in his speech. He trembled, but Ava chalked that up to a sincere worry for Henry.

"And you haven't heard from him since?"

"No. And I wish I had realized sooner that he was gone. Now we're racing against time."

Ava hesitated to pursue this line of conversation, but he'd already brought it up. She threw caution to the wind. "How come it took you a while to realize?"

"Well, I hardly keep Henry on a leash," he replied, taking another swig. "I assumed he got bored with the show and went to the casino or something."

Ava didn't expect Nick to admit to what he and his husband had been up to, but she did expect some cracks to start showing.

"Nick, I saw what happened. At the theater, with Tobias Coen."

Nick's lips thinned into a tight line. He set down his coupe, fingers visibly shaking. "They told us to keep it quiet."

"What? Who?" Ava asked, stunned.

"The Altaire. They didn't want to alarm the guests. Someone dying would cause panic, especially after yesterday's turbulence. That's why I couldn't tell you everything."

"What do you mean? What happened exactly?"

"The show had only just begun when Henry and I heard a crash one box over. We went to look and saw Coen on the floor, having a fit. Henry checked on him, it was a heart attack. I was so stunned, I didn't know what to do. He looked so pale. Henry tried to revive him but—but it was too late. So he left to get someone."

"Where did he go?"

"I don't know where he went," Nick replied, plaintive and frustrated. "I waited ages for him to come back, and when I couldn't stand it any longer, I went myself to grab an usher. I haven't . . . I haven't seen Henry since."

Ava recognized his story for the lie that it was. Those private opera boxes weren't so private that she couldn't see what Henry had done: He strangled Coen until the old man collapsed to the floor. She was impressed by how Nick improvised such an elaborate lie right before her eyes, and equally impressed by how firmly he committed to it.

"I don't want that to be the last time I see my husband, Ava," he said through tears.

This last part at least she knew to be true. These were the tears of a man who feared that he'd become a widower. Nick was devastated, at a loss about Henry's fate just as everybody else was. She couldn't call him out on the lie, not now. Instead, she stroked his back, and said, "It'll be all right. They'll find him."

"I was so busy dealing with Coen and the medics I didn't think about where Henry was. And it took time for things to settle down, for me to even have a single thought about Henry. All the while, he'd been missing. And now he's probably . . ."

"Hush, don't think about that," she replied. "That kind of worrying doesn't help us. And they said he has enough oxygen for hours."

"He doesn't deserve to die like this, Ava."

"No, he doesn't." She continued to soothe Nick, hoping that doing so would also soothe the dread now building up inside her.

"We have so much planned. We have so much ahead of us," he said, sniffling. "And he has so much to offer the world. He's got his flaws but he's as close to perfect as anyone can be."

"Yes, he is."

"Sometimes I wonder what he ever saw in me. I'm garbage compared to him. He's a goddamn saint."

A few months ago, Ava would have agreed with Nick. She saw firsthand the darkness lurking beneath every person in her life, including her closest friends, but she'd always viewed Henry as beyond reproach. That was until she learned more about what happened twenty-five years ago. This afternoon only served to confirm what Ava had recently discovered about Henry's nature, and hearing these praises, even from a grieving husband, made Ava's insides turn.

"He's—he's helped so many people," Nick continued. "So many—do you know many lives he's saved? Him and the company? Millions would die without GDX Pharma. Henry did all that. He did everything right," Nick said, then corrected himself. "He *does* everything right."

"All right, stop . . ."

"No, really. The last thing he did was try and save a man's life, even when it seemed like there was nothing left to be done. That's the kind of person he is, Ava. I . . . he's a good man."

"Nick, please." She leaned away from him, straightened her back. "It wasn't that dark in that theater. I saw what he did. He wasn't trying to save Coen."

A flash of self-righteous incredulity streaked across Nick's face. "Yes, he was. He—"

"Stop it, Nick. I know what I saw."

Before he could say more, the buzzer rang, startling them both. Nick was first to the door, expectant of news from the Altaire staff. He pressed a button and the suite's door slid open with a whoosh.

"Pio, thank goodness. Do you have any updates?"

Ava's blood ran cold upon seeing the Gallaghers' valet. The man likewise looked shocked to see her, but he quickly recovered, flashing a conspiratorial grin.

"Ms. Khan. What a coincidence."

"What's going on?" Nick asked, annoyed. "Aren't you here about Henry?"

"Unfortunately, I'm here about something else." Pio paced into the suite with a self-satisfied bearing. "But if you wanna know about your husband, why don't you ask your friend here?"

"What are you talking about? Ava, what is he talking about?"

She approached Nick unsteadily, as though the ground beneath her feet had cracked open. "I—I don't quite know what—"

"Would you rather I tell him?" Pio asked her.

Nick waited in confounded silence. The valet shook his head.

"Fine, I will—this woman is the reason your husband's out there, Mr. Gallagher."

Ava's eyes widened. She never told Pio to space Henry. When she first heard that Henry was overboard, she almost lost her mind. She loved her friend, and it tortured her to know that he'd been disposed of in such a manner, like garbage hurled into the void.

"What did you do to him?" Nick asked them both, unsure who to turn to. He went for the valet, grabbing him by the arms. "What the fuck did you do?"

"I did exactly what she asked me to do," Pio replied with a devilish smile. "I took care of it."

Nick's face reddened. He pushed the valet aside and came upon Ava. "You better tell me what's going on right the fuck now!"

"It was an accident," Ava said softly. She'd told herself that, over and over again. She never meant to kill him. She'd undo all of it if she could.

Yes, it wasn't that dark in that theater, not even after the house lights went down, and a single spotlight was the only source of illumination in the entire hall. She witnessed Henry strangle Tobias Coen in his private box. Everything inside her screamed, begged for him to stop, but the shock made her lose her voice. She couldn't believe her eyes. Not Henry. He would never. Despite this, she dashed out of the Lonsdales' box to try and stop him.

She called for Henry as he frantically ran down an empty hallway. He saw her for a split second, but he kept running. She managed to catch up to him before he could leave the floor, standing in his way by the grand staircase.

"Henry, what have you done?"

"Step aside," he replied. Ava grabbed him by the arm. "Please, Ava, I don't have much time—"

Owing to their long friendship, she might have given Henry the benefit of the doubt. Yet she'd also learned how everyone around her lied, especially the ones closest to her.

Ava pulled at him. "I saw what you did."

"It's not what you think," he argued, shoving her away. She resisted and he pushed her harder. The impact startled Ava, and she lost her grip. Henry, in turn, lost his balance. He tripped on a step and fell back, rolling down the long flight of carpeted marble.

Ava's mouth gaped in horror. She rushed to the bottom of the steps and knelt beside her friend's lifeless body. Soon, the Gallaghers' valet came to her side. Two others huddled around them—the lobby bartender and Cielo, Laz's valet.

Pio cradled Henry against himself. He felt for a pulse, a breath. After moments of searching, he shook his head gravely.

"It was an accident . . . he just slipped," Ava said, crying. She searched for support in the eyes of the staffers that surrounded her, but she was only met with sly looks. Fear overpowered her shock and sorrow. They might have seen the struggle at the top of the stairs, or heard their argument. There'd be surveillance video too, and then the truth would out.

"I tried to catch him, but . . . we both lost our balance," she continued. "What should I do?"

"That's not for us to decide, ma'am," Pio replied. "The higher-ups will have to investigate it."

Cielo nodded. "For now, we need to get him out of here. We can't risk someone seeing him and causing a commotion."

The woman spoke into her earcuff and asked for assistance. She then directed the bartender and Pio to get Henry to the infirmary, futile as it was. The men lifted Henry by his shoulders, toward a utility corridor that led away from the theater. Ava followed them, tearful and terrified.

"I'm sorry, I'm so sorry," she pleaded, tugging at the hem of Henry's jacket.

"Did you two know each other?" Pio asked.

"Yes. He was my friend."

"Some friend," the older one, the bartender, grunted.

"He was," Ava insisted, seeing the looks the two men exchanged. "And this wasn't my fault."

"You were the only other person on top of those stairs."

Cause was one thing, but blame was an entirely different matter. A misstep, a misplaced arm, loose carpeting, physics and gravity—all of these were causes. Ava admitted to herself that she caused Henry's fall, but she refused to believe she was worthy of blame. Especially not at that moment, as she was trying to do

the right thing, while Henry tried to do the exact opposite. She would not stand to be blamed for that.

"You need to help me. I'll do anything."

"Anything?" Pio asked. He signaled the bartender to
lower their cargo onto the floor. "It's not that simple,
ma'am. If you're asking what I think you're asking, it'll
be my neck on the line. I'm his valet; I'm supposed to be
responsible for him."

"I'll make it worth the risk," Ava told him. "For both
of you."

The old man narrowed his eyes at the valet, who
continued undeterred. "Well, my friend here and I, we
could use some help too . . ."

"Name your price."

The exchange covered too much and too little. Ava
had assumed that her promise afforded her silence,
protection of some sort. An avoidance of risk, in whatever form that solution might take. Her dead friend's
body being pushed out of an airlock was within the
universe of possible solutions, but one that never
crossed her mind. The thought made her heart ache.

"She pushed him down the stairs at the theater," the
valet told Nick now, sneering.

"No, I didn't! We were talking, and, and he slipped—"

"He went tumbling all the way down those steps—"

"—and I tried to hold on to him, but I couldn't,
and—"

"—then she said she'd pay me to get rid of the body."

"You didn't have to throw him overboard!"

"I didn't have to. But I wanted to."

Ava charged at the valet and flung her hand across
his face. Nick pulled her away and gave her a slap of her

own. He then collapsed onto the chaise and bawled, moaning like an animal being slaughtered. Pio watched with his arms crossed, trying yet failing to conceal his sympathy.

"You're a monster," Ava spat at him. "You did this."

"Me? I'm not the one who murdered him then asked to cover it up."

Nick rose from the couch and made to punch the valet, but he lowered his fist as quickly as he raised it. He opened his palms in surrender and slowly backed away from the valet's pointed gun.

"I think everyone needs to calm down now," Pio snarled.

From his pocket, he drew a bundle of zip ties and ordered Ava to tie Nick's hands behind his back. Her hands trembled as she did, and Nick kept flinching, repulsed by the merest contact with her. His gun still at the ready, Pio then told her to bind her own hands.

"Why are you doing this?" she asked as the valet inspected her work. He tightened both restraints for good measure. "What do you want from us?"

"Yeah, didn't she already give you money?" Nick said through gritted teeth. "What's the going rate for dead bodies, huh?"

"Oh, right. That." Pio leaned in and whispered. "He wasn't dead yet. At least not when I put him into the suit and sent him out the airlock. Probably is now, though."

"You motherfucker!" Nick yelled. Pio hit his face with the butt of his gun.

"We could have saved him!" Ava screamed through tears.

The valet responded by pointing the gun at her head, right between the eyes.

"I don't want to shoot you, so don't give me a reason." He shoved Ava into Nick, and motioned for them to walk toward the door. "After all, we still have a banquet to get back to."

Chapter 28
Housekeeping

Every object on the Altaire passed through the cargo holds of the Demeter and the Excelsior. The meats, the wines, the gallons and gallons of water, the linens, the light bulbs, the soaps and sponges, all in pallets and boxes and barrels as the case may be, side by side with the battery packs, the rolls of duct tape, the long-range comm devices, the bags of field-tested heavy-duty zip ties, the bottles of chloroform in mislabeled boxes, the armaments that were overlooked during loading.

Cielo debated their use now, but in the end, her compassion prevailed and she kept her gun holstered under her jacket. On the way back to the hub, she subdued Security Chief Drummond with a rag and the chloroform stowed in her back pocket, then bound his hands and feet with zip ties. Once she was done hiding the unconscious man in a broom closet, she returned to the ballroom.

The first hors d'oeuvre course had just been served, and the Astrarium Hall was raucous in animated conversation. The guests marveled at the tiny plates of exotic seafood set before them, impressed at the freshness of the blowfish and the brine in the uni, despite them being thousands of miles away from the nearest ocean. Amid the oohs and aahs, crystal glasses clinked in celebration. Forks and knives tinkled against fine china. Cielo couldn't keep her eyes away from the silverware. There was a reason they initially planned to set things in motion at ten PM. By then the tables would have been cleared. Now, they had to worry about cutlery being used as weapons. She only hoped that these pampered fools were too soft to even try.

She headed to her post, one of the flanks by the service entrance into the ballroom. She saw that most of the Altaire servers had already formed a ring along its outer wall, with another ring surrounding the circular dance floor. The guests' tables were enclosed on both sides, and, save for the empty stage, all areas were secure. As the last of the servers retreated from the floor, empty trays set aside at their stations, she inconspicuously locked the double doors.

The band slowed their music, hushing into a complete stop that went unnoticed. The rest of the Altaire crew unholstered the handguns under their aprons and took out the rifles hidden beneath their service trolleys.

Two blasts of gunfire erupted, followed by a command to get on the floor. Shrieks rung out in the hall.

"Welcome, Rochford," a voice boomed through the speakers. A stately Filipino woman wearing an Altaire uniform walked on stage, her salt-and pepper hair in a tall bouffant. "Some of you have met me already, but allow me to reintroduce myself. My name is Miren Abaya, and I am the station's chief housekeeper."

"What's the meaning of this?" a man yelled from the crowd. Other guests joined, leaping out of their seats in protest. Cielo steadied her aim at the guests before her. A burly man in a tuxedo stood up to one of the armed crewmen. A guest's security detail, no doubt. Weaponless, he tried wresting the rifle away before receiving a bullet to his gut.

"Everybody on the floor," Miren yelled. "Now."

The guests followed swiftly, and the crew members converged on them, ordering them to crawl on their stomachs toward the center of the ballroom. The ones who resisted received kicks on their backs or the side of their heads. In no time, the well-dressed mass was gathered in the middle of the dance floor, trembling as they lay prostrate on the cold tile.

"We're going to make this quick," Miren announced. A few berifled galley cooks had joined her on stage, and so did the band. "Do what we say and no one gets hurt."

"Yes—yes, we'll cooperate," a guest replied, sniveling. "Please don't hurt us."

"You can't do this to us!" Another said, her outraged tone undercut by the cracks in her high-pitched voice.

Two staffers broke formation and stepped over the guests to locate the ones who spoke up. They shot them both.

"And no talking," Miren said.

Cielo stood side by side with the rest of the crew, standing tall over the Rochford Class of 2064, guns pointed at their backs. She surveyed the room, searching her comrades' faces for the fear she fought to suppress. She only found stolidness, and an occasional glint in one's eyes. It would be a long night, she knew, and she consoled herself with the thought that, no matter how this all ended, this one moment felt victorious.

Laz squirmed in discomfort. His belt buckle dug deep into his waist and his shirt buttons pushed up against flesh and bone. He kept his face away from the dance floor, arching his back to lift himself off the surface. Inches away from his head, the sharp heel of a stiletto was close enough to poke him in the eye.

Though the captors remained at their posts with handguns aimed, they seemed to allow a little bit of movement. Laz craned his neck in search of Ava or Nick, or Sloane, whom he hadn't seen all night. He got no such luck, unable to see much at his level. He thought about Henry and hoped he fared better than the rest of them.

There'd been a hostage incident once, in Santiago. It was a few years before he obtained his ambassadorship, but he studied it nonetheless. Understanding local politics was a critical part of the job, and a hostage crisis at the stock exchange wasn't easily forgotten. The hostage takers ostensibly protested fuel subsidies, but they had demands other than a change in Chilean energy policy—demands amounting to a billion pesos. Cars and helicopters too. The president sent in the Fuerte Lautaro, and they wiped out the terrorists, reporting only three civilian casualties. If only special forces could be deployed up to the Altaire that quickly.

Soon, the ballroom's doors whooshed open, followed by the marching of feet. More hostages. Fearing that his friends were in the group, Laz tried to glimpse the guests being brought in, but all he could see were the feet in front of him. A hostage taker yelled for the new arrivals to get on the ground.

"No sudden movements, and no talking," Miren announced.

From where he lay, his only clear view was that of the elevated stage, where the chief housekeeper lorded over her hostages. She paced around the stage, gathering reports and giving orders. Laz tried to understand who she was, why she was doing what she did. He tried to humanize the woman. This way, he figured, maybe he wouldn't be so scared.

It took Laz a while to unearth, from the recesses of his boyhood memories, the reason this woman struck a deep-seated fear in him. It wasn't just the guns. The woman looked a lot like his great-aunt Geralda, the spinster who raised Laz's grandfather, her much younger brother. Laz had only met her once, on his first and only trip to the Philippines when he was eight. On her deathbed, she wore a lacy black dressing gown, smelling faintly of elemi and champaca blossoms. As a sign of respect for an elder, Laz took her hand and placed the back of her palm against his forehead, for the first time in his life performing the traditional mano. His forehead was slick with sweat, unaccustomed as he was to the heat and the thick humidity of the tropics. The old woman brushed him aside in disgust. She wiped her hand dry of his sweat, and asked that he be taken away from her sight.

An armed man approached Miren, one who didn't wear an Altaire uniform. Laz recognized him from this afternoon's opera. A tenor, the one who played Sportin' Life. Was the entire crew part of this takeover? Why would American actors join in this at all? Judging by the flags on the nameplates, Laz had assumed this plot came from the overseas staff. There were hardly any non-Americans on board, and they were mostly in

Central Command as far as he knew. He shuddered to think that they were in on it too.

Miren scanned the ballroom for someone in the crowd. She waved them over, and a familiar face marched to the stage. The Head of Guest Relations, his personal Altaire liaison, Cielo. She carried a handgun held off to her side. Laz barely knew her, having exchanged only a handful of words over the past two days, but he felt deeply disappointed to see her take part in this. She was better than this.

The women spoke in barely hushed whispers. Miren looked displeased, but Cielo was steadfast. The older one eventually nodded in begrudging agreement, and Cielo marched back down the stage. She made her way to the floor, circling the hostages in search of someone. She shoved the hostages aside with her foot, examining their faces and stepping over them when she was done. Laz's heart sank. He somehow knew, well before she lifted him off the floor by the back of his collar, that it was him she was looking for.

With Cielo on one side and an armed guard on the other, Laz dragged his feet up the stage, his hands tied in front of him. He didn't protest or ask why he'd been singled out. The surrealism of their situation hardened into reality, and courage seeped out of him with every passing second.

Miren walked up to meet him. Laz bowed his head, partly in fear and partly to search the hall from his elevated vantage. He couldn't see Ava or any of his other friends.

The older woman took him in from head to toe, her nose turned up in revulsion. "Him? Are you sure about this?"

"He's the next best thing. And he's the most likely to comply."

"It works better with Lonsdale."

"He's still running around the station. It'll take a while to seize him," Cielo replied, to the other woman's displeasure.

Miren estimated Laz one more time. "Fine, then. Come back as soon as you're done."

Cielo dragged him down from the platform and through one of the ballroom's service entrances. His other captor, a Belizean porter named Elison, trailed him and Cielo as they snaked down narrow passages and utility corridors inaccessible to guests. From the gradual decrease in gravity, Laz guessed that they headed toward the center of the Altaire. They must need him for something. He had a guess as to what, and he hoped it would be enough to save him.

Chapter 29
Lifeboat

Sloane knelt beside the corpse that lay in the hallway, the second one on his journey to the hub of the Altaire. Another Security staffer, a woman this time. She, too, was riddled with bullet holes. The hostage takers must have taken her sidearm but they left her truncheon. Sloane took it from its holster and gave it a forceful flick, extending it to its full length. He felt its heft in his hands. He would've preferred a gun, but it was better than nothing.

"Are you sure we're headed the right way?" Julian whispered.

"Do you want to lead?" Sloane snapped. Julian shook his head. "Then stop asking."

In truth, Sloane didn't know where they were. He'd only been extrapolating their location. The passages in the Altaire's hub weren't labeled, but Sloane knew station design, and he sensed they weren't far off from their destination.

He led Julian down yet another corridor, looking out for threats around the corner. As they turned, a barrage of gunshots echoed ahead of them. They retreated to a nearby stairwell, dashing behind a door as the shooting continued.

When silence fell, Sloane decided to go. "Wait right here."

Julian protested, panicked, but Sloane was already out the door. He stayed close to the ground, heading to the end of the corridor where a bulkhead gave him cover. As he sneaked closer, a hall door started to slide open. He scurried beside it, truncheon at the ready. When an armed crewman stepped through the threshold, Sloane swung with all his might. The man fell to the floor with a thud.

Sloane rolled the body over and searched the man's uniform. A gun. He checked for rounds, then stowed the truncheon back in his pocket.

Once at the bulkhead, Sloane peeked down the service tunnel that led to the shuttle ports. His heart sank when he saw the docking bays. Empty. None of the shuttles were there. Aside from maintenance stations and supply crates, all that remained in the hangar were the dead bodies of Altaire Security, over which stood four hostage takers.

Sloane returned to the stairwell, cursing under his breath. "They've taken the hangar, and the shuttles are gone. We have to figure out another way, and fast."

Julian fell against the wall and slid down onto the floor. His vacant gaze fell on a spatter of blood on Sloane's shirtfront.

"Came upon one of them," Sloane replied. "I'm fine."

"Are they dead?" Julian asked, in a sort of daze.

"I didn't check. But if he isn't, then we really need to get moving."

Julian's eyes began to well. The gravity of the situation was finally pressing on him. Here was a man who'd always been in control, losing it for the first

314

time in who knows how long. This is dangerous, Sloane thought. If Julian fell apart, he could get them both killed.

"Listen, I have a plan," he said gently, joining Julian against the wall. "But it only works if you can keep a level head. Do you hear me?"

Julian struggled to compose himself. "What's the plan?"

"There's a chance they haven't taken Excelsior yet. We head there instead, on the other side of the hub."

"Can't we just use one of the lifeboats?"

"No. They don't have long range comms," Sloane replied. "Besides, they're built to eject from the station and float in space while waiting for rescue. Using one could buy us time, but they've taken the shuttles, which means they'll have no problem retrieving our pod quick and easy. We need the Excelsior."

"What if they've taken it too?"

"We'll deal with it when we get there."

"Didn't you hear all the fucking gunfire?" Julian asked, a quaver in his voice. "How are we even gonna cut through the hangar?"

"Carefully. And there's this." Sloane took the gun out of this pocket.

"Where did you—?"

"You know how to use these things, right?" he asked, handing the gun over.

Julian raised himself off the floor, recharged by the feel of steel in his hands. He studied the weapon, then released the magazine to check the ammo. He slid it back, undid the safety, cocked the gun, and held it downward and to his side, ready to advance.

Sloane whistled, impressed. "Looks like we might have a shot."

A loud rumble shook the stairwell, soon followed by the echo of a low clanging. A klaxon blared in the distance. Frantic yelling came in between its piercing blasts.

"That's an all-clear siren," Sloane shouted through the noise. "One of our missing shuttles must be docking."

"Should we go for it again?"

"I don't wanna risk it. There's still four of them in the hangar, and whoever's on that shuttle will have to come down this tunnel after disembarking. The fight's gonna come to us if we don't leave here quick."

The two of them left the stairwell, gun and cudgel at the ready. They had barely gone halfway through the embarkation tunnel when they heard the docking port pressurize with a loud whoosh. The klaxon stopped and they froze, watching the shuttle port doors begin to open.

A barrage of gunshots filled the air, from both the gunmen in the hangar and the passengers on the shuttle. Julian grabbed Sloane and they sped back the way they came, finding cover behind a maintenance station. If anyone so much as turned the corner, they were sure to be spotted.

"Can you see what's going on?" Sloane asked in between blasts of gunfire.

"Looks like an ambush," Julian replied, craning his neck. "Whoever's getting off, they're not with the hostage takers. Could be Altaire Security. Let's get moving." He dashed out of their post, only to be pulled back by Sloane.

A bullet zipped by Julian's head, then another.

"Fuck, fuck, fuck," Sloane said. "We gotta run."

"I think they're down to two," Julian whispered. He stood against the wall, gun ready and waiting for whoever was coming down. Footsteps advanced toward them. "We got this. Stay where you are."

"Don't be stupid," he replied, none too pleased with Julian's bravado. Mere minutes ago, this man was on the verge of a breakdown. Sloane feared that this display was part of that. "You'll get yourself killed."

Julian peered out again, and another shot rang out. To Sloane's surprise, Julian stepped out from behind their cover and raised his arms.

"My name is Julian Lonsdale. I want to negotiate."

Silence.

"Whatever you want, I can give it to you. I just want to be in one of those shuttles."

"What the fuck are you doing?" Sloane said, spit flying out of his mouth. Julian loosely dangled the gun in his hand, giving Sloane a sideways glance that seemed to say, *I got this*. The man had a death wish.

Julian turned to the tunnel, yelling, "Maybe you can come out and we can talk like gentlemen, huh?"

A response came in the form of a bullet, hitting the wall inches away from him, followed by two more. Julian retreated behind the maintenance station, ready to return fire, but by then, it was too late.

One of the hostage takers had rolled out of cover, shooting Julian in his side. Sloane caught him as he staggered to the floor. Blood seeped out of him, and Sloane scrambled to stanch the flow with his hands.

The shooter stood before them and aimed his rifle at Julian's head. His comrade followed, kicking away Julian's gun.

"Listen. Just let me go," Julian told them, breath heavy and ragged. "I'll give you anything you want."

"This man needs medical attention, now." Sloane's tone was firm, though his hands trembled as he pressed down on Julian's side. "A dead hostage is useless, so you're gonna need a fucking medkit—fast."

"The shuttle should have one," Julian struggled to add. "Take me there, and I'll triple however much you're getting paid."

"How about I just finish the job and shut you up?" the shooter replied. Sloane recognized him as one of the cast members from the matinee show.

His younger partner leaned in, his voice low and furtive. "But we have orders to bring everyone in."

"No one needs to know," Julian continued. His face slowly paled and grew damp with sweat. "I can send the funds right now. Pick a number. Don't care how high."

"This is the problem with you people," said the older one, drawing out each word. "You think everyone can be bought off."

"Isn't that what—this is all about? What—all human—interaction—is all about? Money?" Julian said, mustering his strength.

The hostage takers stepped closer, looming over with self-satisfied grins. "Money's the root of all evil, didn't you know?" said the older one, the opera singer.

"Then what is it you want?" Sloane asked.

"To root out evil."

Julian chuckled, his weak laugh turning into a coughing fit. His breathing slowed, and Sloane tried to shush him, but the man won't be stopped. "Then you've got—the wrong man, my friends."

"Is that right?"

"Haven't you—heard of the Mars program? Of, of the—Lonsdale Foundation? I'm the guy trying to—build a new world. A b-better world."

The older of the two crouched beside Julian, inspecting him like a curious artifact. "You're one of the good guys, huh?"

Julian nodded.

"Your beef isn't with us," Sloane added. "We'll stay out of your way. Just get him patched up. Please, I'm begging."

"And what about you? Are you one of the good guys too?"

Sloane's eyes watered. "I just don't want my friend to die." He hoped that was enough.

"Should we bring them in?" asked the younger gunman.

"Nah, let's give them what they want." He gave his comrade a meaningful look, to which the other responded with a firm nod. "Take them to the shuttle."

The two captors cuffed Sloane behind his back, and once done, they lifted Julian from the floor, slinging his arms over their shoulders. Julian limped along as they carried him down the passageway into the hangar. Sloane followed closely, passing by the bodies strewn on their path. Through the portholes he looked out onto the docked shuttle. The Pollux. Escape was so close at hand, and yet, somehow, never before had it felt so distant.

Chapter 30
A Message for Home

Laz scrambled for a plan. Cielo escorted him down a deserted service corridor with both hands, and she didn't have her gun holstered. If it were just the two of them, he might have a chance at knocking her out and grabbing the weapon from her pocket, even with his hands bound in front of him. With Elison there, he needed to find another way.

"I need water," Laz said meekly. "For my pills. I have this heart condition, and—"

"You must think we're idiots," Elison said without looking at him.

"I'll let that slide this once," added Cielo. "We have all your information and I know you don't take any meds. Pull another stunt like that, and my friend here is going to shoot you."

"If it's money you want," Laz said, taking another tack. "I think you've made your point. Everyone's scared out of their wits. Pick a number and they'll give it to you, no questions asked."

Cielo looked uninterested, bored, like she expected this kind of bargaining from him. Elison merely laughed. They hauled him into a service lift, pressing the button for the bottom deck.

"Then what is it you want?" Laz continued. "Because if it's something else, the people in that ballroom can make it happen, whatever it is."

"How many points do you have?" Elison asked him. "MERIT points, how many?"

"Seventy-two," he answered, confused.

"I have fifty-eight hard-earned points," the porter replied with a note of pride. "Tell me, do you think you deserve to be on Mars more than I do?"

"Is that what this is about? We can help—"

"Yes or no," he replied, each syllable drawn out. "Do you think you deserve it more than me?"

"Everyone deserves it," Laz said, carefully deflecting. "But the system exists for a reason. It's not a matter of deserving to be there, it's resource management. Food, water, oxygen. Mars can only be viable for everyone if we start populating it in the most efficient way and then build from there."

"See, this is why I picked you," Cielo said, pushing Laz out of the lift. "You're very persuasive. You must be great at your job."

The elevator chimed as it halted.

Laz still couldn't tell where he was. All around him were blank walls and unmarked doors. Crew quarters, most likely. With his rifle, Cielo prodded him to keep walking down another long corridor.

"You never really answered his question, though," she continued. "Do you think it's fine to make Elison and his family wait decades for a chance to live somewhere that isn't a hundred ten degrees?"

"In the shade," Elison scoffed.

"In the goddamn shade," she emphasized as she shoved Laz. "And what about me? I got seventy-seven points. I should be ahead of you in line, if the system counted everyone fairly. But none of my training or my work experience on this station matters to them. Labor exemptions, they call it. Is that about resource management too?"

Laz saw an opening at her mention of "them" and seized on the opportunity. "I know those people aren't perfect. But they're pragmatists first and foremost, and I know how to talk to them. I can help you get what you want."

"Oh, really?" Elison asked. "Do you even know what we want?"

"You brought me here to negotiate, right? I'll do more than negotiate," he replied. "I'll tell them to stand down: the US or NATO, whoever's watching. I'll ask for immunity for everyone here. And I'll pull on all the strings to make sure they meet your demands to change the system. I'll be your advocate."

Cielo and Elison slowed their pace as they pondered his every word.

"The MERIT system is corrupt. I've always known, but I've also gained too much from it to question it," Laz continued, contrite. He hoped he looked believable enough. "If you want it changed, I can get that done. You know my background and my influence."

"And what makes you think they'll listen to you?" Cielo asked.

Laz felt a flicker of hope. "Because I'm one of them."

"But are you one of us?" Elison sneered.

"Look at me. Of course I am . . ."

Before he could finish, Elison pinned him against the wall, pressing down on his chest with a thick forearm. "I'm looking at you now and all I'm seeing is a brown man who's too used to double talk," the porter spat, his breath warm against Laz's face. "You're so good at it you've convinced yourself you're better than us because you're one of them. But we see right through you. You're not better than me or her or anyone else who's been serving you on this station. You only think you are because the world you've built keeps telling you so. That all ends today."

Elison pressed a button on the wall and the door slid behind Laz, causing him to lose his footing and stumble. Hands bound, he writhed to get back on his feet, and it took him a while to take in his surroundings. The terminals, the wall-to-wall screens displaying all sorts of navigational data. Strobing distress lights bathed the place in a menacing red glow.

Laz stood on the bridge of the Altaire.

His captors hauled him across the length of the room. Every step he took revealed a new horror: crew members with rifles at the ready, walls riddled with bullet holes, lifeless bodies splayed on the floor, blood seeping through the uniforms of Altaire senior command.

When they reached the far end, Cielo shoved Laz up a flight of stairs that led to the helm. Its viewing deck, lined with a control hub and monitors that wrapped around its perimeter, overlooked the massacre below. She pushed Laz onto the captain's seat and rolled him in front of the comm terminal. Elison established a planetside connection to an unknown address. He adjusted the lights to illuminate Laz's face, holding him by the jaw as he readied him for the camera.

Then, Elison placed a tablet in front of him. It displayed a message in large font intended to be read. Cielo then took out her gun and aimed it at Laz's head.

"When the green light goes on, start reading. This isn't in real time, so if you go off script, you'll be dead way before the message reaches Earth."

Laz looked down at the tablet. The message before him didn't even register as words. They were meaningless figures, as though he had lost all facility for reading, for rational thought.

The green light started blinking.

Laz remained frozen in silence. Cielo's gun inched closer to him, rousing him alive.

"We are the Rochford Class of 2064," he began slowly. "We are bankers, entrepreneurs, statesmen, tech moguls, captains of industry. We rule empires both private and public. We control the world's wealth. We are the one percent."

The script rolled on, and Laz struggled to keep up with its pace.

"For generations we have shaped the world for our purposes. We've conquered every corner of the globe and erected the strongest walls to secure what was ours. We stole and amassed wealth and fed the rest of the world with scraps from our table. We exhausted every resource and took everything we could that didn't already belong to us. After two centuries of rampant capitalism, we've managed to burn the world, and then we blamed it on the poor and ignorant.

"When we saw what we had wrought, we set our sights on a new planet, deciding that Earth no longer had value. With all the money and power and the resources we stole from the billions who needed them, we built on the new planet instead of fixing the planet that we still had the means to save. And we decided that the only people worth saving were ourselves.

"We built a new haven only for those we ourselves deemed worthy." Laz continued, stumbling over the words. "We reduced the value of each human life to a number, and we determined that value according to the standards of extraction. We found the old, the infirm, the queer, and the poor to be unworthy of advancing humankind, as though procreation and wealth creation were the only things that mattered. We took the implicit assumption of capitalism and we made it law: that not everyone deserves dignity, life, a future.

"And when our settlements are inhabited by the people we deem worthy, we will continue to take from the Earth what we want. This is who we are. We are takers. We take what is not rightfully ours, and we continue to do so, even in this promise of a blank slate."

Laz skimmed the rest of the script, steeling himself for the import of what was coming. He finally understood that all his efforts were useless. He was not there to negotiate, and he would never be able to save himself, or Ava, or anyone else on the station.

"We called ourselves visionaries, seeking to ensure human expansion into the rest of the universe. We made it possible and inevitable. At the same time, we also made inevitable the same greed and ruthlessness that has accompanied colonization throughout history. We have made iniquity inescapable. We developed technologies to bring life to where once there was none, but in doing so, we have also consigned most of humanity to its death. For all of these transgressions, there is no ransom, and there is no absolution.

"The staff and crew of Space Habitat Altaire are one with their comrades all over the globe who continue to fight for the end of the ruling class," Laz said through gritted teeth. "They are also one with their comrades on the five other space orbitals floating over the planet: the Palazzo, the Wonderland Resort and Casino, the OASIS, the Sky Citadel, and the Ark Royale, who are in this moment also standing up in collective action to overthrow us."

His eyes welled up in tears, outraged and terrified. Cielo cocked her gun. "Read."

"We are the one percent. We are plunderers, murderers, and thieves, and today is the beginning of our end."

Cielo sensed a shift in her captive. No longer did the ambassador struggle with his bonds, nor did he try to bargain or gain favor. After reading their message, Tom Lazaro seemed to have lost his will to fight.

It gratified her to see one of them so fallen, but she had to admit to herself that he had gotten to her. Maybe it was the way he looked, the way his eyes had become forlorn, like her younger sibling's. Cielo could see Delfin as a diplomat, running the world with the right kind of values, with wisdom beyond their years. Wouldn't that be the dream?

She wheeled him back behind the captain's desk, the bullet-riddled corpses in full view below him. "Now do you get it?" she asked, weapon trained on him.

"On some level, I think I always did." He looked toward the comm terminal, which had since been taken over by Elison. "But it doesn't matter whether I understand or what I believe. You're the one holding the gun."

"This," she replied, brandishing the weapon, "doesn't make me any less right."

"And so what if you are?" the ambassador asked. "We're in range of dozens of defense cannons. The US, the Defense Alliance, someone will have their scopes on the Altaire, if they don't already. You'll be right only long enough until they send their missiles."

"Do you really think they'd blow up Space Habitat Altaire, the jewel of the sky?"

"You might get rid of us, but they won't let you stay here forever," he continued. "You won't get any resupplies from below. You won't last a week. They don't have to blow the station up, they just need to wait you out."

Was this a ploy, an attempt to sow doubt in her? Possibly, but her captive's manner told Cielo otherwise. He wasn't talking to her, not really. It was all idle musing, an attempt to distract himself from what was coming next.

"We're all going to die," he said, his voice cracking.

Elison snickered from across the room. "*We* are not going to die. *We* are heading home on the Excelsior, and *we* will have refuge somewhere no one can touch us," he said, firm on each first word. "*We* will survive *you*."

"And how do you plan on doing that?"

Cielo smiled. "With uncertainty. Chaos."

"Deception."

"The language of your people," she answered. "If there's anything we've learned from you, it's that collateral damage is only acceptable if the lives are dispensable. That depraved belief will be the key to our survival."

"Is that the goal, survival? And then what? You bring everyone to Mars?"

"We don't want your goddamn settlements," she replied with a wry smile. "Going to Mars will always require capitalists. People like you. Our goals require getting you out of the way. You and your orbitals and the Mars program are only the beginning. We'll dismantle everything you've built for yourselves and build anew."

"It's too late for that. It's been too late for a long time now," Laz said, his point blunted by the weariness with which he said it.

"It's easy to delude yourself of that when you have a trillion-dollar backup plan. The likes of us don't have the luxury of giving up. All we have is a clarity of purpose that comes with desperation."

Soon, Elison reported that the message had been sent planetside and would be ready for broadcast by the time they land. Cielo nodded, pleased. The porter then began to approach their captive, but she stopped him, to the surprise of both men.

"Leave him. I'll handle it from here."

"But we need to bring him back with the others," Elison argued. "Miren's orders."

"You go on ahead. I got this," she said firmly. The porter stalked out of the captain's office, doubtful, waiting for her to change her mind. She never did.

Cielo checked the time. The next phase of their plans was underway. She'd expected that her resolve would have hardened by now. Would it really be any different, having one man die by her own hand as opposed to many? Probably not, but still she struggled to quell the pit in her stomach.

"I deal with insurrectionists all the time," the ambassador told her. "I know which methods work and which don't. This one won't. Whatever you achieve will be fleeting, because it's built on unstable ground. Injustice can never fix injustice."

"What we're doing here, what you see as injustice, is the only thing that's ever worked."

"You still have a choice here."

"Didn't you understand what you just read?" she asked. "You have made yourselves unstoppable by any other means. Protests, petitions, laws, elections, pleas, education . . . we've tried everything else."

"Mass murder as a last resort."

"Nothing short of death will stop you."

"That's not what I meant, though." Lazaro leaned in, peering into her eyes with unnerving steadiness. "I meant that *you* have a choice. It doesn't matter if your people think this is the only way. It doesn't even matter if *you* think this is the only way. *You* don't have to be part of what happens next."

"Don't get it twisted," she replied. "Just because it's a last resort doesn't mean I feel forced into taking it. I know I have a choice and I've made my choice, freely and without doubt. I do this for my family, and for the billions who've suffered and who you've deemed unworthy of a future. And you . . . you have a choice too."

Cielo lowered her weapon, taking the seat across the desk. The ambassador squirmed.

"The chief housekeeper doesn't believe your kind is capable of change," she began. "And even if some of you were, she's willing to throw rice out with the rice water. She and I agree on most things, but she is more ruthless than I'd like."

"A necessary trait in these situations."

"More ruthless than I am." Cielo placed her gun on the desk in front of them. Her captive raised his head, as though awakened from a trance. He watched the gun as though it were a venomous snake about to strike. "You could join us, you know."

"Join you?"

"I like you," she replied, shrugging. "And maybe I think you can be saved. You said it yourself: You're one of us. At least on the surface. That's a start. You're not like the others. There might be a place for you in our movement."

"A place for traitors?"

"Converts."

Cielo observed the ambassador, who didn't flinch at her offer and her show of conciliation. Instead, he appeared to consider them. That was unexpected. What would it mean for him to accept? What would she do if he did? She never thought that far ahead. Finally, he spoke.

"It doesn't matter how noble you think your cause is," he said. "At the end of the day, you're nothing more than terrorists. You're just like the people you claim to hate, but at least we know who we are and what we're doing. While you—you're hypocrites. And I'd rather die than stand with you."

Whether he spoke out of pride or principle, Cielo couldn't be certain, but he was clearly willing to die for either.

"I thought you might say that," she said. "Still, I would have loved to see you lie one last time."

"The truth is all I have left. Why would I forsake it now?"

"I meant what I said. I like you, and not just because we're both Pinoy. I do think you're different from the rest of them." She took a deep breath. "Unfortunately, not by nearly enough."

Cielo took the gun and rose from her seat. The ambassador did the same, slowly, not in hesitation but in preparation.

"Turn around."

Tom Lazaro lifted his chin, defiance in his eyes. In them Cielo once again found her sibling. She steadied her aim. She had hoped this would be easier. She prayed that after this, the rest of her actions tonight would be.

Chapter 31
Not Hostages

The Astrarium had completely transformed since Ava saw it last a mere half hour ago. Gone were the holographic stars that glittered down from the domed glass ceiling, and the banquet hall looked stark under the bright white floodlights. The jazzy music and the animated conversation had quieted, in their place a charged silence and the occasional cry from a hostage. On the dais, instead of a brass band and a well-heeled MC, an older Altaire officer stood with a purposeful air of calm, a phalanx of armed crewmen behind her.

Pio shoved Ava toward the dance floor. It looked like a mass grave, with the hostage takers standing guard over a pit of bodies into which she herself was about to be thrown. Gun pointed to her head, she slowly lowered onto the floor. Nick did the same right beside her.

"Welcome to our final stragglers," said the woman on the podium, her voice laced with menace. "With your arrival, I'm told that the station is now completely contained."

An Altaire crewman rushed up the stage, whispering something in the woman's ear. She then walked up to the podium and waved more troops into the ballroom. She directed them to particular posts, pointing to and fro. These troops carried cameras and aimed them toward the hostages, careful to avoid catching their comrades in the shot.

"We'd also like to welcome Captain Edmonia Williams," the woman continued. Two crewmen dragged the captain up the stage. Williams looked bloodied, but her face bore an unrelenting fierceness.

"I wanted to apologize to you personally," the hostage leader said, stepping away from the microphone but not far enough. "You've been a good captain, and a good friend. I'm sorry you're caught in the crossfire."

Captain Williams hung her head low, before leaning back and shooting spit on the other woman's face. She wiped it off, dejected, then waved for the captain to be taken away.

"We can now proceed with the next phase," she announced. "We'll make this as quick as possible."

Armed crewmen moved into the crowd, stepping in between bodies and limbs. One by one they lifted guests by their arms. Ava searched around her, trying to see who was being taken and where. She recognized the terror-stricken faces of her Rochford cohort. Amanda Weston, Isobel Lonsdale, Giannina Weiss . . . Ava's pulse quickened as she realized that only women were being taken.

Right next to her, Nick began to laugh, his face dampened by tears and snot. "This is fucking perfect," he said. "I hope they make you suffer."

Ava's heart dropped. "Nick, truly . . . I didn't mean to hurt him. And I would have tried to save him if they hadn't lied to me. I loved Henry, you know that."

"You don't accuse someone you love . . . of, heh, murder . . . and you don't send them barreling down . . .

a marble staircase," he replied, his patter broken up by disconcerting giggles.

"We have to keep it together, Nick," she replied, even as she started to quiver. "Don't lose your head."

"Hah! *Don't lose your head*," he said. "Was that an execution joke? How fitting."

One of the rebels made his way toward them, and Ava lowered her head. "Nick, please. You need to be quiet," she pleaded in a whisper. "Or else we won't get through this."

"I lost everything today. My chance at Mars, my future, any semblance of a good life. My Henry." Nick sniffled. "My Henry is dead. There is no getting through this for me, or for anyone else."

Nick scanned the ballroom. More women were being lifted off the floor and pushed against a wall in a single file. He shook his head bitterly.

"They're not taking hostages."

"What?"

"We are not hostages, love."

"Don't be ridiculous."

"We don't have much time together," Nick said, suddenly turning somber and lowering his voice, to Ava's relief. "So there's something I want you to know before all this is over."

"What is it?"

"It was Henry."

"What do you mean?"

"He's the one who killed Ashwin," he replied with unsuppressed glee. "And he's the reason your high school sweetheart is dead."

Just then, one of the hostage takers wrested Ava off the floor by her bicep. She kept her sight on Nick, whose face betrayed no remorse, but also no hint of deception.

"No—you're lying. This is what you do, you make shit up. You've lied to me enough times today, Nick."

"On some level, you must've known. It's always the ones closest to you—like what you did to Henry."

"I don't believe you," she answered. "You're just saying that to hurt me."

"I suppose now you can call it quits. You got your man in the end. Yes, you did. Well done, Ava."

Her captor wrapped an arm around Ava's waist and lifted her from where she stood. She fought to break free of his hold.

"No, this is bullshit! Tell me the truth!"

Without warning, a swift jab landed on Ava's side. She doubled over in pain. Her captor then pulled her away from the dance floor and shoved her into the line of women. Mindless of the rifles trained on her, Ava tried to come for Nick, but the others pulled her back.

"Fucking tell me!" she yelled as she got dragged out of the ballroom.

Nick's only response was a tortured rictus, the kind that Ashwin bore on his face whenever he hit her for his own sadistic amusement.

The troops led the women out of the ballroom, snaking through the empty hallways, past the atrium, down one of the spokes all the way to the hub, the beating heart of Space Habitat Altaire. The women pleaded under their breath, plying their captors with offers of money and appeals to families waiting back home. One of them begged a little too forcefully, falling to her knees. Her face was met with the butt of a rifle. Ava tried to help the woman off of the floor but was held back by one of the men.

"Ms. Khan, are you causing trouble again?" asked Pio, pulling Ava out of the line. He walked her toward the front, acting like her personal escort.

"Where are you taking us?" she asked.

"We're not raping you, if that's what you're worried about."

The thought had been paramount in her mind. "Then what do you want?"

Pio pretended not to hear her. He dragged her past all the other hostages, and for a moment Ava allowed herself to believe that she might be getting spared.

"Y'know, we should probably thank you," the valet told Ava, sotto voce.

"Whatever the hell for?"

"If it weren't for you and your friend, we wouldn't have gotten Security off the station. He seemed like a good guy too, but hey, not everyone gets to survive, right?"

Ava's eyes watered in rage, in regret, in self-righteous indignation. Henry could have survived. That was the whole point. He didn't deserve to be sacrificed. Ava believed so, or at least wanted to believe so, Nick's final words be damned.

"The takeover would've been a lot bloodier if they weren't out there on a search and rescue," Pio continued. "So don't cry. Just take comfort in the fact that even as he was dying, your doctor friend was saving lives."

"You fucking bastard."

The marching slowed as they all approached the end of a wide hallway. Two men armed with rifles stood on each side of massive steel doors. The hostages began to scream in terror, finally realizing where they had been taken. Pio pushed Ava onto the head of the line.

"And for all your help," he told her, "you get to be the first to die."

Pio aimed his gun at her head and told her to step into the spacewalk bay.

The chamber was empty and deathly silent. It looked much the same as it did only this morning—a long hall lined with suits and benches and EVA gear, a large steel hatch at the far end—but now, the first set of airlock doors were wide open, like an anteroom to outer space. Ava's breath caught in her throat.

"Don't do this, I beg you," she told Pio, throwing herself against him.

He pushed her into the bay, then did the same to the next captives in line. Once the guests were all in the holding area, Pio and his comrades blocked the door through which they entered. They raised their weapons to drive the message home: there was only one way out.

"Why are you doing this?" cried someone beside Ava.

"We'll give you whatever you want," another shouted. Her indignant tone hushed the room. Isobel Lonsdale looked bold and defiant save for the shiver in her lips. "C'mon, let's work something out."

One of the men stepped up to her, a burly man still wearing his galley apron. He lifted her chin with the muzzle of his rifle.

Isobel edged her face away. "We're no use to you dead."

"Don't you get it, lady? We're not angling for a ransom."

"Well, what's your angle then?"

The door slid open behind the row of captors. Another crewmember walked in, a wisp of a man, slight, barely an adult. He wore the same haughty look of determination on his face, but this one brandished a camera instead of a gun. He swept his device around the room, trying to get a clear shot of every tearful face.

"Once we're done," Pio announced, "there'll be no more orbitals, no more playgrounds for the rich, no more loopholes to exploit for your Mars applications. Hell, there won't be a Mars program at all."

"Best part is," said another, "There'll be a whole lot less of your kind."

"It won't work," Isobel replied, shaking her head. "You need us, you need—our money, and our, our resources—"

"And guess what we'll do with all of those things once you're gone?"

The men marched forward, guns aimed. The cameraman pulled one of the women away from the group and dragged her to the front. Xiomara Harris shook violently, her face streaked with runny mascara.

"Stand up! Lemme get a good look at you," the man yelled. Xiomara's cries grew louder as she got manhandled.

"The face of the Altaire," he commentated as he hovered his device closer. "She's a really good actress, isn't she?"

Xiomara shut her eyes, mumbling frantic prayers. He shushed her, mock-soothing her tears with a hand glancing across her damp cheek. Then, the burly man stepped from behind him and aimed his rifle at Xiomara's kneecap.

Two shots rang out, dulling all sound.

Ava shook, her entire body gripped with terror. The cameraman crouched next to Xiomara's knee, bleeding and mangled, making sure he framed the scene just right.

With rough hands and rifles aimed, the captors forced the women into the airlock. Two of them flung Xiomara into the crowd. They packed everyone tightly, leaving little room between bodies. The cameraman panned around once more, capturing each wail and each horrified look.

Once the chamber was filled, Pio spoke into his comm. "Bring down the next batch."

He pressed a button on the control panel.

As the airlock doors closed, Ava searched the faces around her. These people called her names when she was transitioning; they called her a murderer when her brother died, and they still called her such to this day. No, she would seek no comfort in these women, not even out of desperation.

The chamber was bathed in yellow light as the depressurization sequence initiated. Oxygen whooshed into the chamber, but the process stopped as quickly as it began. The warning light turned red, and the women's cries were drowned by a siren and an automated announcement. *Danger. Sequence incomplete. System override.* The alert repeated itself on a loop, in synchrony with a flashing red light.

This was not how her life was supposed to end. She'd been used and abused, manipulated and betrayed at every turn. All she wanted was the truth: to live her life in truth, and to be afforded the truth, especially by the ones who claimed to love her.

The screams and the cries hushed as the hatch doors slid open. A chill enveloped Ava, taking the air out of her lungs. Finally, the pressure pulled at her, launching her into the void of space. Her dying thoughts lingered on Nick and his vicious parting words. Part of her saw those words as a final act of vengeance; part of her yearned for them to be true. All she wanted was closure, answers. She would never get them now. As in her entire life, in death, all Ava got were lies.

Chapter 32
Orbital Decay

The alert signal went off when the number turned red. Ten percent. Henry only had a few minutes until his O_2 ran out, and already he felt lightheaded. Henry drew an odd relief from knowing that he would die of asphyxiation. At least there wouldn't be any pain. It could have been worse. He could have gotten hit by more debris, or sustained a tear in his suit. The Khafir's missiles could have pushed him at a trajectory toward Earth, pulling him into the atmosphere for a fiery death.

That last one would still happen, he knew; well after he ran out of air, his orbit would decay and he'd spiral down, another space bogey falling from the sky in a blaze of glory.

His throat felt rough with all his worthless yelling, but he had more to say. A few final words to put his mind at ease. He would be orbiting around the planet for hours after he died, and there was still a chance his remains could be recovered. He still held hope that the Altaire had deployed its shuttles, and though they would come too late, he wanted Nick to hear him say goodbye.

He pressed record.

By this time, the events in that darkened theater box had fully returned to Henry. He recalled strangling Coen, and though remorse overwhelmed him, he took comfort in the fact that, faced with the choice at the very last chance, he tried to save the old man's life. Yet this did not comfort him nearly enough. His sense of righteousness cresting as he faced death, Henry tearfully confessed. His admissions would bring him shame, they would stain his name and his legacy, but what did that matter now?

Henry left a message for his parents too, and for his siblings and their children. To his staff at the hospital, to his closest friends. He struggled to recall names and details, his faculties fading.

The number on his display dwindled to one percent. With the little strength he had left, Henry cleared his throat and pressed record one last time

I suffer from a rare genetic condition called erythro-melalgia. I get random episodes of excessive blood flow, which causes my blood vessels to dilate and become inflamed. When I get an attack, my hands, arms, and legs turn red and feel like they're burning. A flare-up can run for a few seconds to a few hours and can happen anytime. My last one was just a couple of hours ago, and let me tell you, it was a fucking whopper.

I've had this condition since I was born, and it's been my biggest secret. I was devastated when my parents explained what was wrong with me. Even as a kid, I understood how this was going to ruin everything. Our family's future was destined for Mars, and a genetic defect is disqualifying. So we kept my condition a secret my entire life.

GDX Pharmaceuticals and the Gallagher name easily managed to erase any mention of my condition from official records, but hiding the flare-ups was the harder part. It's not exactly easy to hide my face or my limbs when they turn beet red, and I couldn't always flee somewhere safe before I collapse from pain. Wherever I went, I lived in fear that I'd have an episode. Just a single attack in public would raise questions.

Of course, I'd had a few of those incidents, rare times when someone witnessed a flare-up. If I could charm them well enough, they'd believe me when I claimed it was an allergic reaction to the lunch I just had. When charm failed, like in middle school when the school nurse had to rush me to a nearby hospital, my parents intervened.

I tried that approach with Ashwin Khan, but it didn't work. All he wanted was to hold this thing over me for as long as he could, money be damned.

The first flare-up he witnessed, I told him I was allergic to the stuff we'd been handling in chem lab. He didn't buy it the second time, though. He saw me cowering in the corner of a shower stall after gym class, red all over. He hounded me, stalked me in an attempt to catch me in another episode. He went everywhere I went—in class, in the hallways, in the dorms.

My parents told me to leave him be. If I act like there's nothing to hide, Ashwin will back off, they said. Bullies get bored easily. The thing is, they didn't know Ashwin like I did. He wasn't just a bully. He was a psycho, and psychos don't get bored. They get obsessed.

It all came to a head when he and Laz got into a fight. It was a stupid idea. I didn't want to be a part of it but I couldn't risk Laz getting hurt. Thank god I defused that situation. I just wish I knew at the time how I'd condemned myself.

Ashwin came up to my dorm the next night after the fight. He said he knew what I had, that he got someone to look into me, a really good PI that his family used. Apparently he'd known my secret for a while, but he'd been waiting for the right time to strike. Standing up for Laz gave him the push, and now he was going to tell. I had to do something, and fast.

Ashwin was predictable. I knew he'd come for me again soon. The next afternoon, I volunteered to do equipment inventory at the training garage. It was a thankless job and none of my classmates wanted to do it, especially after class on a Friday. I made sure all the suits were accounted for and all the buggies had the necessary gear like I always did, and our instructors trusted me well enough to do it on my own.

He came out of the shadows, almost on cue, threatening to ruin my chances at Mars. He said he'd tell everyone what he knew. He said he'd report my parents to the medical board too. He'd destroy me, my family, and our company, and there's nothing I could do to stop him.

I dared him to do it. Ashwin didn't like that. I'd been acting scared until then and standing up to him was something he didn't expect. He also didn't expect that I'd take a swing at him, and that I'd keep going until I knocked him to the ground. I was a ball of adrenaline and rage, but even as he tried to fight back, I could tell that he was amused. I think that's what really brought me to the edge. Up until then, I wasn't sure how far I could go.

I wrapped my hands around his neck and pressed down hard. He struggled under my weight, and it took all my strength to hold him down. I kept pressing down, crushing the mass of muscle and bone under my fingers until he stopped twitching.

Afterward, the plan was to dump his body deep in the salt flats, on the western edge of the school grounds. We had just learned in Exogeology how bodies decompose differently in extreme environments and I thought that'd help me. Plus, no one ever went to that area, and it'd take forever to search acres of Rochford property. That was stupid, of course. People would be looking for him, and with enough effort, it wouldn't even take that long.

I was also supposed to plant some baggies on him to make it look like a drug deal gone wrong. Everyone knew Ashwin dealt. That was the plan, anyway. I brought his body as far deep into the flats as I could, but I forgot to plant the baggies. I also didn't think about the track marks that the buggy left. It wouldn't have been an issue out in the desert, but the salt flats were different.

When the rush and the panic subsided, I realized all the ways I'd messed up. And so when news broke about Ashwin going missing, I volunteered to form the search parties. I needed to be the one to find the body. That way I could drive up to it and manufacture an explanation for the buggy tracks and any trace DNA that might be on him. I needed to plant the baggies too, and I figured it would be easier to slip them into his pockets if I was with Sloane and Laz. They wouldn't suspect a thing. And they didn't.

It should have ended there. It should have been a cold case, killer unknown. I didn't want anyone to suffer for what I did. It wrecked me when they arrested Ava and her girlfriend, and I never wanted Daniela to suffer for my sins. But I needed to keep those secrets, one on top of the other, and I'm sorry that she was the one who paid the price.

This is burden is mine and mine alone. No one else knew, and for decades I alone have carried this guilt. Since then, I've tried to live my life in constant atonement, but it was probably never enough. A longer life of good deeds might never have been enough. And now I will never know.

Chapter 33
Escape

This is how it ends, Sloane told himself. Bruised and blood-spattered, forced into a spacesuit in a tin can hurtling down to Earth. Hey, at least he got a window seat.

Space on the Pollux was tight, uncomfortably so. With him in the open cabin were five Rochfordians and two rebels guarding a high-level Altaire officer who'd been forced to take the helm; seems none of the folks with guns knew how to fly a shuttle.

"How are you feeling?" he asked Julian, seated next to him. Julian attempted a thumbs up. His forehead dripped with sweat and he grew paler by the minute. He was conscious at least. He might not be once their shuttle took off, but maybe that was for the best.

Through his window, Sloane watched as projectiles fell from the Altaire's spokes. Like a string of pearls cut loose and scattered across a stone floor, the bright silver globes shot out one after another, going off in all directions, swiftly at first then slowing to a standstill. The lifeboats formed an archipelago on the already-littered orbit. He doubted that they had any occupants.

Julian shook his head somberly. "I really thought you and I would make it," he said, his voice faint through the helmet comms.

"If it makes you feel any better," Sloane replied, "none of us are gonna make it."

"Not even the good ones." Julian chuckled. "After everything I've done."

Part of Sloane's job was knowing everyone's crimes and transgressions, and he understood that some of his Rochford contemporaries were worse than others. Some wrecked rainforests, strip-mined mountain ranges, spread hate or misinformation or fear. Some profiteered from war, prisons, natural disasters. Did Julian seriously set himself apart? Did he really think he was saving humankind, or was this a delusion brought on by his impending death? Sloane supposed it didn't matter now. Even if Julian thought himself better than the rest of his class, Sloane knew they were all the same.

None of them were good. None of them could be.

His family's stratospheric fall from grace could have redeemed Sloane, set him on a path where he stopped being the kind of person who took more than they gave. But he was so young and so hurt and so desperate, and he'd since survived knowing only one way to live.

For weeks afterward, Sloane refused to believe what he saw with his own eyes that Friday night out on the crags: Henry, driving a training buggy out onto the salt flats. When it became clear that Daniela might be convicted of murder, Sloane mustered the courage to confront his friend. Henry begged him to stay quiet.

"Ashwin hurt everyone. Ava, you, me, and everyone else," he'd told Sloane. "He's just like your father, and the world's better off without him in it."

Henry killed Ashwin for his own sake, not Ava's. Sloane knew as much. Yet being reminded of his father persuaded him that Henry's crime was justified, if only for a moment. That moment was all it took. Yes, Ashwin had been murdered, but if someone needed to suffer for it, it didn't have to be a friend who could help him in his hour of need. At first, Sloane may have kept Henry's secret out of loyalty, but he soon enough decided that he would do so out of gain.

There had been another way for him. Sloane could have been good. But from that moment on, his soul was forfeit.

The cabin lights came on, blinding Sloane with the sudden brightness. The rebels posted themselves behind a bulkhead, away from the helm. One of them had his rifle end aimed at the pilot.

"Ground control, this is Chief Officer J.J. Vaughn of the Space Habitat Altaire," the pilot said, trembling. "I have seven souls on board; requesting clearance for reentry." She explained that hostiles had taken the station, and that the Pollux carried escapees. She transmitted her passengers' implant data and assured ground control that the shuttle carried no hostiles.

Sloane was right; this flight was nothing but a ploy. He looked out the window and magnified his view screen. In the distance, beyond the field of scattered lifeboats, he saw a missile defense array. The pleasure from a sense of validation was a curious thing, given the circumstances.

He gazed at one of the rebels, the older of the two that had brought him onto the Pollux. The furrows that lined his face made Sloane feel equally old and tired. They'd all done horrible things to survive.

"Did you . . . mean what you said earlier?" Julian asked. His breath was ragged, his face ghostly pale. "That I . . . was your friend?"

Sloane nodded, in one last show of compassion.

The cabin rumbled as the shuttle's engines came to life. The pilot continued to feign normalcy at the point of a gun, announcing the countdown to launch. It would be the last voyage of the Pollux, the last flight Sloane was ever going to take. He flicked off his comms, letting out a defeated sigh. He was done. However hard he fought, however far he climbed, it all ended here. None of his efforts mattered anymore. Maybe none ever did. All that pursuit of the pleasurable, the gratifying, the comfortable, and nothing to show for it. He'd only done a single thing that lasted, and it was the biggest regret of his life.

A massive debris field occluded the space, filling it with broken pieces of the Castor and the Pollux. A glass fragment here, a blown-off piece of fuselage there, speeding in all directions alongside the mangled bodies of the shuttles' passengers. Cielo clutched her armrest and braced for impact. Bits of metal pinged off the body of the Excelsior as it flew across the field, scratching its surface and lodging in its side as fast as bullets.

"First wave, folks. More incoming soon," Jin announced from the helm. "And we're about to accelerate, so brace yourselves if you haven't already. It'll be bumpy."

Cielo looked around and saw her friends and coworkers—her comrades—stiffen in anxiety. Their evident fear increased her own. Miren, seated right next to her, placed a gentle hand over her glove and gave her a reassuring wink. The gesture helped little.

The shuttle rumbled and the engine roared as it picked up speed. Cielo couldn't see much through her window, but she imagined everything was going according to plan. Before their group had boarded the Excelsior, they'd been assured that the mutinies on the five other orbitals had succeeded. The speed with which events had unfolded, and the chaos and confusion that followed, would deprive their enemies time to respond. They'd timed the orbits right and the closest defense array, the Vanguard-2, should be out of range. Even if it weren't, its targeting systems would have an impossible time locking onto them past two debris fields, dozens of escape pods, and hundreds of corpses littered across their path.

Cielo sighed in gratitude as she watched the wastes of destruction. That she wasn't in the decoy shuttles was the result of cowardice, really; she could have, but she didn't volunteer on that suicide mission. All the same, she could have been asked. Worse, she could have been commanded. She was lucky to be alive.

She said a prayer for Garrett, Lia, and all her comrades who died in those shuttles to grant the Excelsior safe passage. She prayed for those who died fighting off Security and the guests' bodyguards. Noriega, Wimbo, Queenie, and many more. If not for them, their shuttle would not be as full as it was now. She prayed for those yet to die: Sir Haneef, Junior, Fely, and the handful who stayed behind on the Altaire. When all this was over, they would lose a third of their number. She prayed for their souls to be at peace, but most of all, she prayed that their sacrifice would not be in vain.

Selfishly, she prayed for herself too, that she would find peace after what they'd done. She thought of Delfin and how she might face her younger sibling once she returned. She would be proud; indeed, she was proud of what they'd accomplished, but Delfin would doubtless also see her guilt, and the fear that it might all still be for naught. She hoped that they would understand that she fought for the right cause and had no other choice. She hoped that would be good enough for Delfin, even if their plans ultimately failed.

"Altaire's given us the signal," Jin announced. "Thank you, Haneef and company. Ready to brace. Picking up speed in ten . . ."

In a few seconds, the explosive charges would go off. The Altaire's hub would be the first to go, then each of the spokes that spanned from it, then segments of the upper torus. Twelve explosions in all. Cielo wouldn't get to see it, none of them would, though she imagined it would be a breathtaking sight. By the time the Altaire was obliterated, the Excelsior would be far enough away to avoid the blast and major damage from the cascade of debris.

A piercing scrape tore through the roar of the engine, followed closely by a loud thud that echoed in the cabin. The passengers yelped in fear, their panic growing as the Excelsior took more hits from debris.

Cielo's heart sank as the shuttle accelerated, swerving in one direction then another as it steered to evade

projectiles. She shielded her window and clutched Miren's hand. The tap-tap-tapping of debris intensified. They reminded her of the heavy Manila downpours of her youth, the globs of rainwater pelting their shack's tin roof. Amid the commotion, Cielo closed her eyes and continued her prayers. She wept.

Soon enough, the sounds of impact subsided. The shuttle stabilized and Jin's soothing voice came through the comm.

"We're all clear."

Joyous cheers filled the cabin. There were cries of relief and triumph, there was laughter and applause. They were coming home. They who had lost homes, who had been driven out of their homes, who had once longed to escape the homes they had. They who had once dreamed of a new home among the stars, in the promised land, only to find that promise to be a lie. They who had made homes out of lonely, imperfect places, and who found home in lonely, imperfect people. They were all returning to their one, true home. The one they vowed to save, no matter the cost.

In minutes, the shuttle would enter Earth's atmosphere over Greenland airspace. Its new revolutionary government had pledged to provide temporary refuge for the 142 souls on board, at least until they could make the long journey back to their countries of origin. Cielo hoped that that pledge would be honored.

She understood that their work was not over, and as uncertainty washed over her, she looked to her crew. To the men and women fighting with her. She studied their faces, in various degrees of apprehension and anticipation and glee, and she managed to smile. They made her optimistic for a world that would see what

they'd done and recognize it for the rallying cry that it was. Together they'd rid humanity of its worst and destroyed the Altaire, that shining beacon of inequality.

The road ahead might be difficult, but today they won.

Miles and miles below the Excelsior, in a shanty built from corrugated tin and salvaged fiberboards, Delfin hunched over the stove, filling a kettle for their morning coffee. The sun had barely risen, the waters of the Pasig River still inky dark outside their window, but it was the last day of high school and they were eager to take an early bus before the roads were choked in traffic. Then, from the corner of their eye, they caught a tiny spark cutting through the cloudless indigo sky. A meteor, or so they thought. They turned around instinctively, searching, excited to share the sight with anyone. With their sister who was not there, not really, and yet was always there. Only a week ago, she'd reminded Delfin to always be vigilant for signs. Portents of change. This streak of light, blazing down from the sky, was theirs. They returned their gaze to the meteor. They clasped their hands by their chest, their worn fingers interlaced, and then they made their wish.

For all the advice, the commiserations, and the laughter, thank you to my no-drama crew and to the folks at the pub.

I'm forever grateful to my family: my mom, to whom I dedicate this book; Anika, Benjo, and Robin; Nouel, Cristine, and my grandmother, Josephine; and the wild and wonderful Boco and Manibo clans. Maraming salamat sa lahat.

Finally, and most of all—thank you, Sean Collishaw, for being the perfect first reader, and for planning and sketching the earliest versions of Space Habitat Altaire. Your love sustains me every day. Mahal kita. Sobra.

Acknowledgments

My deepest thanks to my agent, Eddie Schneider, and the rest of Team JABberwocky, especially Susan Velasquez Colmant, Valentina Sainato, and Joshua Bilmes.

Many thanks too, to all of Team Erewhon, most especially to my brilliant editor Sarah Guan. This book truly came into its own because of your instincts and insights; I'm so fortunate to work alongside you on this journey. Viengsamai Fetters—your notes and advice were invaluable; thank you so much. And, of course, thank you to the hardest working publicist in the biz, Marty Cahill, without whom my words would never reach their audience.

Thank you to the smart and generous early readers who guided me in refining this story from pure id: Jose Mari Nava, Jo Ladzinski, Christine Daigle, Chandra Fisher, Sophia Mortensen, and Amanda Helander. I'm especially indebted to Todd Gelbord for teaching me orbital mechanics; to Mikee Inton-Campbell, for her expertise on sexuality and the trans experience; to Ronan Sadler, for their expertise on disability; to Bessie Besana, for helping me make better fashion choices for these characters; and to Elias Eells, for crafting the Ad Martem, a drink that truly captures the spirit of this book.